NOT IN AMERICA

ROBERTA KAGAN

TITLE PAGE

Not In America

By
USA Today Best-Selling Author
Roberta Kagan

Imagine, if you will, that you have boarded a time capsule, and it has transported you to a time and place where life was simpler, where the neighborhood children chased fireflies until well after dark, and folks never locked their doors. It's the late 1920s, and violent crime is unheard of in this small, fictitious town that lies stretched along the Saint Lawrence Seaway in Upstate New York. This quaint little village lies huddled under elms and weeping willow trees far from the sins of the big city.

Let us give this little town a name. Let us call her Medina, with her tree-lined streets, white-wood farmhouses, and heavily scented rosebushes, was divided into two distinct and very different sectors. The larger of the two areas was populated by hardworking folks, most of whom were employed at the local factories. Now, although it wasn't discussed very much, it was true that some of these folks in that very sector belonged to a mean-spirited group known as the KKK, but the KKK kept to themselves, so no one paid much attention.

On the other side of Medina was the smaller section. It was only a few streets away, but once you passed the corner of Main Street, where the synagogue stood, with two stained-glass windows and a large wooden door, you knew you'd entered the Jewish part of town. On Friday nights and on Jewish holidays one might hear the lovely baritone sound of the cantor coming from inside the temple. The people who made their homes here were primarily Jewish immigrants, who were business owners and professionals.

Although there was always an awareness on both sides that an invisible line lay between them that must never be crossed, these two very different groups of people had lived side by side for centuries without much trouble. They even frequented each other's sectors, and often spoke courteously to one another. Sometimes the non-Jewish housewives bought bread at the Jewish bakery or had their shoes fixed by the Jewish cobbler. The Jewish families sometimes ventured to the other side to visit a movie theater or a museum. And . . . all was well. At least until it wasn't.

One day something happened . . . something that rocked that little village like an earthquake . . . something that sent shock waves through the Jewish people who had built their lives in that small, comfortable, protected town, making them realize that even in America, where the streets were surely paved in gold, they must never take their safety for granted. Even here, hatred for God's chosen people lay buried right beneath the oak tree in the village square. And in the time it takes for lightning to flash down from the sky, everything they'd spent their lives building, could be consumed by flames. But this couldn't happen . . . not in America . . . could it?

PROLOGUE

Four-year-old Evelyn Wilson knew it was a bold move to enter the fort that her eight-year-old brother, Ted, and his friends built in the backyard of her family's home. Ted had made it clear that this was a boys-only clubhouse, and she was not welcome. So, she walked slowly toward the fort. It was a structure made of wood and painted with white paint. With a sign outside that read Members Only. Gingerly, Evelyn peeked inside expecting to hear Ted start hollering as soon as he saw her face. But the clubhouse was empty. She was a little surprised Ted and his friends weren't there. However, she knew her brother and his friends often played by the creek that lay just a few feet into the woods behind the family's home. So, she headed there to find him. *Mommy sent me to find Ted. She wants him to come home. He better not be mean to me or I am telling on him,* she thought. *And if I can get him to come into the house, Mommy will be so happy with me that she'll probably give me a whole cookie instead of the half she promised.*

Evelyn loved the forest. In the summer she loved all the different shades of green, the leaves on the trees, the grass, the weeds. But it was autumn now and even more beautiful. She skipped and kicked her way through a blanket of brightly colored leaves that covered the forest floor. *Crunch, crunch, crunch.* The sound of the leaves beneath her feet, as she danced and twirled like a ballerina as she made her way to the little creek, had Evelyn singing softly to herself.

The last of the summer wildflowers grew randomly. Smiling, she gathered a small bouquet. *I'll bring them for Mommy.* Then the little girl spotted a cluster of dandelions that had grown like a pot of gold beneath a tree. Their heads, the color of sunshine, beckoned, and she couldn't resist the opportunity to make a dandelion necklace. Plopping down, Evelyn began to pick the yellow flowers careful not to destroy their beauty. Next, she tore a slit just large enough for the stem of the next flower to fit through. Careful not to break the stem, she pulled it through slowly. To make a perfect dandelion necklace took complete focus, and Evelyn became so engrossed in the project that she momentarily forgot about her brother. Still singing softly to herself, she worked diligently on her project.

"Hello." A voice interrupted her song. It was a teenage boy with wild wavy hair and the soft brown stubble of a splotchy beard. It was the beginning of facial hair that indicated this was a boy who had not yet become a man. He smiled as he peeked out from behind a tree and winked at her with intense blue eyes. "What's your name?"

Evelyn jumped. The boy had startled her.

"I'm sorry. I didn't mean to scare you," he said in a sincere tone, his blue eyes twinkling.

"Evelyn is my name," she said, a little leery. He seemed nice. His eyes and smile were bright. But something about him frightened her, although she could not say exactly what it was.

"Evelyn," he repeated. "That's a very pretty name. What are you doing here all alone in the forest?" he asked as he moved closer to her. She cowered a little and tried to get to her feet. A voice in her head told her to go home. But there were some wet leaves under her, and she slid back down until she was sitting under the tree. She tried to get up again, but the boy was now standing directly in front of her so close that she couldn't move.

Evelyn squinted up at him. The sun was blinding her, so she was unable to see his face clearly. "I'm looking for my brother. I think he is playing here in the woods. I think I should go and try to find him," she said.

"Well, who is your brother because I know everyone in the woods," he said.

"Do you know him?" she asked, confused.

"I probably do." He smiled. "But the only way I can tell you if I know him is if you tell me his name."

"Ted."

"But, of course, I know Ted." The boy smiled again, his tone of voice was warm and reassuring. "Would you like me to take you to him?"

"Yes, I would like that very much. But you're a stranger, and my mommy said I should never go with strangers."

"She's absolutely right about that. You should never go with strangers," the boy said, his face and tone suddenly becoming serious. For a few seconds he was silent as if he were contemplating something. Then out of nowhere, he let out a friendly laugh. "So how about this. I'll tell you who I am, and then we won't be strangers anymore."

Evelyn cocked her head to the side. It sounded logical. "Who are you?" she asked.

"I am the forest elf. I am a friend to all children. I would bet that you have heard of me in fairy tales."

"Maybe. I don't remember any that mentioned you though."

He laughed. "It's all right. Let me tell you a little about me. I am always the hero who saves little children from wicked witches. And who helps little girls to find their brothers. By the way, how old are you?"

Evelyn held up four fingers.

"Four years old! I thought you were at least six."

"You did? My big brother is eight."

"Yes, I did think you were at least six. You look very grown up, and you said your name is Evelyn, right? See, I remembered."

She nodded.

"Good. You see, I know how old you are. And your name too. And you know who I am. The forest elf, right?"

"Yes."

"So now we are officially no longer strangers. Besides all of that, I am also an old friend of your brother's. His name is Ted, right?"

"My brother? You are saying that you know him, but I don't remember seeing you at our house or playing in the fort . . . ever."

"Well, I have been to your home. And I've played in the fort. But I can only come out of the forest once in a while, and I can't stay very long. That's because I have too much work to do in the forest. So we must have missed each other when I was at your house. But as you can see, there is no need to be afraid of me. Ted and I are old friends. And now you and I are old friends, too, Evelyn. Give me your hand, and I'll help you get up," he said, smiling. "Then I'll take you to your brother."

She felt a shiver run down her spine. But she ignored it and gave him her hand. The forest elf turned to Evelyn with a big smile on his face. "I know just where to find your brother," he said as they began to walk deeper into the woods.

EVELYN COULD HEAR her own heartbeat as she opened her eyes in the dark space. But something was covering her eyes. She could not see. And even so, no light filtered in at all. Only darkness. Desperately she pulled at the ropes that bound her hands and feet. Then a sob escaped her lips. She tried to scream but something was choking her, a scarf perhaps. It had been placed tightly around her mouth holding it open so she could not speak. *Mommy*, she thought. *I want my mommy.* Tears burned her eyes. The last thing she remembered was that forest elf. They'd been walking. The sun had been shining. She'd been singing; he had been singing with her, and then she had somehow ended up here. In this complete blackness, alone, tied up, and terrified.

Footsteps came from somewhere followed by whispers. She could not make out what was being said. All she knew was fear. Pure, unadulterated fear—blinding, heart-stopping fear.

Then the door to the small closet opened. A bright light flashed in front of her assaulting her eyes. She winced in pain. But a few seconds later her eyes adjusted. And it was then that she saw them. If she could have made a sound it would have been a scream, the desperate scream of a caged animal. They stood before her, three figures that looked like ghosts with white sheets covering their bodies and black surrounding their eyes. They had enormous doughy-looking noses. She trembled. "Please let me go. I want my mommy," she tried to say, but no words could escape her bound lips.

"Do you know who we are?" a strange, deep, and terrifying voice said.

She shook her head, and again she tried to speak. "Mommy, please, I want my mommy." But again, her words were lost.

"We are the Jews. We've taken you because we plan to use your blood for our Jewish rituals. Remember who we are. We are Jews." Then one of the ghosts removed the gag from her mouth. "Say it. Who are we?"

"I want my mommy. Please, I want my mommy. I want to go home," Evelyn said.

"Shut up." She recognized the voice of the forest elf. "Or say what you are told to say. Who are we?"

"Forest elf, is that you? I want to go home. Please rescue me. You said you rescue children."

"I'm not the forest elf, you dumb child. We are the Jews. Now, if you want to live, repeat it. Who are we?"

"The Jews. The Jews. The Jews. Please, can I go home?" Evelyn cried, and her entire body shaking.

One of the ghosts replaced the gag, and then the closet door closed, burying the child in darkness once again.

"I THINK IT WORKED," one of the three costumed figures said to the other two.

"Let's hope so."

CHAPTER ONE

Medina, New York, September, 1928
6:00 p.m.

The kitchen in the home where little Evelyn Wilson lived with her parents and her brother Ted.

Marjorie Wilson let out a cry of pain when she nicked her finger while cutting an onion for the stew she was preparing for dinner. Grabbing a kitchen towel, she wrapped the cut to stop the bleeding. After a few minutes she looked at the damage. It was only a surface cut. Not too deep. It hurt, but at least it did not need medical attention. She knew she had cut herself because she was distracted. Not paying attention to what she was doing. But she was very worried; it was getting late, and neither of her children were home. They knew better than to be out this late. They knew better. Carefully, she picked the knife up again and went back to working on the onions. *If only I could calm down,* she thought. She wanted to believe Evelyn and Ted were just off playing somewhere and that they had just lost track of time. But she was a mother. And a mother's instinct is strong. *Something is not right. The likelihood of Ted playing with his four-year-old sister is*

slim. He wouldn't stay out to play with her. And Evelyn is afraid of the dark.
She has never stayed out like this before. Never! Where are my children?

Just then she heard the wooden porch steps creak. Her head whipped around to face the direction of the sound. Her heart beat fast. *Footsteps. They are home. Thank God.* Her hands were trembling so badly that she had to lay the knife down. The door opened. She felt her breath catch in her throat.

"Hi, honey," Herbert, her husband, said, removing his hat. Then he turned to look at her. "What's wrong? You're as pale as newly fallen snow in January."

"The children aren't home. It's six o'clock, and the children aren't home."

He glanced at the bloody rag wrapped around her hand. "You cut yourself?"

She nodded. "It's nothing. It's not deep."

"You look frazzled. It's only six o'clock. Ted's been out later than this before. I know we've told him time and again to come in earlier. But he doesn't always listen. Nothing to worry yourself about."

"What about Evelyn? She should be home. She would never do this . . ."

"Have you checked the fort?"

"Don't you think I've checked there a hundred times already. They aren't back there."

"Well, let me just go and check one more time," he said, trying to sound reassuring. But Marjorie knew her husband, and she could see in his face that he was worried too. "I'll just go and have a look. You wait right here, all right?" he said, patting her shoulder.

She nodded as he walked out, the door flapping behind him.

Marjorie put her head in her hands and waited for Herb to return.

The onion juice that stained her fingers was making her eyes water. Between the smell from the onion, the blood-soaked cloth, the nagging fear and uncertainty, she felt sick to her stomach.

The porch steps creaked again. *It is too soon for Herbert to have returned. It must be the children.* Her heart jumped into her throat and began to beat so rapidly that she gagged. The door squeaked open. She held her breath. *It has to be the children,* she thought. *Please, God, let it be my children.*

"Ted!!" she screamed as he entered the house.

"Sorry I am so late, Mom," Ted said, pulling off his jacket and then his cap and hanging them on the coatrack in the living room.

Marjorie jumped to her feet. She slapped him across the face. Then she grabbed him and hugged him to her tightly and began to cry. "Where is your sister? Is she with you?" she asked hopefully.

Ted looked at his mother puzzled. Her body was trembling, her eyes wild. "I haven't seen her since breakfast this morning," he said.

"Oh my God." Marjorie put her hand on her chest and dropped back into her chair. "Oh my God . . ."

The door opened, and once again, for a single second, Marjorie stared at the door with her mouth hanging open. Her body trembling. A drop of blood seeping through the towel and dripping onto the kitchen table. *Evelyn, please God, let it be Evelyn.* She felt as if she were suspended over the Earth walking on a tightrope. Beads of sweat formed on her brow. But it wasn't Evelyn. Herb, her husband, walked in. "They aren't in the fort." He threw his hands up. Then he saw Ted. "There you are, son. Where is your sister?"

"I don't know." Ted shrugged his shoulders. "Like I told Mom, I haven't seen her since this morning."

"Where have you been?" his father asked angrily. "You know better than to come home this late. I oughta take the strap to you."

"I was fishing at the creek with Billy and Fred. I am sorry. I didn't mean it. I lost track of time. Please don't hit me."

"Are you sure you haven't seen your sister? It's important that you try to remember. It's very important," Herb said.

"I haven't seen her. But I promise I won't be late again. Just please, don't take the strap to me. Please, Dad. I didn't mean it."

Herb didn't answer his son. He turned and looked at his wife. "I'm going to go from house to house. I'll talk to all the people in the neighborhood and see what I can find out. Maybe she is visiting with one of the other children, or maybe someone has seen her. Meanwhile, you go to town and tell the sheriff that she's missing."

"Oh my God! Do you think something has happened to her? Oh, Herb. We must find her before nightfall."

"I'm sure everything is fine. She is probably at one of the neighbor's houses." Herbert Wilson tried to sound calm. "But I agree with you. It's best that we find her before dark. So let's get moving," he said and took his hat off the coatrack. Then he turned to his son. "You come with me," he said.

CHAPTER TWO

M arjorie walked as quickly as she could toward the police station. Her heart was beating fast and her thoughts were racing. The darkened streets and the sound of her own heels clicking on the sidewalk unnerved her. Her mind's eye was like the screen of a horror film. Over and over she replayed the last few moments she'd spent with her daughter. And over and over she chastised herself.

Where is my Evelyn? What has become of her? Marjorie Wilson thought. And the movie began again . . .

CHAPTER THREE

Marjorie Wilson remembers what she was doing just moments before her daughter disappeared.

The golden days of Indian summer had slowly descended upon the small town of Medina, which lay along the Saint Lawrence Seaway in Upstate New York. Marjorie Wilson glanced up at the round black-rimmed clock on her kitchen wall. It was almost four thirty in the afternoon, and her eight-year-old son, Ted, had still not come home from school. Sunlight spilled through the kitchen window. It fell upon a plate of cookies that Marjorie had arranged in the middle of the table for the children to snack on. She grunted and shook her head. It was too late for the children to snack on cookies now. If they ate them, they would ruin their dinner. She thought of Ted's lack of responsibility with disgust. He'd promised her he would come home right after school and do his homework before he went out to play. But she could never count on him to keep his word, and this was not the first time he'd run off with his friends and then had to stay up late to finish his schoolwork.

Over the past summer, Marjorie's husband, Herbert, had helped Ted and Ted's friends to build a fort in the backyard, and she assumed that when the boys arrived at the house after school, they'd see the fort and be immediately drawn to it. And so they'd go out to play instead of doing their homework. She took a deep breath. She had to finish peeling the pile of potatoes in front of her. She needed them for tonight's dinner. And Herb would be home soon, so rather than stopping her work to go out to the backyard herself to find her son, she called for her four-year-old daughter, who was busy playing with her doll in her room. "Evelyn," she yelled. "Evey, come on into the kitchen. I need you to do something for me, sweetheart."

A bright little girl with shining eyes and a messy pageboy haircut came skipping into the kitchen. "Can I have a cookie, Mommy?" she said as her eyes landed on the plate of cookies on the table.

"No, it's getting too close to dinner. I'm afraid if you do, you won't want to eat your food. But you can have one for dessert."

Evelyn pouted. "But we always have a snack. Is it because Ted is late getting home?"

"Yes, I'm afraid it is," Marjorie said. "But don't worry. There will be cookies for dessert." She smiled.

"I hate Ted. If he had come home, we could have had cookies."

"I promise you; you can have two cookies for dessert. How does that sound?"

"Good." Evelyn smiled.

"Now, I need you to go out to the backyard to the fort and get your brother. Tell him that Mom is very upset with him. You tell him I said that I want him in this house right now. He knows that he is to do his homework before going out to play."

"Do I have to go, Mommy? I want to play with my dolly."

"Yes, you have to go." Marjorie looked at her daughter's sweet face and it broke her resolve. "All right, I'll tell you what. If you go out back and get your brother for me, I'll give you half of a cookie when you both come in."

"All right, Mommy. I'll go."

Why did I send her? She is only four. What was I thinking? Dear God, please forgive me and bring my child home.

As Evelyn began to walk toward the screen door, she turned to her mother and said, "You know, Ted gets mad every time I go inside the fort. He yells at me and tells me to get out. He says it's not a place for a girl. He says it's a boys-only clubhouse."

"Well, that's too bad for him. You tell him that I said he needs to come into the house right this minute," Marjorie said.

"Yes, Mommy."

"All right. Now hurry back. I want you to come right back in and wash up for dinner before your father gets home. And if Ted can get his homework done maybe we can have an early dinner. Then we can all sit outside on the porch tonight, and you two can collect fireflies. You would like that, wouldn't you?"

"Yes, Mother," Evelyn said as she skipped out the door.

The screen door bounced on its hinges.

I can still hear the sound of the door hitting the wood. Why did I let her go? Why? Marjorie clenched her fists until her nails dug into her palms. She wanted to hurt herself. She deserved to feel the pain. This was her fault. *If something bad has happened to Evey, it is because of me.*

CHAPTER FOUR

6:00 p.m.

The home of Roger, Mary, and Frank Weston.

Roger Weston was fuming. The streetcar had been very late. And he was in a hurry to get home from his job at the aluminum plant because tonight was the weekly meeting of the KKK, and he'd said he would attend. This meeting would be no different from all the others. But because it was an election year, and the Klan wanted to make sure their followers were on board with their support of Hoover, a man they felt represented them, they encouraged attendance at the weekly meetings. It was important, Roger knew, that Hoover beat Smith. Smith was a man who was loved by the immigrants, particularly the Catholics.

If Smith won, it was certain things would change for the true Americans like himself. There would be more attention paid to the needs of the Italian and Irish immigrants. And he'd come to truly hate the ones he worked with at the plant. They were Catholics, and Roger, like his fellow Klan members hated Catholics almost as much as they hated the Jews. And he had to say they truly despised and feared the small

Jewish community in Medina. The men with their long beards and their strange curled sideburns. The women with their covered heads. Whenever he was forced to walk past their little Jew temple, he spit on the ground.

In order to reinforce their shared hatred of the Jews, the KKK meetings always concluded with one of the members reading aloud from Henry Ford's book *The International Jew*. Roger wasn't much of a reader; in fact, he didn't set much store in education. He considered it to be a waste of time. A man needed to be working not sitting in a classroom wasting time. But Ford's book was one book he had read. And after he read it, he'd read all the articles he could get his hands on about Jews. After what he considered a thorough investigation, he couldn't see how anyone could disagree with Ford. The Jew was a menace to society. That was why the KKK was such a necessary club. They were needed to keep the Jews and Catholics in line. Besides that, they were his friends and his extended family. In them he'd found a group of men who shared his same values.

The streetcar finally arrived in front of the aluminum plant. It was fifteen minutes late. He hopped on annoyed at the delay and plopped into a window seat. Staring out at the familiar landscape, he thought about his son, Frank. Frank had always been a strange child. But lately he seemed to be getting worse. When Frank was eight years old, Roger had brought home a puppy. A stray dog had given birth in the back of the factory. Since Frank had never had any friends, Roger thought it would be good for him to have a pet. At first it seemed that Frank loved the puppy, who was a sweet and devoted little bundle of black fur. But then one day, Roger had returned home from work to find his wife, Dotty, distraught. She insisted that they give the dog to her sister because she found Frank torturing the poor creature.

Dotty loved her son. She loved him so fiercely that she covered up his strange behavior as much as possible. Whenever Roger mentioned that he thought it might be good for Frank if they put him into some sort of institution before he got into serious trouble, Dotty refused to listen. But Roger knew his wife was as worried as he was about their son. Frank had no friends. He spent all of his time alone building his collection of butterflies whose wings he'd pinned to a thick paper.

Roger knew Frank was treated badly by the other children at school. Frank was an outcast. And it saddened Roger to know that some of the men who were his sworn friends in the KKK didn't care for Frank. He overheard a group of them at one of the KKK picnics telling their children to stay away from Frank. But how could he blame them? At the KKK gatherings that included family, Frank would often laugh hysterically for no apparent reason or purposely spill his punch on one of the girl's dresses. It seemed like Roger was always apologizing for his son's odd and often cruel behavior.

The streetcar arrived at Roger's stop. He got to his feet and raced down the stairs and onto the sidewalk. Then he walked as fast as he could until he arrived at home. Looking at his watch he frowned. Only a half hour until the meeting was to begin, and he still had to wash up, eat, and walk three blocks to the meeting. Dotty was not in the kitchen waiting for him, and he was too rushed to search for her or his son. Instead, he gobbled the plate of stew she had left on the stove for him, splashed his face with cold water, and then ran out the door to go to his meeting.

CHAPTER FIVE

6:30 p.m.

Schatzman's bakery located two blocks north of the Jewish synagogue in the Jewish sector of Medina.

Goldie Schatzman bagged up the challah bread that was left over from the day's sales. She would sell it tomorrow at a cheaper price as day-old bread. Quickly, she washed down the counters while her eighteen-year-old son, Samuel, swept the floor and her husband, Irving, did the financial calculations for the day. Even in her apron and baggy work dress, Goldie was a beautiful woman, tall and slender with long legs, slim hips, tiny breasts, and golden hair. When she was a child her mother loved to tell her the story of how shocked she was the first time she saw her daughter: "You were a tiny baby with a full head of hair the color of sunshine," her mother, Esther Birnbaum, would say.

As Goldie grew up, she became even prettier. But then something happened when she began to menstruate. The wonderful gift of being a gorgeous child became the dangerous curse of being a stunning young woman. Everywhere she went, she turned the heads of all the boys and men. The opposite sex pursued her relentlessly. And at first it was exciting and lots of fun. Goldie and her best friend, Leni, went to parties and to dances, where Goldie never sat out a single dance. Everything was glorious until she met Paul. And to this very day, she cursed his name, blaming him for ruining her life.

Goldie took a quick glance at her husband, Irving, and her heart sank. She was so unhappy with him. She'd always been unhappy with him. Irving was a plain-looking man with a good, solid work ethic and gentle personality. He had bulging eyes framed by dark-rimmed glasses with thick lenses. His hair was salt and pepper, wavy, and thin. There was nothing alluring. Shorter than Goldie and too skinny, with rounded shoulders, he looked like an old man even when they were young and first married nineteen years ago. And for the past nineteen years, each time she looked at him, she cursed Paul again. How different Irving was from Paul. She'd met Paul when she was just a young girl and still living with her family in Germany. He'd swept into her life with his handsome face and roguish charm. It hadn't taken him very long to steal her heart and then her virginity. It had been a whirl-wind romance. He was not only fiercely handsome, but he was clever and witty. He wrote her poetry and read it to her as they lay under the stars after they made love. But he had no trade, no money, and to make matters worse, no desire to marry anyone ever. She knew he would run away once she told him she was pregnant. He'd never lied to her. He'd told her from the beginning that he was not the kind of man to marry and settle down. But when he found out she was pregnant, he said, "I want to see the world, and I want to write beautiful stories. I can't do that with a wife and child hanging around my neck." The next day he was gone. He'd left Berlin.

Her parents were livid when she had to tell them she was expect-ing. And to make matters worse, the father of her unborn baby was not Jewish. Her parents had warned her about the shaygets. The non-Jewish boys who only wanted one thing from a good girl. She had refused to believe them.

Goldie's father was a pillar of the community, wealthy and admired. He had to hide the family's shame by marrying his daughter off quickly. So when he heard that the baker's son was planning to move to America and already had a possible sponsor who was going to help him open his own bakery, Goldie's father thought this would be a good match for his daughter. At first her father did not tell Goldie that she would be going to America. But he felt it was important to get her out of Berlin, away from the prying gossip, which was sure to start any day. And since Goldie's father was wealthy, it was easy to offer the baker a sizable dowry to agree to a marriage between his only son to their daughter, who was now too soiled for any other suitor.

The marriage between Goldie and Irving was little more than a marriage of convenience. He needed money to open his own bakery, and she needed a husband to quiet the gossip as her belly grew larger. Her rich father had made all the arrangements. She had not even met Irving until everything had been decided. Then once her father had agreed upon the match, Irving was invited to her home for dinner. She could still remember the moment she first saw him sitting at the dinner table. She walked in and went to her seat. Their eyes met; she was repelled by the thick lenses of his glasses. Her heart sank as he told her about his dreams of owning his own bakery. And she thought, who has dreams of opening a bakery? That's not a dream; it's a nightmare.

She didn't want to marry him, and she begged her father to let her out of the match. But her father was insistent. "Irving Schatzman is a good man. He has a good profession. He's a baker. A baker will always have a job. This is all your own fault, Goldie; it was you who got your-self in trouble. You've brought this upon yourself. You are lucky to have this man. He is willing to marry you with another man's child growing in your belly. You should be grateful. Most men wouldn't give you a second look."

She wept. But the date was set. They would marry quickly to quiet any gossip. But then miraculously something exciting had happened. Irving had come to see her one afternoon. There was a worried look on his face when he told her that he was afraid she was going to break the engagement when he told her the news. "What news? Just tell me," she said, annoyed. Knowing that if she could have broken the engagement, she already would have.

Poor Irving squeezed the fabric of his suit jacket with sweaty palms. Then he took a deep breath and said, "Goldie, my cousin had arranged to sponsor me to come to America. He lives in a small town in Upstate New York called Medina. He will help me to open my own bakery. More than anything, I hope you will consider going with me. I believe we will have an opportunity to live a very good life in America," he said, then he looked down at his black shoes. They were old shoes, but Goldie could tell that he'd shined them to come and see her." Then he added, "I promise you; I will be a good husband to you if you will only come with me."

Goldie stared at him. She didn't realize she'd been holding her breath. He didn't know she had no choice but to go because she was certain that no matter what happened, her father would not let her out of the marriage. She had no interest in baking bread or in owning a bakery. But Goldie knew she was stuck, and she had to find a way of making the best of a bad situation. The idea of going to America was exciting to her. And so instead of focusing on her unwanted marriage, she kept her thoughts fixated on America and what wonderful things might await her there. Still, she wept on her wedding day. She wept because she wished it was Paul instead of Irving who was standing beside her under the chuppah. And at that time, with Paul's baby growing inside her, she still loved him. Yes, he'd left her, but she still loved him. And the following day when her mother came to see her and found her crying, her mother had promised her that over time she would learn to love Irving. But it had never happened. As time passed, she found that she had stopped loving Paul, although she often wondered what happened to him. And she had to admit, Irving had never treated her badly. He had always been respectful and kind even if she'd had to work alongside him, baking bread in a hot oven, a way of life unknown to her social class.

At least she didn't have to lie when Samuel was born. Irving knew the boy was not his biological son. Sam was handsome, and he looked just like Paul, the artist from whose loins he sprung. But Irving didn't hold that against the boy. Instead, he raised him as if he were his own son, never letting Samuel even sense the truth. In fact, Sam and Irving were the best of friends, and sometimes Goldie felt Samuel was closer to his father than he was to her.

On the day of Samuel's bar mitzvah, Irving gave him a gold Star of

David necklace, which his father had given him. "Be proud that you are a Jew," Irving said, his eyes shining with love as he put the necklace over his son's head. "Our people have suffered through the ages for the privilege of wearing this star. But even though we have suffered, we are God's chosen people."

"I will wear this with pride, Dad. I'll never take it off. Never." Samuel put his hand over the Star of David, and he held it tightly in his fist. And so far, Sam had kept his word. He wore that necklace every day of his life.

Now, Alma was different. She could not be mistaken for being the child of any man other than Irving. She looked just like her father. For this, Goldie mourned. Alma, at fifteen, was no beauty. But she had a good and kind heart, and so she found love by doing community service. When her grandparents sent her money as birthday or Hanukkah gifts, she bought food and made baskets which she distributed to the poor. Goldie admired her daughter's generosity, but she could not, in any way, relate to it. When Goldie received letters containing money from her parents, she took the money and ran out to the shops eager to buy pretty dresses, handbags, and shoes. And as time passed, she found herself waiting for those small checks, which became her brightest moments. They were tiny reminders of the way things were when she had been the daughter of a wealthy man in Germany. As soon as one would arrive, she would tell Irving she was ill and could not come into work that day. Then she would doll herself up in her finest dress and shoes and make a day of pretending she was still a rich, single girl without a care in the world. Oh, how she waited for those gifts with anxious anticipation. She found being the wife of a baker to be like a prison sentence. It was filled with hard work and limited rewards. And because she was forced to stay with Irving, she felt justified in grabbing for any small amount of happiness even if it meant stealing from her own children.

Sometimes when Goldie couldn't sleep, she would glance across the bed at her husband as he slept and think to herself that she and Irving had been married for nineteen years, and she still could not honestly say she felt any love for him. When they'd first come to the United States, she'd found it exciting. But now, after having spent eighteen years in America, she longed to return to Berlin. Everything she wanted, she realized, was everything she had before she'd gotten married. Goldie bought magazines and newspapers and read every piece of news she could find about Berlin. Since she'd been gone, the city had grown even more fascinating. In fact, artists of all kinds from all over the world were traveling just to experience the wonderful uniqueness of the city.

At thirty-six, Goldie was a stunning woman with thick golden, wavy hair and bright blue eyes, which twinkled with a zest for life. She longed to flirt and to dance and to laugh. But all she did was bake, cook, and clean. As time passed, her resentment toward Irving grew. She felt guilty about her feelings toward her husband. But she couldn't help but dream of how much fun it would be to be rid of him and his dreary lifestyle. And how glorious it would feel to sit in a café in the center of town in Berlin, surrounded by world-renowned painters, writers, and musicians, flirting madly.

"Mother, you can go. I'll finish up here," Samuel said, interrupting her thoughts.

"Are you sure?" Goldie asked. *Sam is such a good boy. He can see how tired I am.*

"Yes, we're almost done. I am just going to mop the floor and take out the trash."

"I can wait for you if you'd like," she offered, knowing he would tell her to go home.

"No need. Go on home. I'll be along soon."

"All right. I'll get your dinner ready."

"Sounds good," he said as she picked up her handbag and walked out the door.

CHAPTER SIX

7:00 p.m.

The alleyway behind Schatzman's bakery.

Betty Howard's heart raced as she waited for Samuel Schatzman behind Schatzman's bakery. She was excited to see Sam again. But she knew she had to be careful that no one saw her here, because if her parents found out, they would be livid. They would never approve of her feelings for Samuel because he was a Jew. They were not as bad as some of the non-Jews in her neighborhood. They didn't hate the Jews. In fact, they had nothing against Goldie and Irving Schatzman, the owners of the bakery. But they would have gone mad with anger if they even suspected their daughter was in love with Sam. *They would lock me in my room until John Anderson and I were married. John Anderson, now, he is another problem,* she thought. It was all but expected that she was going to marry him, whom she'd known since they were small children. They had played together when they were very young and had been dating since they were fourteen. He was a nice boy even if he was member of the KKK. And he'd always treated her well. He'd been very respectful never expecting more than a few kisses on their dates.

She knew he loved her, but she never loved him. And when he'd put his arms around her, she'd never felt the passion with him that she felt when she was in Sam's arms.

The lights of the bakery were turned out, and the inside of the building was now dark. Betty felt her heart skip a beat. The door opened, and there he was, tall, glistening just slightly from sweat. His long muscles were flexed as he carried the heavy trash, and his thick dark hair caught the light of the moon. His dark eyes were immediately drawn to her. She could feel the fire ignite within her. He smiled as he tossed the trash bag out with ease. She trembled. "Come in, we're alone," he whispered. "Let me wash up before my hands grace your pure beauty," he said. She was mesmerized by his gaze as she followed him inside.

Little did Betty know that John Anderson had missed the KKK meeting that night in order to follow her. Last week after his meeting ended, he had gone to her home. He wanted to see her if only for a few minutes. But when he knocked on the door, her parents said she wasn't home. "She's at the library," Betty's mother told John.

John walked to the library and went inside. It was a small building, so he walked through every aisle. Betty was nowhere to be found. That was when he became suspicious. So he stood outside her home waiting for her to return, hidden from view. When she arrived a half hour later with her hair looking less than perfect and her lipstick smeared, he felt sick to his stomach. He had to know where she'd been and with whom. So he decided that the following week he would forgo his meeting. He would wait outside her house and follow her. Then he could find out exactly where she went and who had smeared her lipstick.

CHAPTER SEVEN

8:30 p.m.

The only Jewish synagogue in Medina.

Rabbi Jacob Goldstein was helping his wife, Rasa, prepare the food that would be served to break the fast at the synagogue on Yom Kippur, which was only a few days away. He knew she was doing her best, but there was a lot to be done. Rasa was a balabusta, a wonderful Jewish homemaker, but she was still very young. And he knew the holidays were hard on her because during that time she found herself missing her family back in Lithuania. He wanted to do whatever he could to help her feel cared for and less overwhelmed.

Even though theirs was an arranged marriage, there had been an instant bond between them, which had grown into a deep affection, especially since they'd left their families and beloved homeland to travel to a new country together. He knew she was skeptical of the modern ways of this new land called America. She told him often how different the Jews here seemed than the ones she had grown up with in Europe. But he'd promised her several times that the move was a good one. "In America we will never have to face the pogroms that our ancestors suffered. Here we are treated like equals. It is a good place to live, Rasa. We will be happy here. Our kinderlach and their kinderlach too will be happy here."

Rasa had smiled at him. She trusted his decisions. And so she was doing her best to be happy in this strange and fascinating country.

"I wish mine shvester could be here with us on the high holidays," she said wistfully.

"I know, Rasa. I know how much you miss your sister."

"They would love to come, but they don't have enough money, and we don't have enough to send them. We will never have enough to send them." She sighed.

"Never is a long time. We can't say never. Right now, it's impossible. But only God knows what the future holds."

"Of course, you're right."

Just then one of the temple's congregants came into the downstairs kitchen of the synagogue. He had been a part of the ten men who had come to complete the minion an hour earlier. When he'd gone home his wife told him some very disturbing news, and he rushed back to tell the rabbi.

"Gut tog," he said to Rasa.

"Gut tog, Saul," Rasa answered

"Rabbi," he said.

"Yes, what is it, Saul?" The rabbi stopped what he was doing and turned to look at the young man.

"Have you heard the news?"

"What news?"

"The whole town is up in arms because a four-year-old girl has gone missing."

"One of ours?" Rasa asked. "A little Jewish child from the shul?"

"No. It's not one of ours. It's a little shiksa. Her name is Evelyn Wilson. The goyim are arranging a search party. I've offered to help."

"Oy, Jewish child or not, it's a rachmones, a terrible pity. The poor child. I pray she is not hurt. And there are no words for the pain that poor mother must be feeling. May Hashem give her strength," Rasa said.

"I, too, will help," the rabbi declared. "Let me wash my hands, and I will join the search party with you."

"Vey iz mir." Rasa sat down wringing her hands in her lap. "How horrible this is."

CHAPTER EIGHT

9:00 p.m.

I t was dark outside, and little Evelyn Wilson had still not returned home. A search party was formed consisting of the sheriff, the child's brother, her father, and many of the neighbors. Mrs. Wilson was told to stay at home in case Evelyn returned. The search party scanned the woods for any trace of the girl including the creek where it was feared she might have drowned. The sound of coyotes and the howling of wolves were a constant reminder that Evelyn might have been killed by wild animals. Herbert Wilson had the irrational hope that Evelyn had fallen asleep under a tree and that soon they would find her unharmed. The search party was relentless working through the night, but when there was still no trace of the child by sunrise, Herbert Wilson began to fear the worst. *How am I ever going to live with this? Our lives will never be the same without our little girl*, he thought. *And how can I ever tell Marjorie that there is a good chance Evey is dead? My poor wife.*

CHAPTER NINE

5:00 a.m. the following morning.

The home of Frank, Roger, and Dotty Weston.

Roger forced himself to get out of bed. He hated mornings. The bed always felt so warm and comfortable when the alarm clock rang, but he needed to eat a substantial breakfast, get dressed, and then walk a mile to catch the streetcar so he could make it to the aluminum plant by 7:00 a.m. In the past, his wife had been pretty good about bringing the laundry up from the basement and folding it. But the previous day she had arrived home late from her job at the lingerie factory. She told Roger when he got home from his meeting that she had not been feeling well all day. So instead of filling his drawers with clean clothes, she'd prepared dinner and washed. Then she went directly to bed where he found her reading a magazine when he got home from his meeting.

Roger stared at the empty drawer and cursed what he saw as her newly found independent streak. Before she'd started this job at the factory, she would never have been so arrogant. But now since she was working, she thought she could neglect her duties in the house. He would have preferred she not work. The problem was they needed the money, and he felt she was ignoring her wifely chores as a punishment because he didn't earn enough to support her.

He lit a kerosene lamp, and then slowly he descended the stairs into the dark basement to get his clean clothes. Roger walked over to the clothesline. He pulled down a few pairs of underwear and two pairs of matching socks. Then he heard a noise. Something was moving inside the cedar closet. *A rat probably got in here again,* he thought as he carried the lamp over to the closet. He set it down on the concrete floor and then opened the heavy wooden closet door. What he saw shocked him so much that he dropped the clean clothes he had been carrying. The color ran out of his face leaving him white as porcelain. His mouth went dry. All he could think of was Frank.

CHAPTER TEN

Roger ran upstairs. He was no longer lethargic. All the soft memory of the night's sleep had drained out of him. He was frightened. Truly frightened. He opened the door and looked into Frank's room. Frank was not there. Then Roger raced back into the bedroom he shared with his wife and sat on the edge of the bed. Shaking Dotty's shoulder, he said, "Wake up, Dot."

Dotty Weston stirred in her bed. "What is it?" she said, annoyed. "Please don't tell me you are waking me up to go downstairs for you and get your laundry. I told you when you got home from your meeting that I was feeling sick last night, Roger. That's why I didn't bring your clothes upstairs for you."

"It's not the laundry. Come with me."

"Is it your damn breakfast again? I don't have to get up for another hour. I stayed late last night, so I don't have to punch in until eight today. I'm very tired. And I still don't feel well. I have a horrible headache."

"It's not my breakfast. It's nothing like that. Get up. Please Dot, it's important. I need your help."

She glared at him, but she got out of bed. Then she followed him down the stairs.

He opened the door to the cedar closet. Inside was a child. A little girl with a pageboy haircut, the pink bow she'd been wearing hung on by just a few hairs. Her eyes were covered with a cloth that was tied tightly around her head. Her hands and feet were red from being tied with rope. Another scarf had been pulled across her mouth holding it open so she could not close it, but she could not speak, and her face was swollen from crying. She wore only her underpants.

"What is this?" Dotty said, looking at Roger.

"I don't know. But it looks like this is something Frank is responsible for."

"What are we going to do?" Dotty said. She was shaking all over. "If we let the child go, she'll tell the police that Frank did this to her. He'll be arrested."

"Come into the other room. We have to talk."

The little girl kicked her legs, but she couldn't free herself.

Roger looked at his wife. She closed the closet door even though she could hear the child who was locked inside. The little girl was moaning.

"I don't know what to do," Dotty said. "But we have to protect our son. We can't let them arrest him. He is strange. We know that. We've always known it. But if the authorities find out, they'll put him in the insane asylum, and we might never see him again. He is our only child, Roger. We can't let this happen."

"Maybe he would be better off in an asylum," Roger said.

"How can you say that? He is your son. Do you know what they do to people in the nuthouse?"

Their conversation was interrupted when they heard the door upstairs open. Frank came bounding down the stairs. He still had his jacket on, but he carried a long hunting knife in his hand.

"What have you done? And where have you been?" Roger asked his son.

"I was helping the search party look for poor little Evelyn Wilson. Four years old and she's missing. Have you heard the news?" he said, his voice dripping with sarcasm.

"She's not missing, you idiot. She's down here in the cedar closet. I found her." Roger slapped his son hard across the face.

"Not for long. I am going to kill her. Then I am going to feed her to the wild animals in the forest. No one will ever know what happened to her."

"You are insane." Again, Roger slapped his son hard across the face. Frank's head snapped back. Then Roger spit at his son and said, "I should turn you in myself."

"No!" Dotty screamed. "No. We can't do that. But as for you, Frank, you are not going to kill anyone. Do you understand me?"

Frank looked at his mother. "If I let her go now, she'll tell her parents what happened."

"She won't if we scare her," Dotty said "We have to scare her. We have to tell her that if she ever says a word, we will come to her house during the night and kill her entire family. She'll be too afraid to speak."

"I can't be a party to this," Roger said, shaking his head, disgusted.

"You can and you will. He is your son. Can you imagine what your friends would say if they found out the truth about Frank? We have to do it this way. It's better than killing the little girl," Dotty said. Roger glared at her. She glared right back at him, but tears ran down her cheek. "Do you think I like this? I love children. But I love our son more. I can't let anything happen to him, Roger. Help me. Please help me."

For a few minutes Roger paced the basement running his hands through his hair. Then he stopped and looked at Dotty. "I have an idea," Roger said, rubbing his chin. "There is some big Jew holiday that is coming up in a day or two. How about if I start a rumor that the Jews took the girl? What if I tell the other fellows in that KKK that I think the dirty kikes have the kid? I can take it even further. I'll say that I think they are going to use her blood to make their Jew crackers for their ceremonies for the holiday."

"Interesting idea. I think it could work. But what can we do about her being able to identify Frank?" Dotty said.

"All right, hear me out," Roger said, taking charge as he had always liked to do. "Here's how we'll do it. We won't release the kid right away. We'll keep her here until late tonight."

"She's already been gone one night," Dotty said.

"I know, but we need time to complete our plan. So here's the next step. Are you listening?"

"Yes, go on." She nodded.

He liked that she was listening to him again. He enjoyed feeling important, and he hadn't felt important since she'd started working.

"All right. So when you and I get home from work, all three of us—you, me, and Frank—will dress up as Jews. We'll put black scarves over our heads, and we'll smear coal dust under our eyes. And we can make big noses out of dough. You have red lipstick, don't you?"

"I do," she said, looking encouraged.

"We'll smear it on top of our eyes. I'll bet that she's never seen a Jew, so she won't know what to expect. We'll scare the hell out of her. We'll tell her over and over that we are Jews and that we plan to kill her for her blood. We'll keep repeating it until it sticks in her young mind. Then we'll tell her that we need it to celebrate our holiday. The child is only four. She'll be so frightened that she won't remember anything else. And most importantly, she won't remember Frank."

"That's true. A little child of that age has a very short memory. And just to be sure she doesn't recognize Frank, we will cut all of his long hair off. Then we'll get rid of his stubbly beard and make his face clean. She won't recognize him," Dotty said. "Did you tell her your name?" she asked Frank.

He laughed. "Of course not. I told her I was the forest elf."

"Oh, Frank." Dotty shook her son until she was out of energy. Then she sunk down into a chair and curled up like a frightened kitten. Tears fell freely down her face. "Why did you do this, Frank? Why? I've protected you all of your life. But I'm so afraid that someday you are going to do something so terrible that I won't be able to protect you from the consequences." Dotty was trembling.

Frank shrugged. "I did it to see if I could get away with it."

Roger looked at his son and his eyes shot daggers. "Don't say another word. Don't make me hurt you. You stupid bastard."

"Go on, Roger, I want to hear the rest of your plan," Dotty said to her husband.

"We'll keep the kid locked up here in the closet until late tonight. Kids are scared of the dark. So night is the perfect time for us to release her. But before we do, we're going to have to make sure that she is really terrified. And most important, we have to make sure that she pees in her pants when she hears the word Jews. If we can do that, she won't be able to think of anything else. She'll be so scared she won't remember Frank's face."

"Especially after we clean him up," Dotty said. She was wringing her hands in the fabric of her nightgown.

"My thoughts exactly," Roger said, and he continued. "We'll scare her, then we'll lock her back up so that she is sitting in the dark thinking about the Jews coming to kill her. Then late tonight we will take her out of the closet, still blindfolded. I'll borrow a truck from one of the fellas in my group. I'll make up a story that he'll believe."

"Can you drive it?"

"Sure, I drove a tractor when I was a kid on my parents' farm. Can't be much different," Roger said. "So, anyway, we'll throw her in the back seat and drive until we get close to her home. Then I'll take her out of the truck and walk her for at least a block through the forest in the back of her house, and that's where I'll release her. My bet is that the poor thing will run home as fast as she can and tell her parents that Jews took her. And if all goes as planned, her parents will go to the police right away, and they'll tell them that the kid has come home. And, of course, they'll tell them that the Jews had her."

"You think she'll be able to find her way out of the woods?"

"She'll have to. But don't worry, I'll make sure she can see her house when I let her go. Then tomorrow I will start another rumor among the fellas at the KKK. I'll say that I think the Jews did have her and that they must have released her because their evil plan to kill a Christian child and take her blood had been discovered."

"You think they'll believe all of this?" Dotty asked.

"Oh yes, I'm sure of it. I'd bet that your folks told you about this story of the blood libel. When I was a kid, my parents told me to be careful of Jews because they take Christian children and drink their blood. I've even heard that Jews have tails. These stories have been going on for centuries. And who knows, they might be true. I wouldn't doubt it. You know what they say, where there's smoke, there's fire."

"I've met Jewish girls at the lingerie plant. They don't seem so different than us," Dotty said.

"That's because you don't really know them. They are different. I'd bet money on that. Anyway, I have no doubt in my mind that everyone will believe this story. The folks in town will be wild with anger. There will be so much chaos that the focus will be completely on the Jews. And once again, we will have gotten our son, Frank, off the hook." He sneered at Frank. "And if we do this thing right, we won't have to kill the little girl."

"Yes, I really believe you're right," Dot said. "I think everyone has heard tales of the blood libel when they were growing up. It sounds like a good idea, Roger. That poor child will be so frightened that she won't recognize Frank if she sees him in the street. Poor little thing." Dotty shook her head. "But at least our son will be safe. And with his hair short, and without his beard, he looks so different."

"I like this idea. I like it a lot," Frank said, grinning.

"Shut up before I kill you," Roger growled at his son. "And let me tell you something, boy . . . if you ever do anything like this again, it will be the last time. Because I promise you, I will kill you."

Frank glared at his father; his eyes were filled with hatred. Then he turned away from his father and nuzzled into his mother like a small babe. She put her arm around her son, but her face was lined with worry, and tears were falling down her cheeks.

CHAPTER ELEVEN

An hour later.

On his way to work Roger stopped at the home of the leader of his KKK group and asked if they could arrange an emergency meeting.

"What's this about?" the leader asked.

"You must've heard about that little girl that went missing?" Roger said.

"I have. I think I heard that she went missing last night while we were having our meeting."

"As you know, it's two days before the big Jew holiday. They are walking all over their part of town in their long black coats and with those curly long sideburns. They hide in that temple of theirs and do unimaginable things. Just look at them; they look like some evil tribe. Anyway, I'll bet the Jews took the kid. You know they need the blood of a Christian child for their rituals on those Jew holidays."

"Nothing like this has ever happened in Medina before. But you could very well be onto something. I'm going to call an emergency mandatory meeting tonight. I'll see if Mack can have it at his house. Can you be there after work?" the KKK leader said.

"I'll be there," Roger said.

"Spread the word."

CHAPTER TWELVE

A house in the neighborhood.

The KKK meeting was held in the early evening when everyone had just gotten off work at the home of Mack Jenkins, a man who was a good friend of Roger's. Mrs. Jenkins put out a platter of cheese sandwiches because many of the men had come right from work, still in their work uniforms, and they were hungry and tired. They stood around impatiently; they wanted to get home, but this was an emergency meeting, mandatory too, so they waited to hear why they'd been required to attend. Once everyone was present, the leader of the group called for Roger to stand up and explain why they were having an emergency meeting. "I'm sure all of you have heard about the little girl that's gone missing," Roger Weston said.

There were several responses from the crowd. "Yeah! Yes . . ." Roger could hear the impatience. He knew the men wanted to get home to their dinners and their sofas, so he got on with his story quickly. "I know you are all tired and you want to get on home, but it seems to me that this thing with the little girl is a Jew job. The Jews have some kind of a holiday coming up. I have a feeling that they took that little girl so they could drain her blood to use it for their rituals."

"I've heard of that," one of the men said, with a serious look on his face.

"Yeah, me too. The Jews do that, don't they?" another man said.

"We ain't seen it here yet, I mean, in America, but I heard they did it all the time in Europe. My father told me all about it when I was young. You gotta be careful of them," someone else offered.

"We have to stop them," Roger said. "This could be the start of them doing this stuff in America."

"Yeah, we sure do have to stop them as soon as possible. I have kids."

"Me too."

"I heard about some kind of a case in Chicago a few years ago. In 1924, I think it was. There was these two Jew boys who kidnapped and killed a little boy on his way home from school. Did anyone else hear about that case?"

"I heard about it," one of the members, who was eating a cheese sandwich, said. "That was the Leopold and Loeb case. But the kid they took was a Jew too. This is different."

"Maybe they didn't know he was a Jew," someone else said. "Maybe they thought he was a Christian, and they were planning to use him the same way they were planning to use little Evelyn Wilson, for her blood."

"Could be. Could very well be," another KKK member said, rubbing his cheek.

"But wasn't that little boy, who those two Jews killed, their cousin?"

"Who the hell knows," the leader of the KKK said. "All I know is Jews kidnap children because they need their blood."

"I have three little kids. Hell, most of us have children," one of the men in the back called out.

"I'm sure you all remember that case last year about that little girl in California. It made all the papers," John Anderson said.

"What was her name again?"

"Parker. Marion Parker. She was taken right out of her class in school. A man took her out of her school and killed her," John answered.

"Who did it? Did they catch 'em?"

"Yeah, they caught him," the chief of police answered. "I remember the case very well. But I have to tell you fellas the truth; I don't think he was a Jew. Could have been. But I don't think so."

"What was his name?" Roger asked.

"Hickman."

"Hell, that's a Jew name," Anderson declared, his face red and wrinkled in anger.

"How old is the girl that's missing?" one of the other members asked.

"Three or four. A little thing, or so I heard," Roger answered.

"You think she's dead already?" It was a small-built man who worked in the office at the factory with Roger.

"I couldn't say," Roger said sincerely. "But I sure do hope not. I feel for the poor mother."

"Yeah, me too," someone said, taking a bite of one of the sandwiches that had been put out for the meeting.

Then John Anderson stood up. He was handsome, tall, strong, and the ideal of every man in the room. His voice was deep as he began speaking slowly. "As you all know I wasn't at our meeting last night. It was because I wasn't feeling too good. I had a blasted headache all day at work," John said. "After I got off work, I walked over to the pharmacy right down the street here, but it was closed. My headache was so bad that I couldn't stand it. I walked all the way to the Jew pharmacy because I thought Steinberg the Jew, would be open. You know how the Jews are always open because they'd do anything for money. But I was surprised to find that Steinberg was closed. But anyway, what I think I had better tell all of you is that on my way back home, while I was walking through the Jew neighborhood, I saw the Jew baker's son, Samuel Schatzman. He was walking toward that Jew temple; you know, the scary building where they all gather to do their rituals. He was holding hands with a little girl," John lied. He saw an opportunity to pin the crime on the man who had stolen his girlfriend.

"Maybe the kid was his sister. Doesn't the Jew baker have a daughter?" one of the men asked.

"If I am right, and I think I am, the Jew baker has a daughter, but the daughter is much older than the missing kid. She's a teenager. I saw this child. And I am telling you that she was no Jew. She was white. She looked like one of us, like a Christian child. Like one of your kids. And the poor little thing was only about three or four years old. My bet is that Schatzman was luring this kid to the Jew temple so those filthy rats could sacrifice her to whatever kind of God they believe in and take her blood for their Jew holiday," John said.

The men liked him. They rallied behind him, most of them yelling out, "Yeah," or "John's probably right."

"I'd wager that you're right, Anderson, and that little girl you saw walking with the Jew was the child that's missing," one of the younger men, who worked with John, said.

"Well, what Anderson is saying sounds logical. I think we had better look into it further." The leader of the group nodded his head.

CHAPTER THIRTEEN

After the meeting ended and everyone went home, the leader of the KKK went to see his friend, who was the mayor of the small town of Medina. "Hey, sorry I missed the meeting. I've been working with a search party that's out looking for that little girl," the mayor said.

"That's why I came here. I want to fill you in on what happened at the meeting," the leader of the KKK said, sitting down in a chair opposite the mayor's.

"Go on, tell me. I'm listening."

"Mind if I smoke?" the leader asked.

"Not at all; go right ahead."

The KKK leader lit a cigarette then said, "It's a dirty shame about that kid going missing. Dirty shame, I tell you. And between you and me, I don't think we'll find hide nor hair of her. My guess is she's already dead. But at the meeting, me and the fellas talked about something we think is very important. We all think the Jews took her for her blood to use for a ritual. Some kind of Jew holiday is coming up. I wonder if they needed the blood of a Christian kid. Pity for her folks, ain't it?"

"Sure is." The mayor bit his lower lip and scratched his head. "You know, I've heard of things like that happening in the old country. But it mighta happened here, and we just didn't realize it. Kids have gone missing before. Who knows? Coulda been Jews all along." The mayor sucked air through his teeth, then added, "I'm gonna have the police chief send an officer over to that Jew temple, and see what we can find out. I'll have their rabbi brought in here to the police station, and I'll talk to him myself," the mayor said. "Meantime, I am going to start a boycott on them Jew businesses. I been wanting them Jews out of our town for a long time. This could be just the opportunity I've been waiting for. If we can starve 'em out, maybe they'll leave."

"After you talk to their rabbi, I think you oughta talk to the son of that Jew baker. One of the boys said he saw the baker's son walking with a little girl about the same age as the missing kid. They were walking toward their Jew temple last night."

"You mean Goldie and Irving Schatzman's son?"

"Yeah. I think his name is Samuel."

CHAPTER FOURTEEN

The Jewish synagogue.

The rabbi was counseling a young couple who had come to speak to him when two policemen walked into the synagogue. They found the office of the secretary, who was the rabbi's wife, and demanded to be taken to the rabbi's office."

"I am sure that you are mistaken. My husband has done nothing wrong," Rasa Goldstein said, shaking. Her husband had promised her that America was different. Her husband had promised her that in America Jews were safe. She'd never believed him. And now, the police wanted to see him. Why would they want to see her husband? *Should I lie? Should I say that he is not here? It is a sin to lie. But I feel such a terrible danger lurking right around the corner . . .*

"Take us to the rabbi," the officer said, his voice raised loud enough for the rabbi to hear.

Rabbi Goldstein came out of his office, which was only a few feet away.

"I am Rabbi Goldstein," he said. "What can I do for you?"

"You're coming with us to the police station."

"For what?" the rabbi asked, his voice still calm but with a small element of fear. Then he glanced over at Rasa and saw the panic in her face. He offered her a smile of confidence.

"The police chief and the mayor want to talk to you."

"To me?" The rabbi sounded genuinely surprised. "Why?"

"You'll find out when you get to the station. Now, come with us."

Rasa put her hand over her heart. She looked into her husband's eyes. "Jacob . . ." she said.

"It's all right. It will be all right. We have done nothing wrong."

"Jacob . . ."

The officer pulled the rabbi's coat roughly, and then grabbing his arm, pushed him forward until they were out the door of the synagogue and on the street.

CHAPTER FIFTEEN

The police station.

The mayor and the police chief were waiting in a small examining room when the rabbi arrived.

The young officer shoved the rabbi into the room where the men waited for him.

"I am the mayor, and this is the police chief of Medina. Tell us your name."

"I am Jacob Goldstein."

"Are you the rabbi from that Jew temple?"

"Yes."

"Do you swear to tell the truth, the whole truth, so help you God?"

"Of course."

"Don't get smart," the police chief said. "Just answer yes or no."

"Yes."

"Do the Jews use Christian blood in their religious rituals?"

"Never."

"I said, don't get smart. If you answer anything other than yes or no, I am going to make you sorry. Now, do you use the blood of Christians, mostly children."

"No."

"Never."

"Never."

"I've heard differently."

"No," the rabbi repeated. "May I say something?"

The police chief eyed the mayor, who nodded his head. "Go on. Say what you gotta say."

"We Jews do not use blood of any kind. We don't eat blood either. It is against our religion."

"You know that there is a little girl who lives here in our town that has gone missing from her parents' home."

"I was informed about it, and I was part of the search party last night. It is a terrible thing."

"Yes, very terrible. So . . . where are you hiding her?"

"Me? I am not hiding her. I would never do such a thing."

"And what about that boy, Samuel Schatzman. Did you send him out to find a Jewish child and kidnap her and bring her to the Jew temple?"

"Samuel? What does he have to do with all of this?"

"He was seen walking with the child before she disappeared."

"Samuel?"

"Yes."

"We are pretty sure you have the little girl hidden away, and you are planning to sacrifice her and use her blood for your Jew holiday."

"This is madness. Pure madness. There is no such thing taking place, I can assure you. I will speak to Samuel, and if he has any information, I will let you know."

"Well, that sure is convenient because he was arrested an hour ago. We have him in custody," the police chief said.

"Bring him in here," the mayor said. "Let these two talk . . . alone."

Samuel was brought into the room. He was flung into a chair. The force pushed Sam and the chair into the wall. The rabbi gasped as he could see that Sam had taken a beating. Already his eyes were bloodshot and the skin around them was turning purple. His nose was bleeding and twisted. *Most likely broken,* the rabbi thought.

"Samuel, what is going on here?" the rabbi asked.

"I swear I don't know."

"Were you walking with a little girl last night?"

"No! Never. I swear it, Rabbi. I swear it."

"Where were you?"

"I cleaned up the bakery, and then I went home."

"You were seen walking with the child," the rabbi said gently.

"I was not with any child. I am not lying, Rabbi. I would never lie to you."

"Where were you? Were you at home?"

Sam hung his head. "I cannot lie to you, Rabbi. I was not at home. I got home late. But I was not with a little girl. I never saw any little girl."

"Then where were you?"

"I can't tell you. If I do, it will hurt someone very dear to me."

"You must tell me. The safety of the entire Jewish community relies on it. Tell me, son. Where were you?"

Samuel put his head in his hands. "I have a girlfriend who I am in love with. She is not Jewish. She is betrothed to a gentile boy. But we are in love, and so we meet . . . and . . . we hold hands . . . and we talk in the back of my family's bakery when the bakery closes."

"What is her name?"

"I can't tell you. I am sorry, Rabbi. I can't do that to her."

The police chief returned to the examination room. "So what did you find out, Jew Rabbi?"

"Nothing. The boy knows nothing. He did not take the child."

"But he has no alibi."

"I'm afraid not," Rabbi Goldstein said as he glanced over at Samuel.

"Then we can't let him go." The police chief lit a cigarette. "And as for you"—he pointed at the rabbi—"how about we come and take a look around your Jew temple. How about we come and see if we can find a child hidden somewhere behind a trapdoor or something."

"You are welcome to come and look around our temple. You can look wherever you like. We have nothing to hide," Rabbi Goldstein said. "We do not do these things you accuse us of."

"I have heard different stories," the police chief said as he took a puff of his cigarette. "I've heard that for centuries, after you all killed Christ, you have been using the blood of Christian children for your Jew magic rituals."

"You are so very wrong. We would never do things like this. I just want to say that I felt so blessed when I came to America. I believed that for the first time my people would be treated fairly. I thought that people would be more intelligent. I would never have thought that an old and wicked fairy tale like this would have found its way to such a great country."

"Shut up, Jew, before I slap the lies out of you. I'm going to bring a couple of policemen with us. We'll go and take a look around that Jew temple. Let us just see if we can't find that little girl," the police chief said.

CHAPTER SIXTEEN

The synagogue.

When the rabbi returned unharmed, his wife broke into tears. She fell to her knees at his feet. "Thanks be to Hashem for your safe return," she said as she looked him over to be sure he'd not been hurt in anyway.

"It's all right, Rasa," Jacob said, lifting his wife up from the ground and holding her in his arms. "I'm here."

The police had come with the rabbi, and now they were in the process of ransacking the synagogue. They threw the Torah on the floor. They tore the prayer books out of the cabinets.

"What happened when you went to the police station? And why are the police here now?"

Jacob told his wife what had transpired. "They are here looking for the missing child. They think we have her."

"Oy. Pooh, pooh, pooh. It is just like Europe and Russia. They hate us here too, Jacob. If they only knew that we would never do such a terrible thing."

The rabbi nodded. "It will be all right. They will look around, make a mess. Destroy some of our things. But then with God's help, they will go. And we can clean up."

Rasa took his hands in hers. The rabbi mustered a smile. Then he went on to explain what had happened with Samuel Schatzman. He told his wife how Samuel was protecting the reputation of a non-Jewish girl whom he'd fallen in love with.

"The baker's son? Do they still have him?" Rasa asked.

"Yes, he is still in police custody. They won't release him because he has no alibi."

"Oy vey, this is what happens when one of our Jewish children thinks about marriage with someone outside of our religion. Here in America our Jewish children think that they are safe and accepted. But this proves they are not. I hope they don't kill him."

"Oh, Rasa, so do I. So do I," the rabbi said.

After the police left, Rasa and Jacob cleaned up the mess and destruction the police left behind in the beloved synagogue. Once they'd finished, they went home to their humble apartment to have a light dinner.

"I was so worried, I didn't prepare anything," Rasa said. "Forgive me?"

"Of course," the rabbi said. "Let's have some bread and some tea. Yes?"

She nodded.

There was a fierce knock on the door of the rabbi's apartment. Rasa moved the kitchen drapes to see five police officers. She turned to her husband. "The police are here. They probably want you to come with them, back to the shul."

"Then I'll go," the rabbi said, smiling at his wife.

"I want to go with you."

"No, you should stay here."

"Please, Jacob, take me with you."

He nodded. "All right. Grab your shawl." Then he opened the door.

"Come on, Jew priest," one of the policemen said. "We looked around earlier, but now we want you to show us around your temple."

Rasa held Jacob's hand as they watched the police rummage through the Jewish synagogue destroying artifacts for the second time. They combed through the small temple until they were certain the child was not there. As they turned to go, one of the officers whipped around to face the rabbi. "This ain't over. We know you have the child. We just don't know where. But we'll be back to look around again, so even if you keep moving her, we'll find her. We're watching you. And I promise you . . . dead or alive, we'll find her."

CHAPTER SEVENTEEN

G oldie Schatzman was working at the counter in her family's bakery when she received the news that her son, Sam, had been arrested. Mrs. Morgenstern walked into the bakery and discreetly whispered to Goldie, "Come outside for a minute. I must speak with you."

"What is it, Mrs. Morgenstern? I have a shop full of customers," Goldie said.

"I need to speak with you. I think you'll thank me for being discreet."

Goldie knew Ruth Morgenstern since she'd moved to Medina, so she excused herself and followed Ruth outside.

"Your son was arrested," Ruth said. Then she explained everything Sam was accused of. Without thanking Ruth, Goldie ran inside and grabbed her husband's shirtsleeve.

"Sam is in big trouble. He's been arrested for kidnapping a little girl. He's at the police station. I'm going there," she said.

"Let me go, just in case there is any danger. I'll close the store and go. You go home and wait for me. I'll be there as soon as I can."

"Are you sure?" Goldie asked.

"Yes, I am sure. You stay at home and be safe. Let me find out what all of this is about."

"All right. I'll go home. But please let me know as soon as you can."

"You know I will. Alma is in school, so you won't have to explain anything to her."

Goldie nodded and then she left.

As he always did, Irving handled the customers with kindness and tact. He told them he was going to have to close the bakery due to a family emergency. He gave each of them some free cookies and a challah. After the store was empty of customers, he headed for the police station to find his son.

When Goldie arrived at the empty house, she was unnerved. She missed her family in Berlin, their influence, and their money. She missed her home in Berlin, and she missed her best friend, Leni. Over the past nineteen years, since she'd moved to Medina, she and Leni had corresponded by letter at least once each month. Goldie wished she could talk to her friend. But since that was not possible, she sat down at her desk and began to compose a letter to help calm her nerves.

Dear Leni,

I am looking out my bedroom window at an elm tree. It is lovely, but I am wishing I were at home in Berlin. I can't stop crying. You see, my son was arrested today. He's accused of kidnapping a child. I am certain he didn't do it. My Sam would never do such a thing. I know for sure that he would never hurt a child. I am terrified of what might happen to him. If he goes to jail, I don't know what I will do. My dreams of returning to Germany are ever stronger now that I am facing these problems with Sam. He is wild, like I was at his age, and fearless. My own fearlessness got me into trouble. If I had been a little more tame, I am sure I would not have ended up here in America getting up before dawn to bake bread every morning. I might have been the wife of a man with money, or if I had been truly fortunate, you and I would still be running around all night with fascinating lovers. Oh, how I long for those sweet days when we had no responsibilities. Now, all I have is work, work, and more work. And a son who is in terrible trouble. Oh Leni, pray for me. Pray that somehow I can save my son and return with him and my daughter to Berlin. I know Irving would never go back to Europe. And I don't care. If he wants to stay here, then let him. As soon as I finish writing to you, I am going to send a letter to my father asking him for money for passage to return to Germany. I will tell him that it is only for a short visit because if he even suspected that I wanted to leave Irving, he would never give me the money. But he doesn't need all the details . . . at least not until I am back in Berlin.

Please write soon. Every time I receive a letter from you, I feel as if I am inhaling a breath of fresh air.

Love always, your friend,

Goldie

CHAPTER EIGHTEEN

The home of Roger, Dotty, and Frank Weston.

Roger was shocked at how easy the plan fell into place. The entire town, including the police, the firefighters, many of whom were Klan members, and even the mayor rallied together against their common enemy, the Jews. After the meeting, Roger borrowed a truck from one his friends. He drove it carefully to his home. Once he arrived, he, his wife, and his son all got dressed in long white sheets with black fabric over their heads. They smeared their faces with soot, and they rimmed their eyes with red lipstick and black coal.

"This is fun," Frank said. Roger punched him in the stomach. Frank bent over trying to catch his breath. "He hates me, Mommy," Frank said in a childish voice.

"I'm warning you. Keep that son of yours mouth shut. I can't stand to hear his voice," Roger said to Dotty. "He caused us all this trouble for no damn reason at all."

Once Frank caught his breath, the three of them walked toward the cedar closet. Frank walked behind Roger; he stuck his tongue out at his father when he knew his father couldn't see him.

Dotty opened the door to the closet. Little Evelyn had fallen asleep, and for a few seconds Roger felt sweat pool in his arm pits, and his heart began to race. He was afraid the child was dead. Gently, Dotty took the blindfold off Evelyn's eyes. The little girl stirred awake. When she saw the three ghastly figures, she jumped and then began to cry.

"We are the Jews. We have come to sacrifice you to our God," Roger said, trying to disguise his voice as best as possible.

"Sacrifice means kill. We are going to kill you," Frank said disguising his voice and then laughing in a high-pitched tone.

The Westons spent the next half hour terrifying poor little Evelyn Wilson. They repeated the word Jew as many times as they possibly could. Then before they closed the door to the closet, Dotty asked the little girl, "Who are we? Do you know who we are?"

Evelyn's small face was bright red and covered in tears; snot hung from her nose. She was crying so hard that she was coughing. She shook her head unable to speak.

In a deep, resounding voice, Roger said, "Who are we? If you can tell us who we are, we will let you go home without hurting you."

Evelyn's body trembled.

"Who are we?" Frank said, letting out a high-pitched howl. "Who are we?"

"Jews?" Evelyn whimpered. "Jews. Please, please, Jews, can I go home? I want my mommy."

They closed the closet door.

EVELYN SAT IN THE DARKNESS. Her body trembling. Urine ran down her leg, wetting her underpants. She vomited into the scarf and almost choked as the vomit backed up into her mouth. *Mommy, I want my mommy.*

A few hours later when it was very dark outside, Roger went back to the cedar closet. He blindfolded Evelyn. Then he picked her up and began carrying her. She was kicking her feet and flinging her arms. "Stop it, or I will kill you," he said. "Now, behave because I am taking you to your mommy. So shut up. Once we get to your house, I am going to take this thing off of your mouth. But if you scream, you'll be very sorry. Do you understand me?"

"Yes."

Then although he was disgusted by the vomit-soaked scarf, Roger pulled the scarf down so Evelyn could speak. "And just so I am sure you have not forgotten . . . do you remember who we are?"

Trembling, Evelyn said, "The Jews."

"That's right. Now be still." He put the gag back into her mouth. *Damn Frank*, he thought.

The child did as she was told.

CHAPTER NINETEEN

In the woods behind the home of Evelyn and her parents.

R oger put the little girl down on her feet. Evelyn was crying. He looked at her, and he felt bad for what he and his family had done. But his son had left them no choice. "All right," Roger said more gently than he'd intended. "We are in the forest right behind your house. I am going to leave you. I am going to remove the rope that is binding you and the gag in your mouth. When I am gone, you will be able to take off your blindfold. Then turn around slowly in a circle until you see your house. The lights in your kitchen window are on. That will make it easy for you to find your way. Follow the lights and go home. When you get there make sure you tell your parents who took you. The Jews. The Jews. The Jews."

Evelyn was shaking so hard she almost fell. He removed the gag.

"Do you remember who took you?"

"I don't know," Evelyn said. She was crying hysterically now.

"You have to remember. If you don't know who we are, then you can't go home."

"Jews," Evelyn cried. "Jews."

"Right," Roger said, then added, "Now, wait for a minute before you take off the blindfold. Then you are free to go home." Roger ran deeper into the forest and hid behind a cluster of trees where he watched as the child took off the blindfold. Withing seconds, little Evelyn was running toward her house. She tripped and fell but got up without crying and continued to run. She ran inside the kitchen door. From where he stood Roger saw a woman come into the kitchen. The woman lifted Evelyn into her arms. Roger couldn't hear anything that was going on inside the house. But he knew instinctively the woman and the child were both weeping. An owl hooted. Roger slipped away and quietly returned to his apartment.

CHAPTER TWENTY

The home of Evelyn Wilson.

W hen Marjorie saw her daughter standing in her kitchen, she couldn't believe her eyes. She was sure Evelyn was dead, and still she prayed every night that her little girl would come back to her. So strong was her fear that she would never see her child again, she almost thought Evelyn was a ghost. For a moment she stared at her child. It was Evelyn. Her heart beat faster. Sweat pooled on her brow. It was Evelyn. She was dirty, and there was a large bruise on her arm. But it was her, and she was alive. *Thank you, dear God, thank you,* Marjorie thought. Trembling, Marjorie took her daughter in her arms. She fell to her knees and held her daughter tight to her body because she knew it was by some miracle, an act of God, that Evelyn had been returned to her. The young mother wept tears of joy, tears of relief, tears because she would never again be carefree when it came to her children. She could never again be naïve enough to trust that her children were safe when they went out to play on a sunny afternoon.

"Herbert," Marjorie cried out, her voice cracking "Herbert . . ."

The intensity in his wife's voice brought Herbert Wilson racing into the kitchen. When he saw Evelyn standing there, dirty, disheveled, but alive, and his wife on her knees holding their little girl close to her, Herbert bent his head and sobbed. Marjorie turned to look at him. She'd never seen her husband cry before.

"Where were you?" Ted asked, angry with his sister as he came into the kitchen. "You had Mom and Dad crazy with worry."

"The Jews had me."

"The Jews?" Herbert said, puzzled. "What Jews?"

"I don't know. They called themselves the Jews."

"I'm going into town to tell the police chief that Evey is home. I'm going to tell him what she said about Jews. Meanwhile, you keep the children inside, all right?" Herbert said to his wife.

"Yes." Marjorie nodded.

CHAPTER TWENTY-ONE

The police station.

Herbert walked into the station and asked to see the police chief. Within minutes he was escorted into the office.

"Evelyn came home. Thank God," Herbert said.

"What? When?" the chief of police asked.

"Right before I left the house. I'd say about a half hour ago. But she said something very strange. She said the Jews took her."

"How would she know that? She's only four," the police chief said.

"She says that the people who took her called themselves the Jews. She must have heard them talking."

"Hmmm. Now, if all that's true, I wonder why they'd let her go."

"Don't know. But the wife and I are sure glad that they did. Poor child, she's been through a lot. And we've been through a lot too."

"This doesn't make sense. If the Jews took her to use her for some kind of ritual, then why would they let her go home?"

"Beats me. I'm just glad she's home and safe. And I thought I should tell you what she said. Who knows, this kidnapping of children might be a new problem here in Medina. Jews might start taking children for their rituals. I'd hate to see that happen."

"Do you believe that stuff about Jews stealing children to use their blood for Jew rituals?" the police chief asked.

"I never did before. I thought it was nonsense. After all, I'm an educated man. I have a year of college under my belt. But after this happened to my daughter, I'm questioning myself. I hate to say it, Chief, but it just might be true about the Jews. You know what they say? The Jews are just different than regular folks. They just are not like us."

"Yeah, I know. I've heard the stories about Jews using the blood of Christian children in their rituals. Hell, my grandparents used to warn us to stay away from Jews. They used to tell us all those scary stories, and I've heard them many times since from folks in town." He lit a cigar then continued talking. "Now, I don't much care for Jews. I don't trust them. They are sly and sneaky. And sure as I'm sitting here, they'll con you out of every penny you have. But I never paid much attention to the stories about the kidnappings, the murders, and the blood. We've lived side by side with that Jewish community for as long as I can remember. Some of our residents even go there to buy some of their Jew food. I figured they were harmless. But now I find myself looking back at every time there was a missing child, at every time there was an accident. I'm asking myself . . . were the Jews responsible for a lot of this stuff, and we just didn't know it?"

"Can't say, Chief. But I'll tell you this, I won't go near their neighborhood. My wife used to go and buy clothes at one of their dress shops. I am going to forbid her to do so in the future. And I will make sure my children never go out unsupervised again," Herbert said.

After Herbert Wilson left the station, the chief of police went to see his friend who was the head of the KKK. He told him the child was home and safe. "Why would the Jews let her go? It doesn't make sense."

"I don't know. Maybe they found out from that Jew priest that we knew they had her."

"Very possible. And when they found out that we knew it was them, they let her go," the police chief said.

"Besides, it had to be the Jews who took her. Where would a four-year-old learn the word Jew?" the leader of the clan asked.

"I have to agree," the police chief said. "I think we oughta call another KKK meeting," the police chief said. "Let's make it tomorrow evening. Spread the word. I'm going to ask the mayor to join us."

"Good idea."

CHAPTER TWENTY-TWO

The home of a member of the KKK.

T he men in the KKK looked irritated. They were used to weekly meetings. Nevertheless, these emergency, mandatory meetings were becoming annoying.

"I don't know how many of you have heard, but the little girl who was missing has returned home," the chief of police said.

"Good, that's good news. Then I guess we can figure that it wasn't the Jews," one of the Klansmen said.

"Well, I wish we could say that was true. But when the child's brother asked her where she was all night, she said she was taken by Jews," the police chief said. "She used the word Jew."

"Very strange indeed." The mayor shook his head. "It sounds like the Jews had her and then let her go."

"Maybe, just maybe, the Jews got scared. They realized we were onto them, that we knew they had the kid, so they turned her loose," Roger said.

"Is that Jew boy, Samuel Schatzman, still in police custody?" John Anderson asked.

"Yes," Chief Horn said. "He has no alibi for the night that the child disappeared. So we can't let him go."

"Right," Anderson said. "I'll bet he kidnapped the girl and then gave her to the rest of the Jews. They were probably going to kill her, but then, like Roger said, when they found out that we knew they had her, they had to let her go."

"Now, unfortunately we can't prove anything. So we can't put the Jew baker's son on trial for kidnapping. Truth is, I don't much care for Jews either. So I think we oughta punish them in another way. I say we set a boycott against all Jewish businesses," the mayor said.

"That would hurt them financially for sure. Might even drive 'em out of here," the police chief said. "And we could still prosecute that Jew kid for the kidnapping. After all, he has no alibi. I am kind of sure he took the little girl."

"I'd like to see them out of our town," John Anderson said.

"Good idea," the president of the KKK said, then he added, "Let's set up the boycott."

CHAPTER TWENTY-THREE

The police station.

The following morning on her way to work, Betty Howard stopped at the police station. Her hands were sweating as she held her handbag while she waited to speak to an officer.

"Miss Howard." A tall, slender young officer came out of the back of the police station. "I'm Officer Johnson. How can I help you?"

"I am here because I have to tell the police chief something very important."

"The police chief?" Officer Johnson said, raising his eyebrows.

"Yes, sir. May I please see him?"

"I'll see if he's busy. Why don't you have a seat over there. I'll be right back."

Officer Johnson knocked on Chief Horn's door.

"Come in."

"Sir, there's a young lady here to see you."

"Oh? About what?"

"I don't know."

"Bring her back to my office," the police chief said, sighing. He thought it might be the girl he'd met at a local bar a few nights ago.

He'd had plenty of indiscretions during the course of his marriage. And some of those girls appeared at the station when he didn't call them. They were usually embarrassed and hurt. But most of all, he found them easy to get rid of. All he had to do was tell them that if they spoke out, their reputations would be ruined. And they always backed down. Some cried a little. Others got a little angry. But in the end, they never told his wife.

Betty wore a simple brown dress and matching hat. Her eyes were cast downward as she entered the police chief's office.

The police chief was surprised and pleased to see that it was Betty Howard and not the girl from the bar. "Aren't you William Howard's girl?"

"Yes, sir."

"I've known your father all my life. We went to school together. What can I do for you?" The police chief studied Betty. She was a pretty little thing. But he'd been friends with Bill Howard for many years, and out of respect for his friend, he wouldn't dare try to seduce his daughter.

Betty cleared her throat. She kept her eyes glued to the floor. Shame spread like a red blanket across her pretty face. "You have a boy by the name of Samuel Schatzman here in jail. He's in police custody."

"Yes, that's right. And what about him?"

"Well . . ." She hesitated for several moments. Then she scratched the back of her neck. "I . . . never mind. Never mind. I'll go now." She stood up and fiddled with her handbag. Then she turned to leave.

"Why don't you just sit down?" the police chief said. "You came to talk to me, didn't you? Well then, let's you and I have a little chat."

Betty sat tightly gripping her handbag with both fists. "I don't know how to tell you this. I mean, my folks are going to kill me when they find out what happened. They are going to blame me for ruining their good name around town. But I feel like I have to come forward. It's the right thing to do. And yet . . ."

"Now, just what are you trying to say? Has that Jew boy done something to you? Has he forced himself on you?" The police chief's voice was gentle as he continued, "You can talk to me. I know it's not your fault. I know you're not to blame. Go on, girl. Tell me what you have to tell me. Get it off your chest."

Betty took a long, deep breath. Then still looking down at the hardwood floor, she said, "Samuel has never hurt me in any way. And I know for certain that he didn't take that little girl. Because, well, you see . . . I was with Samuel that night that the little Wilson girl disappeared."

"You? What were you doing with him?" The shock in his voice made her silent.

She shrugged, but tears had begun to fall down her cheeks.

"Did it have anything to do with the little Wilson girl?" the police chief asked.

"No, nothing. We had nothing to do with the child. We never saw the little girl," Betty said.

"Well then, what happened?"

Betty shrugged. The police chief handed her his handkerchief, and she blotted her tears.

"Now, Betty, like I said, you can talk to me. Are you sure that the Jew boy didn't do something bad to you? I know sometimes when things happen to a girl, folks will mistakenly blame the girl. But I won't blame you if he did something to you. It's not your fault. Now, come on, girl. You can tell me what happened."

"No. Sam has never done anything bad to me. He and I . . . well . . . he and I . . . we have been keeping company."

"You have been keeping company with this Jew boy?" The police chief looked at her shocked. "This is a small town. I thought you were engaged to that Anderson fella."

"Yes, I am. But . . . Samuel and I. Well, Samuel and me. We are in love."

"In love? You're damn right your folks will have a fit when they find out." The police chief took a cigar out of the drawer of his desk and lit it. Then, shaking his head, he added, "Maybe we ought to keep this a secret. Maybe we shouldn't tell anyone. Let the Jew rot in jail. Let him be tried for kidnapping."

"I can't. I won't leave Samuel here in jail to be punished for a crime he didn't commit," she said as a tear trickled down her cheek.

"You know that the whole damn town is going to turn against you if you say you were with this Jew boy, now, don't you?"

"Yes, sir. I am aware." She wiped her nose with his handkerchief.

"And you still want to go through with this?" He scratched his head. Then he looked her square in the eyes. "Well, let me give you one more chance. And I'm only offering this to you on account of the friendship between me and your pa. So take a moment and think it over real good."

She looked at him. "What are you saying?"

"I'm saying that out of respect for your father, I am willing to pretend that you never came here. I'm willing to bury everything you told me and go forward with prosecuting the Jew boy for kidnapping."

"I have to tell the truth. I know it will destroy my reputation in this town. But I can't sleep, and I can't eat as long as Sam is in that cell. I won't let Sam pay for this. He did nothing wrong. He had nothing to do with that little girl going missing. I am sure of it."

"So you want me to tell the world that you, Betty Howard, are Samuel Schatzman's alibi for the night that the Wilson girl disappeared? You want me to say you were with the Jew boy?"

"Yes, sir."

"All right, then, I'll put out a notice that the Jew has an alibi."

CHAPTER TWENTY-FOUR

Samuel was released later that afternoon. Before he was released, he was informed that Betty had come to see the police chief and that she'd told him she and Samuel were together on the fateful night in question.

He left the police station, still trembling, and rushed home. His clothes were filthy and disheveled, and he was exhausted from spending two nights trying to sleep on a wooden board in the jail cell. But he could have endured all of it, all except the terrible heartsick feeling of guilt he had. And this feeling of guilt was because he knew Betty was going to face terrible consequences for her actions.

His parents were at work, and his sister was at school when Sam arrived back at his parents' home. He was sure the news of his release had not yet reached his family. Soon they would hear about him and Betty. They would be shocked. They would wonder how he could keep the secret from them. All the customers in the bakery would flood him with questions. And the truth was that Sam was too tired to explain. He dreaded going back to the bakery where he would be forced to face all his Jewish friends and neighbors. But he longed for Betty. He had so much to say to her. He racked his brain. *If only I could somehow find a way to speak to Betty. She is going to go through hell once her family and friends find out, and she needs me. How can I go to her? What can I do for her?* he thought. But he dared not go into the gentile sector of town and search for her.

Samuel fell asleep on the sofa. He slept for two hours before there was a knock on the door. Groggy, he got up, wiped his eyes with the back of his hand, and opened it. There stood Rabbi Goldstein.

"How are you, Samuel?"

"I am all right. The two nights I spent in jail were brutal."

"Yes, I am sure they were. Can I come in?"

"Of course. I'm sorry. I had fallen asleep, and I am still a little sleepy. Come in. Sit down."

Before the rabbi walked inside, he kissed the mezuzah that was mounted over the side of the door. Then he sat down on the sofa.

"Can I get you a something to drink?" Samuel asked.

"No, thank you," the rabbi said. "I came to talk to you because there is a lot of noise about you and a gentile girl. The girl's name is Betty Howard?"

"Yes, Rabbi," Samuel said, not looking the rabbi in the eyes.

The rabbi nodded. "You were with her the night the child was taken?"

"I was."

"She loves you. She loves you enough to put herself and her family through a lot of shame in order to save you."

"I know. I love her too."

"This is not good for either of you. You are a Jew. I realize that this is America. But believe me, even here we are only a step away from another pogrom," the rabbi said.

"What can I do?"

"Once you are declared innocent, you must leave Medina. You must go where no one knows you. Where no one equates you with the blood libel. Where no one can look at you and remember the terrible things you were accused of. Because even if you are declared innocent, you will never outlive the stigma. The gentiles will always look at you with fear, and that fear is what has caused pogroms in the past."

"But my life is here in Medina. My family is here. The Jewish community I grew up with is here. Rabbi, you are here. You performed my bar mitzvah. This is my home."

"I know. And I am asking a lot of you. But the Jewish community is suffering. There is a boycott on our businesses. And, who knows, things could get worse. People could get hurt. It appears that you have been singled out by the non-Jews as the enemy. A dangerous enemy."

"Why, do you think? Do you think I am the enemy? Do you think I am dangerous? I've done nothing wrong. I've never hurt anyone intentionally. The love Betty and I feel for each other just happened. We didn't plan it."

"No, you haven't done anything wrong. Not really. And you are not dangerous. But it is difficult to be a Jew. When one of us steps away from our religion and wants to marry a gentile, there is always trouble for the Jews. The gentiles are appalled at what they feel is a crime. You have taken one of their own as your girlfriend. And from what I understand, this girl was engaged to a gentile boy."

"Yes, I know. I knew about it."

"And you were seeing her anyway?"

"Yes, Rabbi. At first it was innocent. And then . . ."

"I wouldn't be surprised if her boyfriend started this horrible rumor about our people taking the little girl to use for her blood. This could get bad, Samuel. It could get very bad for us, for your Jewish friends and neighbors. I am ashamed that I must ask this of you. I wish I had the courage to stand up and fight. But it is not only me I am worried about. It is our entire community."

"Then I will do as you say, Rabbi."

CHAPTER TWENTY-FIVE

After the rabbi left, Samuel could not go back to sleep. He was still worn out, but he gazed out the window instead. A half hour later, his mother came home. Goldie was red faced and out of breath, practically hysterical.

"The rabbi came to the bakery and told me that you'd been released. For God's sake, Sam, what happened? What did you do? Look at you—just look at you. Are you all right?"

"Yes, I'm fine, Mother," he lied.

"I have had it here. I want to go home to Berlin. You and your sister will come with me," his mother said.

"But, Mother . . ."

"I don't want to hear a word out of you. Not after what you have done." Then she took a deep breath and continued, "Do you have any idea what is going on here in town? The goyim are boycotting our businesses. The bakery is sure to suffer. All I know is that if you had been in Berlin, you would have never been with a shiksa. You did that because there just aren't enough Jewish girls here. This is all my fault. I should never have come here." Glaring at him, she continued, "As soon as I receive money from your grandfather for our passage, we are leaving."

"What about the bakery?"

"Your father refuses to leave. We've been fighting since your arrest. He can stay if he chooses. I don't care. We are going. You are my child; you will do as I say."

Samuel stood up and began to pace. The last thing he wanted was to be the reason his parents separated. But he also had no desire to leave America. He loved this country. He was born here. And that made him as American as the goyim, who hated him, didn't it? "I'm sorry, Mother. I don't want you and Father to fight."

"By the way, who in the hell is this Betty Howard? This is the first I am hearing of her."

"A girl I've been seeing."

"Not just a girl, Sam: this girl is a shiksa."

"Yes, but you already knew that, didn't you?"

"I did. I heard everything. Not from you, of course. But the whole town is talking about you. They think you are the reason for the boycott of their shops. They blame you for all of this. Sam, just look at the trouble you've caused for me and your father and for everyone else. This could get worse. The goyim could decide to hurt us, even kill us, like they did in Russia and in Europe. My grandmother used to tell me about the pogroms in Russia. You can't imagine the terrible things the Russians did to the Jewish people. You might have brought down the wrath of the devil on us all. Oh, Sam, tell me, please, that you had nothing to do with taking that child."

"Of course not. I would never do anything like that. You should know me better, Mother."

"I thought I knew you. But, of course, I never knew about this Betty Howard girl. So I had to ask. I had to hear it directly from you. I wanted you to say it."

"I've said it. I had nothing to do with the child's disappearance."

"And about the shiksa? What about that? I don't understand you, Samuel. You have always been able to tell us everything, haven't you? How could you have kept such a thing from us? How could you have lied to me?"

"I didn't lie to you. I just didn't tell you. I knew it would upset you, and so I just didn't tell you. Look how you are responding now that you know. This is what I thought you would do."

"Oh, Samuel, what were you thinking? When you play in the goyim's playground, you get into trouble. They don't like us. They don't trust us. And now . . . just look what you've done. Do you love her?"

"You really want to know?"

"Yes." She whirled around to look at him.

"Yes, I do, Mother."

Goldie shook her head and wrapped her arms around her chest. "Well then, I'm sorry for you. But you are still my son, and as long as you are living under my roof you will do as I say. And I am telling you that you will have to forget about her. You will come to Europe with me. I promise you that you will love Berlin. It's a very modern city. And from what I hear, it's become a home for artists of all kinds. We are going home."

"But what about Father?"

"Your father can do as he likes. I don't care what he does. I come from a wealthy family. I was too good for him when we were married. I am just waiting to hear from my papa. The sooner we get out of here, the better."

"I don't want to go to Europe, Mother," Samuel said. He held open the blood-red velvet drapes that covered the big picture window in the living room, so he could gaze outside.

"But you will go with me. Whether you like it or not," Goldie hissed, her face firm like a mask. Her parents had made decisions for her. Now she would make decisions for her children.

CHAPTER TWENTY-SIX

S amuel didn't have the strength to fight. He went to his room. He did not wish to talk to his parents anymore that evening. Sitting down on his bed, he sighed. *I must speak with Betty.* Then he looked up at the clock. She would be leaving the factory where she worked, in a half hour. If he left now, he would be able to catch her on her way home.

"Where are you going?" Samuel's mother glared at him as Samuel grabbed his coat and hat from the coatrack.

"I'll be back soon."

"Samuel, you . . ." She started to speak, but before she could finish her sentence, he was out the door.

Sam had never ventured into the gentile part of town before. Betty had always come to the bakery to see him. He was certain that with all that had transpired recently he would be recognized and not welcome. So instead of taking the streetcar, he walked, staying away from the main roads. When he got to the row of factories, he found the lingerie factory where Betty worked. Then he hid behind the building until he heard the whistle indicating the day's work had ended. Groups of girls came flooding out of the door. Samuel could hear some of their conversations. A group of three were discussing a trip to the movies to see

Charlie Chaplin in his new film *The Circus*. They were followed by two girls who were talking about the latest fashions in *Vogue*. Another group were giggling, something about a boy named Harry.

Samuel was trembling. He knew how dangerous it was for him to be here hiding behind a building after what he'd just been accused of. *Where is she?* he thought. Another two girls came out of the factory door. They were discussing a recipe. "No, don't boil the potatoes. Shred them then put them in with the carrots," one of them said.

Samuel ran his fingers through his dark wavy hair. How much longer? What if Betty was not at work today? After all, she'd been to the police station. Perhaps she had not gone into work. He felt panic rising inside him. He didn't know where she lived. He had no other way of finding her. But then, there she was leaving the building with another girl. A tall, slender girl with a hint of mischief in her blue eyes. The girl's raven-black hair shimmered as it caught the rays of the sun.

"Psssst," Samuel whispered. "Betty."

She whipped her head around and saw him. She looked at the girl with the black hair who was walking beside her. "That's him, isn't it?" the girl asked.

"Yes, Joan. It's him."

"He's handsome. Very handsome. Can I meet him?"

Betty nodded. She nervously scanned the crowds of employees to see if anyone was paying attention. Then once she was certain no one noticed, she grabbed Joan's arm and pulled her behind the building. Before anyone said a single word, Betty and Sam fell into each other's arms.

Taking a breath, Betty remembered Joan was with her. "This is my friend, Joan," she said. "She wanted to meet you."

"Hello. Nice to meet you," Sam said, but his eyes never left Betty's face.

"So you're the cause of all the trouble around here," Joan said, slightly joking.

"Yes, I suppose I am."

"Well, you two, be careful. Betty and I have been best friends since we were kids. I am fairly sure I was the only one who knew about the two of you," Joan said.

"Yes, it was a well-kept secret. At least until today." Betty looked down at the ground.

"I probably should be going," Joan said. Then as she turned to leave, she added, "Well, nice to meet you."

"Yes, nice to meet you," Sam said.

"What are you doing here," Betty asked as soon as Joan left.

"I had to see you."

"You shouldn't have come."

"I know," he said. "Why did you do it, Betty? Why did you do it for me? You ruined your life. You were engaged."

She shrugged. "I love you," she said. "And if you put it that way, I guess I ruined my life the first time I kissed you. I knew then that I would never be happy with John. But you don't want to marry me."

"Oh, Betty. It was never that I didn't want to marry you. Heck, I would give anything to marry you. But I can't see how it is possible. I mean, me being who I am, and you being who you are in a little town like Medina. So I figured I had to be satisfied with the crumbs you were able to throw me. A few stolen minutes here or there." He squeezed her tighter.

"Tell me you love me," she said, hugging him tightly.

"I love you," he said, squeezing her. "Oh, Betty, every time we met in secret, I felt guilty. Guilty for what I was doing to your future. Guilt for my parents. I am so drawn to you. I love you more than I can ever say. And I am drawn to you like I have never been drawn to any other girl."

"And now you know because of what I did today that I love you too. Actions speak louder than words," she said.

"Oh, Betty. I appreciate what you did. And I know you love me. You rescued me. But I never wanted to see you put yourself in harm's way like this. Things aren't going to be easy for either of us. We are in a mess."

"You're telling me. I think they're going to let me go at the factory. I don't know how the people I work with have already found out about this but they have and they're talking. And the papers haven't even come out yet."

"And your parents—what did they say?"

"I haven't seen them yet. But they'll be livid when they find out about us. And . . . John! You know he belongs to that KKK. They hate Jews. Just wait until he hears about this."

"The first thing he'll do is break off the engagement. Then he'll probably come after me," Samuel said.

"I am glad about the engagement. I didn't have the courage to do it. I don't want to marry him. But, my God, Sam. I would die if he hurt you."

"Yes, well, now you won't have to marry him. I can't promise what he will or won't do to me. You know him better than I do."

"I'm scared for you," she said.

"I knew what I was getting into when we started. I am afraid. But I wouldn't change it for the world. Your love has been worth whatever price I may have to pay. I would marry you in a minute. In fact, I plan on it. I just don't know how we will live. Where we will live. I need time to think everything through. We will not be accepted easily. But give me a chance. Let me see if I can find a way. Will you do that for me?"

"I would do anything for you. And I don't care what other people will say. I just hope that John will handle this like a man. I pray he won't get violent."

Sam gently pushed her against the building and kissed her. Then he nuzzled his face into her hair. "Have I ever told you that you smell like spring?"

"Spring? What does spring smell like?" she asked.

"Like flowers, like sunshine, like promise . . . like you."

She giggled. "I can't imagine what sunshine smells like."

"Well then, you'll just have to find a way to nuzzle your own face into your beautiful hair and you'll know."

"You're being silly."

"I suppose," he said. "You make me feel like somehow everything will be all right."

"It will. You'll see," she said, purring at his touch.

"I wish there was somewhere we could be alone," he said, holding her hand in his and gently placing kisses on each of her fingers.

"I don't know of anywhere. My parents will be home in a half hour. I wish I could invite you to come over for dinner . . . but . . ."

"I know. It's all right. I am going to go home. I'll come back, though, in a day or two as soon as I have some ideas of how we might be able to work this out."

"I would run away with you," she said.

"That's what I am thinking. We could run away together. But I need a job. I have to find a way to support you. As much as I would like to think we could live on love, I know it's impossible. So give me a chance to find work. And then I'll be back for you."

"I love you, Samuel. In spite of all the hatred and cruelty we might face from other people for being together, I love you."

He held her close to his chest for several long moments. Then he whispered, "I love you too, Betty. And God help us. Things could get a lot worse than we realize."

CHAPTER TWENTY-SEVEN

On the walk back home, Samuel thought about his relationship with Betty. His mind was restless as he remembered how it all began. He'd never planned on dating a non-Jewish girl. It had just happened. They'd met when her mother sent Betty to the bakery to purchase his mother's, Goldie's, famous challah bread. It was a rich braided egg bread that many of the gentiles had come to enjoy. Samuel, who was working behind the counter, was drawn to the pretty blonde with her expressive blue eyes. She had a friendly and open smile. Betty was not like the other gentiles who came into the bakery. She treated him like an equal. And for the first three months that they knew each other there was little more between them than a few comments about the cold winter weather and a few short conversations about the baking of bread. But then one day Betty came in just as Samuel's father took a batch of rugelach out of the oven. The fragrance of the freshly baked dough filled with homemade apricot preserves filled the small bakery.

"Would you like to try a piece of my father's famous rugelach?" he asked her boldly.

"What is it?" she asked, curious.

"It's a delicious cookie." Then even more boldly, he said, "Here, do you trust me?" as he handed her a small, round cookie.

She took the cookie. Their eyes met. She was not smiling. There was a serious expression in her deep-blue eyes. The subtle question "Do you trust me?" was not lost on her. And somehow it meant far more than just do you trust me that you will enjoy this cookie. It meant do you really trust me. And her eyes were saying yes. She took a bite. He watched her lips as she chewed, and his heart longed to lean over the counter and kiss her. "It's delicious," she said, her voice trembling.

"Here." He put a handful of the cookies in a bag. "Here, take these home. They are my gift to you," he said.

"Oh?" she said, flabbergasted. "Oh."

Betty's lips trembled as she smiled. Then she took the bag of cookies, but she was so flustered that she forgot the bread that she'd originally come to the bakery to purchase.

A few minutes after Betty left, Samuel saw the bag with the bread inside still sitting on the counter. "Dad, I'll be right back," he called out to his father, who was in the back of the store working the oven.

"All right," Irving said.

Samuel took the bread and began to run toward the streetcar. As soon as he turned the corner and saw the streetcar coming, he saw her. Betty was standing alone waiting for the streetcar to stop. His heart skipped a beat. *She is so pretty*, he thought as he walked up. "You forgot this," he said, suddenly feeling foolish that he had come after her.

She took the bread from him. "Oh dear. I did, didn't I. How foolish of me," she rambled. Then she added with a bright smile, "Thanks for bringing it out here. My mother would have killed me."

He knew he should turn to go. He felt foolish standing on the corner where the streetcar stopped, in his white baker's apron. But he wanted to stay longer. He wanted to talk to her. If only for a few more minutes. But he had no idea what he might say.

"I'm glad you liked the rugelach," Samuel stammered.

"Yes. It's delicious," she said, her face turning a soft shade of peach, the color of a blush rose.

It was early spring, and tiny blades of grass were peeking up between the cracks in the sidewalk.

"I have been learning how to make some of the traditional Jewish cookies and pastries. I can make rugelach, too, but not as good as my father's," he said, trying to find something to say. He was feeling more and more foolish. "Do you bake?"

"I try. But I am not very good," she said.

And then the streetcar arrived.

"I have to go," she said quickly.

"Yes, I see," he said, nodding his head toward the streetcar. "By the way, what's your name?"

"Betty Howard."

"I'm Sam Schatzman," he said. His heart was beating wildly. He watched her climb the steps onto the streetcar. As the streetcar began to pull away, he said, "Enjoy the rugelach."

"Thank you again . . ." she called after him.

For the rest of that afternoon his emotions vacillated between fearing that she thought him ridiculous, and giddy feelings of intense desire to see her again. He wondered what it would be like to kiss her. It wasn't that he had never been kissed before. He had. And he wasn't a virgin. About six months before Sam met Betty, he and two of his friends had slipped away for an evening. They'd gotten drunk and then spent a few hours with some prostitutes. It was fun and exciting, but nothing like this. That was pure lust. The feelings he had for Betty, well, that was something more.

Samuel never expected things to go any further. To him, Betty was a dream, a fantasy. She was not a part of his world, and he was not a part of hers. The best he could hope for was an attraction from afar. But the next time Betty came to the bakery, she came when the store was closing. Samuel's parents had left for the day. All the shelves had already been cleared. He was doing the final mopping when she knocked on the door.

"Hello," she said. "I'm sorry I'm so late, but I got off work late. Is there any way I can buy a bread?"

"I don't have any here," he said. "But come in. If you can give me a few minutes, I'll go home and get you a bread."

"You don't have to do that," she said.

"I don't mind at all. Please come in." He ushered her into the back room and pointed to a chair. "Please, sit down. I'll be right back."

Then without thinking about how foolhardy it was to leave a stranger alone in his family's bakery, Samuel ran all the way home. His mother was setting the table for dinner. "Go wash up," she said, thinking he was done for the day.

"I have to go back to the bakery. I need one of today's leftover breads."

"Who came so late to buy bread?"

"Some lady. I don't know her," Samuel lied. Then grabbing a bread, he wrapped it in a clean white towel and quickly ran out the door before she had an opportunity to ask him any more questions. After all, if it had been one of the Jewish women from the neighborhood, Samuel would have recognized her. So his mother had to assume it was a shiksa.

"Hurry back," his mother yelled out the door after him. "I'll hold supper for you."

"No, don't. I want to go by Anschel's house after I close the store. I owe him some money."

"Money? What kind of money?"

"It's nothing, Mom. He loaned me money last week to buy a book. I didn't have any cash when we went to the bookstore. But I have to go, Mom." He was still yelling back his answers to her, but he was already halfway down the street.

Anschel was his best friend. They'd known each other since they were young children. But they were not close until they were about to turn thirteen when they found themselves in the same bar mitzvah class. Samuel was the smarter of the two, and if Samuel had not helped his friend, Anschel would never have made his bar mitzvah. From that time on they'd been inseparable. If, by some miracle, the girl wanted to stay and talk for a while, Samuel knew that Anschel would cover for him.

Sam ran as fast as he could back to the bakery with the loaf of bread tucked under his arm. From the street he could not see the back of the shop as he approached. His heart raced. He wondered if she'd left. Pulling open the door he said, "I brought you the bread." Then he locked the door and went to the back room. She was standing by the table where he rolled out the dough every morning.

"Here. Betty, right? Your name is Betty," he said, feeling foolish again, not knowing what to say.

"Yes, you remembered." She smiled "And thank you for the bread. Sam, right?"

"Yes, Sam." He blushed. "You remembered."

"I did." She smiled. "So how much do I owe you?" she asked, taking the bread.

"It's all right."

"I don't understand."

He shrugged. "I mean . . . well . . . it's a gift."

"You are so kind." She smiled, and his heart lit up. He could almost feel it glowing and lighting up the entire room. "By the way, do you own this bakery?" she asked.

"My parents do. Someday, I will," he said.

"Oh, I didn't realize. I thought you just worked the counter."

"I do. My father bakes. I help sometimes. So does my mom. My sister too. It's a family effort."

She smiled. "That's really nice. It must be fun to have a family business where everyone chips in together. It's not like that in my family. My father works for the aluminum factory. My mom is a housewife. I guess that isn't really relevant." She giggled.

"It's all right. I would love to know all about you." Even as he said the words, he could hear his own voice, and he felt that he sounded foolish. Why do I always feel silly around her? Maybe it's because she's so pretty.

"What would you like to know?"

"Anything you want to tell me."

"I'm eighteen. I work at the lingerie factory. Someday I want to design women's clothes. How old are you, Samuel?"

"Nineteen."

"And what are your dreams? What are your wildest dreams?" She smiled at him fetchingly.

"I haven't any dreams. I guess I just always thought I would take over the bakery. Get married. Have a family. I never thought anything else was possible for me."

"Everyone has dreams," she said. There was a note of sadness in her voice, but she continued. "All right. Let me put it like this. What would you do if you could do anything you wanted to do?" she asked, and her eyes caught the light from the single bulb that hung in the back room.

"I would be a big-game hunter and go on a safari to Africa." He smiled.

"I wouldn't. I would hate to hunt and kill animals." She shook her head.

"Yes, you're right. I'd have to agree with that. I love the idea of doing something brave, but I wouldn't want to kill anything. Maybe I could be a hunter who hunts with a camera instead of a gun. What do you think about that?"

"I like it. I like it a lot." She looked up into his eyes. "But you don't really dream of going on a safari, do you?"

"No, fact is, like I said, I don't really have any dreams. I guess I never dared. How about you, Miss Betty Howard? What are your dreams?"

"You really want to know?" she asked.

"I wouldn't ask if I didn't." He smiled.

"Well . . ." She hesitated. "If I could really have anything I wanted. I would want to be very rich. I'd want a big house and plenty of money. I'd want so much money that I would never have to listen to my father or to my boss again."

He smiled at her. "That would be nice."

She gazed into his eyes. He wanted to kiss her. But he was afraid. The gold cross she wore on her slender neck twinkled in the light reminding him that they were from different worlds. He was just a Jewish kid from a small, often loud, and very Hamish Jewish neighborhood. He came from a place where everyone knew each other and said Good Sabbath to each other as they scrambled to prepare for their Shabbat dinners each Friday before sundown. And she . . . this beautiful blonde, Betty Howard, had magically materialized into his life from another world altogether. Her world was as foreign to him as life would be at the bottom of the ocean. Betty hailed from a mysterious and forbidden world that he hardly understood. Although her home was only on the other side of town, it might as well have been on the other side of the globe. Here in Betty's world, girls wore golden crosses like the one Betty wore today. She attended Sunday dinners which followed church sermons where he assumed, she'd eaten ham or bacon, both of which had been forbidden to him his entire life. There was no denying it; they were different.

While Sam had been lost in thought, the moment to kiss Betty was lost. She looked away. "Thank you for the bread," she said. "I'd better go now."

"I hope you enjoy it," he answered, wishing she would stay just a few more minutes.

"My family loves the challah from your parents' bakery." She said the word challah, and he smiled because her voice inflections let him know she wasn't Jewish. Halla, she said, not knowing how to pronounce the guttural "ch" sound. *She is so cute that she sounds like a shiksa.* He smiled at her.

She returned the smile. "You have dimples," she said.

He nodded. "I know."

"Well, thanks again. Bye."

"Bye."

For a few minutes he stood alone in the semidarkness of the back room of the bakery, a smile lighting up his face and the sweet smell of Betty's perfume still lingering in the air. He liked this girl. He really liked her.

From that day on she came every Tuesday at closing, always after his parents had gone, always while he was mopping the floor. And each Tuesday he saved a challah for her which he gave to her at no charge.

As time passed, their meetings grew longer. They shared stories about everything they'd done the previous week. One Tuesday Betty told Samuel about the movie she and her girlfriends saw at the local cinema. She told the story with such animation that he laughed as if he were sitting beside her in the theater. In turn he told her that his mother had a new recipe for black-and-white cookies, and then he took out a small box with several that he'd saved for her. "I guess I am boring. I don't have anything exciting to tell you. But as soon as those cookies came out of the oven, I thought of you. And I put these away for you," he said.

"I don't find you boring," she admitted. "In fact, I've never met anyone like you."

He let out a short laugh. "I'm your first Jewish friend?" he asked.

"Yes. And . . . you're different than the boys I know."

"Am I? How so?"

"You're serious. I mean you make jokes. Like wanting to go on a safari, but behind it all, your eyes say to me that you're serious about life."

"I suppose I am," he said. "I grew up knowing that it will be my responsibility as a man to take care of a wife and family someday. So I have been working toward that goal all my life."

She looked down.

"What is it?" he asked.

"Nothing," she said, shaking her head. Then she repeated, "Nothing." But when she looked up at him, there was a deep sadness in her eyes. And in that single moment he felt bold and strong even though he was trembling. Then gently he kissed her. *Forbidden fruit*, he thought. *So sweet. So very sweet.*

"I would love to take you to the movies," he said, touching her chin and gently running his hand along the perimeter of her face.

She smiled. "What would our parents say?"

"I can just imagine." He let out a laugh, but there was no joy in it. "Still, I would love to take you none the less. I'd love to show you off to everyone I know," he said, then he took her hand and looked into her eyes. "Has anyone ever told you that you are very, very pretty, Betty."

They kissed again. And again.

Over the next two months, their meetings grew more intimate with long, warm kisses and soft, gentle exploration of their bodies.

Then one night Betty came to the bakery with a tear-stained face. "What is it?" Samuel said, throwing the mop to one side when he saw she was upset. "What's wrong? Is it something I said or did?"

She shook her head. "I've been lying to you. I've been leading you on. Our relationship has to end. I never told you the truth, but I'm engaged to be married."

"You were dating someone that I didn't know about and you got engaged?"

"No, worse. I've been engaged the whole time we've been seeing each other."

He was stunned. He felt as if someone had just shot an arrow through his belly. "Who is it?" he asked, his voice cracking. *As if that really matters*, he thought. *All that really matters is that Betty is going to marry someone else. She will never be mine. I've always known it, but somehow I allowed myself to believe . . .*

"His name is John Anderson. And to make matters worse, he's a member of the KKK. This relationship between you and I can come to no good, Sam. I am so very sorry. I know I am a terrible person. I should never have started this with you, knowing I belonged to someone else." She hesitated, clenching and unclenching her fists. Then softly, she added, "I've come to say goodbye."

"Betty . . ."

He felt as if his entire universe crumbled in that moment. Her eyes were the color of the ocean, and her skin was as soft as a blanket. Her kisses made him feel like he could conquer the world. He loved her. With all of his heart, he loved her. And here she was telling him that he would never hold her in his arms again. Samuel could not speak. He just stood there looking at her, and his hands reached out to her. But she turned away from him, and then the door swung open, and she left the bakery. Once Samuel was alone, he let his knees buckle as he sunk to the floor behind the counter and let the tears roll down his cheeks.

Three terrible weeks passed. Every Tuesday he would hope against hope that somehow she would walk into the store. But she didn't. Sam couldn't eat. He hardly slept. And he thought of nothing but Betty. One evening after work he needed to talk to someone, so he went to see Anschel. His friend could see Sam was distraught, so they went for a walk, and on that walk Sam told him everything that happened between Betty and himself.

"A shiksa?" Anschel said, putting his hands on his temples.

"Yes," Samuel said. "She's not Jewish."

"Oy, Samuel, what are you thinking? You're asking for trouble." Anschel stopped in his tracks to look into Sam's eyes. "And you say her boyfriend, the one she is going to marry, is a member of the KKK? Are you crazy in the head? Those people hate us. They are just looking for a reason to kill Jews."

"I know. I know everything you are saying is right. But I am crazy about her. I love her."

"Love! You might love her, but you can just as easily fall in love with a Jewish girl. You must forget about her. This is the best thing you can do. Maybe you should think about getting married soon. Listen, we are lucky; Rabbi Goldstein is a modern rabbi. He isn't forcing arranged marriages on us. We can choose our future wives. This is nice, huh? You can go to the dance that is coming up this weekend at the shul. There, you'll meet a nice Jewish girl. I was planning to go. So why don't we go together? What do you say?"

"All right. I'll go with you. I'll give it a try."

The weekend came. Samuel dressed in the only suit he owned and reluctantly went to the dance with Anschel. There were plenty of girls. And many were very pretty. If he'd never met Betty, he could have easily found at least one who he would have liked to talk to. But as things stood, he could not divert his mind from Betty.

After the dance Sam and Anschel walked home in silence. When they arrived at Anschel's home, he turned to Sam and said, "It didn't work, did it?"

"No. I'm smitten with her. I don't know what to do. I love her, Anschel. But she doesn't come to see me anymore. I am devastated."

"It will take time, but you'll get over her. Perhaps you should go and talk to the rabbi. He's very understanding. Maybe he can help you."

Sam nodded. "Zei gezunt, be well," he said.

"You too," Anschel answered as he walked up the walk to the door of his home.

Sam had no intentions of speaking to the rabbi about this. He knew the rabbi would say the same things Anschel said. And as much as he would have liked to comply, he couldn't bring himself to date another girl.

Samuel's parents were growing concerned about him too. He had always been on the slender side, but now he was dropping weight rapidly.

"Maybe you should see a doctor?" his father suggested.

"I'm fine," Samuel insisted.

"You hardly eat," his mother complained.

"Maybe it's a phase. I just haven't been very hungry."

But it was his sister, Alma, who offered him the most practical advice. She knocked on the door to his room. "Can I talk to you Samuel?" she said.

"Sure, come on in."

Alma sat down on the edge of her brother's bed. She gazed at him with her serious dark eyes. "It's a girl, isn't it?" she finally said.

"What do you mean?"

"I mean you are in love with some girl, and that's why you're losing weight; you can't eat . . ."

"How did you know?"

"Because I am a girl. I know what it's like to be heartsick over someone. Does she know how you feel?"

"I think so. But we can't be together."

"Why not?"

"It's complicated."

"You can tell me."

Samuel looked at his sister. Then he took her hand in both of his. "Alma, this is not one of those romance novels you are always reading. This is real life."

"I know it is, Sam. But I believe in love, not only in books but in real life."

He sighed. "You are a hopeless romantic."

"I know," she said, giving him a little smile.

"All right, then. Do you swear to me that you will keep it a secret?" he asked.

"Of course." She nodded. "Haven't we always kept each other's secrets?"

He nodded back. They'd always been good friends as well as siblings. "Then I'll tell you everything." And he did.

She wasn't shocked like Anschel. Instead, she just listened quietly. Then once he'd finished speaking, she said, "Would you still want to be with her even though you know she is going to marry someone else?"

"I would want to marry her," he said.

"But as it stands, you can't. So would you want things to go on the way they have been?"

"It's a sin," Samuel said.

"Then you should let her go."

"I want to, but I can't."

"Then be with her on her terms. Go and see her, and tell her that you'll continue to meet with her in secret even after she is married."

"Oh, Alma, I don't know. This is such a terrible sin."

"What else can you do?"

"Do you believe in God? Do you believe that God would think this was right?"

"I don't know what I believe about God and what's right. But I believe in love and you're in love," Alma said, her eyes warm with sympathy.

He looked at her and bit his lower lip. She was fifteen and such a romantic. But what she was suggesting was against everything he believed in. "Thanks for the advice, Alma. I'll think it over."

She squeezed his upper arm. "Follow your heart," she said, then she left his room.

At that moment, Samuel had no plans of following his heart. But Alma had planted a seed in his mind, and the possibilities of it began to grow. He felt a surge of hope as he began to believe there might be a possibility that if he could accept things as they were, he might hold Betty in his arms again. He dreamed of her kisses. And then finally he gave in to the strong desire that pulled him to her and went to the factory where she worked. He waited outside behind the building until the whistle that ended the workday sounded. Bunches of girls came rushing out the door. As soon as he saw Betty, he made noise to get her attention. She turned at the sound. Her eyes flew open when she saw him. Her hand went to her throat as she ran to him where he hid behind the building. They fell into each other's arms without speaking. Then they kissed.

"I've missed you so much," she said breathlessly.

He kissed her again, so swept away by emotion that he couldn't speak. Sam pressed his lips to her forehead, her eyes, and her cheeks; he kissed her lips and her hands. Finally, he stopped for a moment. He held her face gently in his hands and gazed into her eyes. "Do you remember that you once asked me what my dream is?"

"Yes," she whispered.

"My dream is you. My dream is to be your husband."

She turned away from him. A tear slid down her cheek, but he didn't see it because she'd buried herself into him and hugged him. He squeezed her tighter. "I'll come to the bakery this Tuesday, like before," she said. "You best be going now before someone sees us."

And from that day on they saw each other every Tuesday night when the bakery closed. Their short but painful separation had only brought them closer. In the back of his mind, Samuel knew that this forbidden relationship posed a real danger to him. But there was a romantic desperation to their love affair, and both of them found themselves caught up in it. The clandestine meetings continued through the spring and summer, and their kisses grew more passionate.

But still, without fail, every Saturday night Betty would go with her fiancé, John, on their weekly dinner date. It was always the same; they ate at the local diner. And even though on the inside Betty had lost any feelings she once had for John, on the outside nothing changed. They were still to be married that fall. John wanted more from her and she knew it. He constantly asked to see her. She gently refused, telling him that her job was physically taxing, and she was too tired to see him during the week. Occasionally, when he was exceptionally insistent, she would agree to accompany him on a Friday night walk. His kisses were passionate, but too hard and forceful. He kissed her neck and held her tightly. She could feel his hardness pressing against her thigh. But every time his hands wandered to her breasts, she reminded him that she was saving herself for their wedding night. It was only an excuse. She felt guilty about lying to John because she and Sam had been physical for months. They had lain naked together, kissed each other all over their bodies. They had not actually had intercourse, so Betty could make-believe that she was technically still a virgin.

Each time Sam and Betty lay naked together and held each other close, in Samuel's mind they were lovers; intercourse was not important to him. He loved Betty with his heart, his mind, his soul, and his body, like the famous lovers in Greek tragedies. There was no other woman for him. He simply did not see them. Pretty girls came into the bakery. They smiled at him flirtatiously. He returned their smiles, but to him they were just pretty girls. Betty was his everything, his secret wife. And it drove him mad to know when the chill of autumn came, Betty would stand beside John in front of her friends and family and say vows that would make her John's wife. From that day forward she would sleep beside John in the home he provided for her. She would prepare his meals, wash his clothes, and bear his children.

Sam would be nothing. He would be no one to her. All he'd be able to do was watch from the shadows as her life with John progressed. And each night, he would go home to his bed, alone. He knew he should break this thing off. He should marry and have a wife and home of his own. He knew all of this. But still, he could not walk away. Now it had been a year since they broke up and went back together. A year since Sam had learned of Betty's engagement. However, it had not pulled them apart: if anything, the breakup had only brought them closer.

CHAPTER TWENTY-EIGHT

After Sam left Betty outside the factory, on the day she'd declared herself his alibi, he walked all the way back home. It was growing dark outside when he put the key in the lock of the back door. He turned the knob and then returned the key to his pocket, when he felt himself being grabbed from behind by a pair of large rough hands. A pillowcase was flung over his head. He let out a scream, but someone punched him in the side of the face. "Make another sound, and it'll be the last sound you make, Jew." It was a male voice. Then Sam was lifted, flung over someone's shoulder, and carried away. He felt his stomach lurch as fear came over him. He tried to get away, but the man who held him was far too strong. The walk was only a few minutes. Then Sam was tossed onto a hard surface, landing solidly on his hip. His head was still covered. He tried to remove the pillowcase from his face, but someone who had been standing over him kicked him in the stomach. He struggled to get to his feet. But something, he thought it was a man's knee, was pressing hard on his back. His heart pounded. *John has come for me. I've been expecting this, but I'm still so terrified. What can I do? How can I get away? There are more than one of them. I heard several different voices. It's got to be the KKK. And they are going to kill me,* he thought as his panic grew. Samuel could hear the sound of his short, raspy breath inside the pillowcase. *I can't breathe.* Someone grabbed his hands and tied them so tightly that he could feel the rope cutting into his flesh. Then the same was done to his feet. A horse whinnied, and he realized he was in the back of a wagon that had begun to move. *Where are they taking me?*

Again, the horse neighed, followed by the sound of a whip cracking. The wagon began to move slowly at first but gained speed as it left the paved streets. Within a short time Sam could feel that the wagon was traveling on a dirt road. Sam lay flat on his hip in the back of the jolting and tumbling wagon as it rumbled along. Minutes turned into what seemed like a lifetime. The pain in Samuel's jaw where he'd been punched intensified with every bump. *I think they broke my jaw,* he thought, trying to open his mouth but finding it far too painful.

Without warning the wagon came to an abrupt halt throwing Samuel forward. He moaned from the pain in his jaw, but he didn't say a word. Someone pulled his foot until he fell off the wagon and onto the ground. The pillowcase that covered his face moved around, and he realized it was wet. *Blood,* he thought. *My blood.* Samuel tried to stand but his hands and feet were bound. Then he was being dragged by his feet through the brush. He could hear twigs snapping and felt what he thought were branches scraping his bare forearms.

Someone tossed him against a hard object and then pulled the pillowcase off his face. Samuel saw that he had been correct, the pillowcase was covered in blood. His back was against the bark of a large oak tree, and in front of him was a cross made from wood. The group of men all had white hoods covering their heads with small spaces that had been cut out for their eyes. *Oh dear God. I knew the KKK were coming for me. But please give me courage. I am so scared.*

"We're gonna burn you, Jew boy. But first we're gonna cut your balls off and stuff 'em down your throat."

There was no one around. They were in the middle of some sort of clearing surrounded by forest with only one dirt road running both in and out.

The anger and hatred that the group felt toward him was so strong that Samuel could feel it in the air. He wanted to beg. He longed to plead with them for mercy, but he knew they would not grant it. He was certain his pain and begging would only feed their bloodlust.

"You took that little girl, didn't you? You took her, and you gave her to that rabbi of yours. You Jews were going to kill her, but you decided against it once we figured out that it was you who took her. Didn't you?" Samuel didn't know who was speaking. But it was Roger Weston, Frank's father. His face was covered.

"No," Samuel managed to say. "I never even saw the child."

"Liar." Sam didn't realize it was John Anderson, Betty's fiancé, who was speaking. And his head was also covered. "And you had the balls to force a good Christian girl to act as your alibi. You filthy kike." He kicked Sam in the stomach. Sam doubled over trying to catch his breath. Then John continued, "I don't know what you did to that girl to make her lie for you. But I know she wasn't with you. I know it because I know you were busy kidnapping that child for your Jew rituals." John Anderson looked down at Samuel and spit on him and then kicked Samuel in the chest. "You were a real idiot to mess with that girl. She's my girl." Even though he wore the hood, John Anderson had just revealed his identity to Sam. But Sam knew it didn't matter because even if he lived long enough to go to the police, they would side with the KKK. Most of them were members. Everyone in the Jewish section of town knew that. They also knew that those who were not members of the KKK always seemed to be sympathetic to their cause. *So many Jew haters,* Samuel thought.

Then one of the hooded men lit the cross on fire. The smell of burning wood filled the clearing in the forest. Samuel gagged. He felt bile rising in his throat. He had to speak in spite of the pain in his jaw and chest. "I didn't take the little girl."

"Where was she, then, if you Jews didn't have her?"

"I don't know. I never saw her before this all started."

"Liar," Roger said.

They started beating him with sticks and baseball bats. He felt the life oozing out of him. Then someone kicked him in the head, and he fell unconscious.

CHAPTER TWENTY-NINE

The crisp September air smelled of smoke. Samuel lay on a blanket of multicolored leaves in a clearing in the forest. It was two o'clock in the morning when he opened his blood-encrusted eyes to see a full silver moon illuminating a star-filled sky. Every inch of his body cried out with pain. But he was alive. And he knew they had purposely left him alive because his hands and feet were unbound. *They want me to go back and tell Betty that we can't see each other again. They want me to cower with fear and shame. I think John is responsible for this whole thing. He wants me to look like a coward in her eyes.*

Sam struggled to his knees then to his feet. For a moment he leaned against a tree. He was dizzy, and his head ached. Vomit rose in his throat he let it spew from his lips onto the ground, taking deep breaths until he felt strong enough to go home. Once he could walk, he began to slowly head down the path, each painful step leading him back to town.

Gripping his chest, Samuel arrived at home just as his parents were getting ready for work at the bakery. His mother was in the kitchen making coffee when he walked into the house. Her face became a mask of horror when she saw him. Her hand went to her throat and she let out a scream. His father who had been shaving dropped the razor and came running out of the bathroom. Then his sister, hearing the commotion, came running into the kitchen wiping the sleep from her face. His father ran over to his mother who was collapsing and helped her into a chair. "Goldie, are you all right?"

She nodded.

"What happened to you?" his father asked Sam.

"I was at the door to our house when the KKK came up behind me and grabbed me. They took me out to an open field and then they beat me, with sticks and baseball bats."

"I let you take off from work because I thought you needed to rest. Why were you out of the house anyway? You should have been home in bed. Where were you coming from?" His father was rambling quickly. Then he took a deep breath and continued, "You went to the other side of town, the goyish side of town, didn't you? Didn't you? I just know you did. OY, Samuel, what are you thinking? Don't you see you put yourself right in the lair of the dragon. You must leave that girl alone. They will kill you, Samaleh. They have no respect for Jewish life. And you are playing with fire," his father said, his eyes heavy with fear.

"Your father is right. You must leave that girl alone. These boys will kill you, Sam. They will. They almost have. Look at you. Just look at yourself. I was talking to you, and you ran out of the house to go and find this good-for-nothing shiksa, and this is what happened. These boys grabbed ahold of you and they beat you. They probably thought you were dead. But look at what they've done to your face, your shana punim. Your Grecian nose. I can't stand to look at you. You're covered in blood. Have you learned? Have you? Or are they going to have to kill you for you to stop? You tell me, Sam!"

"I'm sorry, Mother."

"Sorry, you should be sorry. Better you should cry than I should cry. Because if I cry it means that you're dead. Sam, please, don't go there anymore.

"But I had to. I had to see her."

"NU? You had to see her? Samuel . . . Samuel," his mother said, then she hit him hard on the shoulder and wrung her hands together. "Kleine kinder lozn nit shloffen, grosse kinder lozn nit leben. Little children don't let you sleep, but big children don't let you live." She clenched her fists then went on. "I can't believe it. I would have thought you, of all people, would have had a bissel seichel. But you have no common sense. You have let yourself fall in love with a shik-sa," his mother said. "You went there to see her. Oy, Samuel! You should have known better. Now, just look at you. My son, my son, a bloody mess . . ."

"I'm sorry, Mother. I didn't do it to hurt you. But the girl has a name. Her name is Betty. And Betty stood up for me. She put her future and her reputation on the line for me. I had to go and thank her."

"And you, you put your life on the line for her. That's more than a reputation, mine kind. You know better; you know that you should not have anything to do with the goyim." His mother pointed her finger at him.

"They love each other, Mom," Alma said. "They are in love."

"Love? Love between a shiksa and a Jew is only trouble by another name. There is no possible love between the two of you. Why would you ever start something like this? Are you crazy?" his mother asked.

"Maybe I am. I don't know. Love is a strange thing. It just happens. It's not something I planned," Samuel said, sinking down into a kitchen chair still holding his ribs.

"Are you wheezing?" his father asked, moving closer to Samuel. "You are. You must see a doctor. Lift your shirt up."

"I'm all right."

Samuel's father lifted his shirt to reveal a large purple bruise. "You have to go and see Dr. Plotnick right away. He has to see if your ribs are broken."

Samuel didn't argue.

"I'll go with you if you want me to," his father said.

"No, I can manage, Dad," Sam answered.

"I'll go with you," Alma said. "I don't want you to have to go alone."

CHAPTER THIRTY

Goldie found a letter from Leni waiting for her in her mailbox when she returned from work. She had always loved hearing from her friend, but this time she was disappointed that the letter was not one that contained money from her father. Without explaining anything, she walked past her husband and daughter and took the letter to her bedroom where she could read it privately.

Dear Goldie,
When I got your letter that said that you were going to ask your
parents to send you money to return to Germany I stood up and did
the cha cha all alone in my flat. I do hope you return. I have missed
you so. I would send you the money myself, but alas, I am just a poor
artist. And to make matters worse, if I do make any money it seems to
lose its worth before I can even spend it. The economy is crazy here.
But Berlin is still the most exciting place in the world. Last week I
went out with the most handsome, passionate man. He belongs to some
silly political group, I think it was called the Nationalist German
Workers Party. I don't know much about it. It really doesn't matter
anyway. All I know was that he was a fabulous lover. We spent an
entire weekend together. Then in conversation I mentioned that I am

Jewish. Well, you can't imagine how he changed. His face became distorted. It was almost as if he went insane while he was telling me how the Jews are responsible for Germany's downfall. He even slapped me when I laughed at him. So that little affair is over. I am not too worried about his small political group. I've seen them ranting in the streets in their brown uniforms. But no one seems to pay them any attention. Still, I must admit, I was hurt that he had such nasty things to say about Jews. And I was even more hurt that he pushed me aside so easily. Enough about that stupid bastard. You know what they say about men, don't you? Men are like streetcars, and there will be another one along in about ten minutes.

I was sorry to hear about Sam, and I am very concerned about him. I hope that by the time you receive this, the mail being as slow as it is, things will have resolved themselves in your son's favor. I would pray for him, but I have recently joined a new order. We study Nietzsche, and I have decided to become an atheist. But you know me, and I can't promise how long this romance with atheism will last. After all, last month I was fascinated with Hinduism. That is, of course, until one of my author friends from Paris took me out for a steak.

I send you my love. Please keep me posted on everything. Remember when we were children, and your parents would forbid you from seeing me for a while? They never liked me. But I am sure you must remember how we used to close our eyes and send each other mental messages? Whenever you feel alone, Goldie, just close your eyes and speak to me. I will always send you back a mental answer.

Leni

CHAPTER THIRTY-ONE

After Samuel and Alma left, Goldie turned her attention to her husband. They were sitting at the kitchen table. She poured them both cups of tea. "Irving, I was serious when I told you that I am going home to Germany. I've sent a letter to my father asking for money for passage for me and the children. I would write another letter and ask him to send money for you, too, if you change your mind about coming with me. I don't want to be here in America anymore. I want to go to a more civilized place." Goldie was an internal battlefield of emotions. On the one hand she would be glad to go home again and to be far away from Irving and the bakery. The very idea of Berlin with its artists and musicians excited her. But on the other hand, when she thought about actually leaving her husband, she felt insecure. They had been together for a long time, and even though he bored her, the idea of never seeing him again was a little frightening. In his quiet way, Irving had been her rock. He managed the finances, finding ways to provide her with a few of the luxuries she had always longed for by denying his own needs. When she gave birth to each of the children, they had not been able to afford a nurse, so when Irving got home from work, he took over the care of the children so his wife could rest. *He is not a bad man*, she thought. *Just not an exciting one.*

"I really wish you'd stay here in America with me, but I can't keep you against your will. I've done everything I can over the years to make you happy. But I've always known that you were less than satisfied, Goldie. You came from money. You came from cultured people. I could never give you the life you expected. I have often regretted marrying you. Not because you didn't make me happy. You did. But because I knew how much I failed you." He hesitated, then he took a deep breath. "Meanwhile, I think we should close the bakery and move out of Medina. If we stay here and Samuel continues to see that girl, those boys from the KKK will eventually kill him. It's a terrible shame because I worked my whole life to build a business like the one we have now. In the past I would sit outside and smoke my cigar and think about how lucky we are. We have our own home. Our own home, Goldie. For a man like me that is something! We always have food on our table and clothes on our back. I know that I can't give you the furs and diamonds your mother had. But I have given you the best life I can. And not only am I losing you, but now I must give up the bakery too."

"Are you sure it's necessary for you to close the bakery?"

"Yes, the rabbi came to see me. He asked me to move away from Medina. He said that the situation between Sam and that shiksa caused problems for all the Jews in town. I have to go. I have to close the business and go."

"Where do you want to go? Where can we go?"

"So you will go with me?" he said, his face lighting up.

"I have to go with you until I hear from my father. If he sends me money, I'll return to Germany. If not, I'll be stuck going wherever you decide to go."

"You'll hear from your father. Your parents will send you the money."

"Are you sure you don't want to go back?"

"I'm sure. I am staying here in America. There is opportunity here for a man like me."

"You did as well as you could in Medina," she said.

"I tried," he said.

She nodded. "You did."

"Don't look at me like that," he said.

"Like what?" she said, turning away from him.

"Like you pity me."

"I do. I know how hard this is for you."

"Do you, Goldie? Do you have any idea? I grew up poor. My father worked for a baker his whole life. Then I worked for the same lousy goy who treated me like dirt. Every day I went to work. I had to give most of my money to my parents to keep up the small, dirty rat-infested apartment where we lived. But that didn't matter. Every penny I could save I saved so I could have my own bakery someday. Then what good fortune! I met you! Never in my wildest dreams would I think a girl like you would even speak to me. But you needed help, and I was more than happy to be the man to help you. I was so honored to be your betrothed. More than you could ever know. I was walking on air, Goldie, walking on air."

"I know," she said, looking away from him.

"And then I felt like God himself had kissed my forehead when my cousin agreed to help us come here to America and to help me open the bakery."

She felt tears form in her eyes. She cared for him deeply, but love? She didn't love him. And having once known love, with the man who fathered Samuel, she knew the difference. *Yes, I pity you. I pity you because you love me so damn much,* she thought.

"And now, look at us. We have a terrible choice to make. Either we give up the small house and the bakery that we worked so hard for, or we risk the possibility of some hoodlum killing our son. So what do we do? You tell me? I will not throw my son out of our home just because other people want him out of town. If he is forced to leave Medina. I will go too," Irving said firmly.

"I want to go home to Germany. Go home to my parents. Ask them to help us. They have the money to help us open a bakery in Berlin," she said, but then she thought, *Samuel is not your son, yet you treat him as if he is your most precious boy. I could not ask for a better man than you, Irving Schatzman. And . . . yet . . . why can't I be satisfied? Even if you came home to Germany with me, I would never be satisfied with you. There would always be that nagging, deep longing for more. I am a terrible woman, a woman who should be ashamed of herself. A part of me will be lost if Irving doesn't come with me, and another part of me tingles with excitement at the thought of finally being rid of him.*

"We are living in the greatest country in the world. Do you have any idea how much I had to beg my cousin to sponsor us to bring us here? I never want to go back to Europe. Besides, if I go with you, we will be dependent completely on your father. And I don't want that. I feel that a man must support his own family and I am a man. It is my responsibility to take care of you and the children. So if you are coming with me, then I think we should move to Manhattan. To a place I've heard of called Delancey Street. I hear there are a lot of Jews there. I have a little money saved. Not much but enough to open a small bakery."

"Delancey Street? What is it?"

"It's a primarily Jewish area right in the middle of New York City. I hope that somehow you will like it there. Perhaps you'll change your mind about going back to Germany and decide to stay. Manhattan is a big place. Not a small town like Medina where everyone is in everyone's business. And besides, there will be concerts and theater, and museums with art, all the things you love, my sweet Goldie."

"You've always been such an optimist, Irving. You've always had a way of looking on the bright side. Even when there is no bright side. I know you think that moving to the city is the answer for us. And even after this terrible thing happened to our son, you still trust this country. Don't you?"

"America? I never said I trusted it. I am a Jew. I know that I must always be watching behind me. But I believe that this is a good country. One of the best, especially for Jews. It's a civilized country. I mean, we haven't seen any Cossacks on horseback wielding swords as they kill everyone in our neighborhood, have we?"

"The KKK are the same thing as the Cossacks. Only they come in the night instead of the middle of the day. Besides, the Cossacks were in Russia, not in Germany."

"And you think Germany is better?" he said.

"You don't? Germany is the home of culture. It gave the world wonderful composers like Beethoven, Brahms, and Strauss. Incomparable artists like Leutze, and Nast. And brilliant writers like Hesse and Schiller. America is all shiny and new, but it has no culture."

"I have to agree with you there. But Germany is no friend of the Jews either."

"Who is? But at least the Germans are far too advanced of a people to act like this. They would never employ Cossacks like the Russians. Or allow groups of men with white sheets over their heads to attack innocent people."

"You could be right. I don't know. I know that there is no land where a Jew is safe. Perhaps someday there will be. Perhaps someday we will have a homeland. But for now, I will tell you this, America is the land of opportunity. It's a place where a man like me can open his own business and earn a decent living."

"Don't you ever miss being home? The delicious authentic food, the music? All of it?"

"Of course I do. I miss my parents, my sisters, my older brother, and his wife. I know they have a son who I have never seen. I sometimes feel bad about that. But, Goldie, our lives are here now. People in Europe would give anything to be here in America."

"The poor, yes. Not the rich."

"Like your parents."

"Yes, like my parents."

"Well," Irving said, hanging his head, "if you want to go home, and your father sends you the money, there is nothing I can do to stop you." He looked at her with pain in his eyes and continued, "I think you should know that I'm going to sell the bakery to Shlomie Jacobson."

"You've already talked to him about this? I would have thought you would have talked to me first. I mean at least you would have included me in the discussion."

"It wasn't that I didn't want to include you. It just happened. I saw him when I went to the butcher shop after work this afternoon. I knew he always wanted to buy the bakery. He's told me before. So when I saw him, we talked. I mentioned that we were thinking of moving. He was very interested in buying the bakery. It wasn't that I went to him before I spoke to you . . ."

"But you did. You've already put all of your plans into motion. And now you come to me to tell me exactly what they are. You don't ask me what I think. You just tell me that this is what you are going to do." She folded her arms across her chest.

"Goldie, why are you always looking for a reason to fight with me?"

She shook her head and stood up. Then she walked out of the room leaving her cup of cold tea on the table. She went into their bedroom and slammed the door. Irving was right. She was always picking fights with him. It was because nothing about him made her happy. Then she lay down on her bed and slammed her fist into her pillow. *Why is it taking my father so long to send the money? What if he never sends it?*

CHAPTER THIRTY-TWO

Before the sale of the bakery was finalized, Irving took Goldie into the city to see the store he planned to rent and the area where he planned to move his family.

Delancey Street was a lower-class neighborhood. The streets were cluttered with vendors of all sorts. Scrappy children ran and played in the streets between the shoppers and the workers. Goldie looked around her. A woman in a housedress, that was so worn it had lost its color, was haggling over the price of potatoes with a fat man in a filthy white apron. Two young boys ran through the crowds almost knocking an old woman over as they dashed by with apples they stole from an apple cart.

"Goniffs! Thieves!" Goldie said in disgust as the two boys ran past. Then she grimaced at the piles and piles of horse manure that had collected on the streets.

"This is it?" Goldie asked her husband. "Feh! This is like the poor section of Berlin. Why would we want to move here?"

"There are a lot of Jewish families here. We are good bakers. We offer a good product. Our bakery will be a success here."

Goldie glared at him. "This is horrible. It's dirty, and these people are prost; they are low class and ignorant. I hate it here already." *As soon as I get that letter from my father with money for passage home, I am leaving. I will die if I have to live here. What if my father refuses to help me? What if he still hasn't forgiven me for getting pregnant out of wedlock,* she thought and felt a terrible pang of despair shoot through her.

A vendor yelled out, "Fresh ripe strawberries, firm cabbage, and leafy lettuce."

"Come, Goldie. Please, give it a chance. Just let me show you the store I want to rent," Irving said hopefully.

She nodded, but she felt hot tears stinging the backs of her eyes.

They walked for half a city block until Irving stopped. "This is it," he said proudly.

She nodded with a bitter smile on her face. *How can he be so optimistic about this? He's losing everything, our family business, our home, everything. And he's doing it all for Sam. Even though he knows Sam isn't his. I should be happy he loves Sam the way he does, but I can't help but think of him as a fool.*

It was a big storefront with a large picture window perfect to display cakes and breads. The wood floor was clean and polished.

"Do you like it?" he asked. "It's right on the main street. There will be lots of potential customers walking by." Irving took his wife's hand. "Please, stay here with me. Don't go back to Germany."

She shrugged her shoulders. She might have to stay. If her father didn't send money, she would not be able to leave. Manhattan was a dirty, congested place. She didn't like it. But she tried to think of some of the good things it offered. *At least it is full of life, and it's not boring like Medina. And if we have a nice home I might be able to tolerate it.* "Where would we live?" she asked.

He was so encouraged by her question that his eyes lit up. "We won't be able to buy a house right away. But if you trust me, I promise you, I'll buy you a home of our own as soon as I can."

"So if we can't buy a house, then where would we live?" she asked again.

"For a while"—he hesitated, then he took a deep breath and continued—"we would rent an apartment."

"In one of these tenement buildings?" she said, her face screwing up into a grimace.

"Just for a short while," he said, his voice tender. He smiled softly and caressed her shoulder gently.

She wanted to shake him off, but she resisted the urge. "Can we go inside and see one of these apartments?"

"Yes, let's walk up the street and see if we can find a For Rent sign."

They walked for less than a block, and there stood a sign that read Rooms for Rent Upstairs, with an arrow pointing to a door. It was in the window of a storefront that read Aronnson's Delicatessen.

Irving led Goldie to a small separate door which was located outside the deli. It creaked as he opened it for his wife. Goldie walked inside. There was a pungent odor of garlic and salami in the hallway which made Goldie gag. To the left there were two rows of three mailboxes totaling six in all. On a door to the right hung a large crudely written sign that read Apartment Manager.

Knocking three times on the door, Irving turned to his wife and mustered a smile. She did not return it. Then a young woman, with greasy blonde hair wrapped in a knot at the base of her neck, wearing an old, shapeless housedress and carrying a baby on her hip opened the door.

"Yes?"

"Hello, I'm Irving Schatzman, and this is my wife, Goldie. We'd like to see the apartment you have for rent."

"One minute," she said in what sounded like a Polish accent. Then handing the baby to a boy of about twelve, "Avi, watch your brother. I'll be right back."

"Yes, Mama."

Then she turned to Goldie and said, "It's nothing fancy, but it's clean." They walked up three flights of stairs, and when they got to the top, the woman opened a door. As soon as she flipped on the light switch, cockroaches scattered. "Well, this is it. Come on in." Goldie turned to Irving, who nodded. Then they followed the woman inside.

"There are two bedrooms. Bathroom's down the hall. It's for the whole floor. It's not my place. I mean, I don't own it. I just work for the fella that does, so I can tell you the truth. You won't be likely getting much heat in the winter or hot water," she said, "but at least, it'll cost you a little less than two dollars a month."

Goldie looked around the room and imagined her furniture in this place. The very idea was appalling.

"When would you want to move in?" the woman asked.

"About a week," Irving answered.

"Well then, I am going to need some kind of security deposit to hold the place. Apartments that are this cheap go fast around here. So if someone else comes and I don't have a deposit, I'm going to rent it. By the way, I'm Miriam Finkelstein."

"Nice to meet you," Goldie managed. "Would it be all right if my husband and I took a moment alone? We'd like to discuss this," she asked.

"Sure," Miriam said. "I'll go back down to my apartment. Just knock on my door, and let me know what you want to do."

Goldie thought she might cry. "This apartment is horrible. I can't believe how horrible. At least we had a nice place to live in Medina." *On the one hand there is a lot of activity on the street and a lot going on. That should bring us plenty of business. And there will be a lot of things to see and do. I do like that, at least, until I can return home to Berlin. But on the other hand, we are living in a dump.* She groaned. "This apartment is so small and dirty. And can you just imagine if our friends back in Medina saw this place? What would they think of us? Where will we put the children? It's not big enough for the two of us, let alone the children. Alma and Samuel each need their own rooms. They are too old to share a room. I'm sorry, but I can't stay here. I want to go home to my parents. If my father sends the money, I am leaving as soon as I can."

He took her hand. She tried to pull away, but he held it tightly. Then he begged her, "I know you are not used to living in an apartment, but it won't be for long. I will work hard. I will find a way, Goldie. I will buy you a house."

She just shook her head and gritted her teeth. "We do have to move from Medina, don't we? Are you sure that we can't stay in Medina anymore?" she said more to herself than to him. *Please Papa, please send me the money. If you don't, I am doomed to live in this horrible place.*

"I'm afraid so. It wouldn't be safe for our family. And it wouldn't be fair to the Jewish community. We must move," he said. "Perhaps I should go and talk to Mrs. Finkelstein and give her a deposit down on this place. Then we will know for certain that we have somewhere to go when we leave Medina."

Goldie nodded but she turned away. She couldn't look at him. Right now, she hated him and everything he stood for. *Shlemiel*, she thought. *He is a real shlemiel. Completely worthless.*

CHAPTER THIRTY-THREE

G oldie couldn't wait to get home so she could write to her friend. She needed someone to talk to, and it was certainly not Irving. The entire way back to Medina she sat beside Irving on the train with her arms crossed over her chest. He tried to make conversation, but she let him know that she had no desire to speak with him by responding to his questions with one-word answers. As soon as she was alone in her room she threw herself on her bed and wept. Squeezing her eyes shut, she thought of Leni. *Leni, I am so miserable.* Then she got up from the bed and sat down at her desk. Taking out a fresh sheet of stationary she wrote.

> *Dearest Friend,*
> *Sam has been released. It turns out that he was with some shiksa, and she actually vouched for him. So he is off the hook, thank God. But a group of lousy shaygets, boys from a terrible group called the KKK, beat my Sammy up so badly that he is in the hospital. I was sick with worry. But once I learned that he would be all right, I was angry, and I refused to visit him. Irving goes to the hospital often. He has always treated Sam like he was his own. Poor Irving. You always said he was a nar. And he is. Anyway, Sam is doing fine, but the Jewish population*

in our town paid a steep price. The goyim organized a boycott of their businesses, and some of them lost so much money they were forced to close. Then our town rabbi came to see us and suggested, or shall we say, insisted, that we leave Medina. I suppose he is right. As long as we say here Sam is in danger. Irving thinks the best place for us is New York City. Because it is so large, Irving feels we will have anonymity. But I think it's also because he is afraid we won't be able to afford to live anywhere but a cheap apartment on the Lower East Side. I went to New York with him to see it. I am forced to stay with him until I receive the money from my father to come home to Berlin. New York is exciting, but only if you have money. And as you know, Irving is a nothing, a baker. If you saw the apartment where Irving left a deposit, you'd be appalled. It's filthy and the hallway stinks. I'm on shpilkes, waiting on pins and needles for that money from my father. Damn my papa for having so much power even now, and it's been nineteen years since the last time I saw him.

Write to me soon, Leni. I need to hear from you,
Love, your friend,

Goldie

CHAPTER THIRTY-FOUR

Betty Howard's parents were livid when the news of what their daughter had done reached them. Her mother screamed and cried declaring she was too embarrassed to face her neighbors. "People will stare at me and whisper every time I have to go to the market."

"I'll go for you," Betty said.

"Haven't you done enough, young lady?" her father said. "You are an embarrassment to this family."

The following day the newspaper came out with Betty's picture and an article about her and Sam Schatzman on the front page. When Betty's father went to work that day, he got into a fistfight with a coworker at the factory because the man called Betty a Jew-loving whore.

The article was shameful. It made Betty look like the kind of girl her parents had always warned her about. It stated that Betty and Samuel were alone in the back of Samuel's parents' bakery, and there were strong insinuations that they were engaged in sexual relations.

Since Betty's father punched the other man first, he was suspended without pay for two weeks. And to make matters worse, a lamp was broken during the altercation and it was decided that Mr. Howard would pay for it. The sum of two dollars would be deducted from his already insufficient pay.

Betty's twin sisters were so furious with her they wouldn't even speak to her. They had been ostracized at school. The other students didn't want anything to do with them. And even the girls whom they had lunch with every day for years were no longer sitting with them.

Betty lost her job. The gossip spread even before the newspaper was released. But the following day when the papers came out, Betty's boss called her in the office and handed her the last pay envelope she would receive from the lingerie factory.

"I'm sorry, Betty. You've been a good worker. But we just can't have this sort of thing going on at our plant. It's just not good business. We have an image to keep up. I'm sure you understand."

She nodded. He handed her an envelope and said, "I'm sorry."

Then she left.

Betty's father insisted she take her meals in her room. He told her he couldn't bear to be in the same room with her. "The sight of you makes me want to puke," he said. "I never dreamed that my daughter, my own flesh and blood, could be so stupid."

She looked away so he wouldn't see she was crying. His vicious words hurt her more than anything that anyone else had done to her. But she said nothing. Instead, Betty was careful to stay out of her father's way. Since she had no job, she spent most of her time alone in her room only leaving when she was sure no one else was in the house. Nights were harder than days. Something about the darkness made her loneliness more unbearable. Often, she lay on her bed looking out the window at the night sky and wept. She longed for Samuel. *He must be searching everywhere for me. He has probably been going to the factory looking for me. And, of course, I am not there because I don't work there anymore. He couldn't come to my house because he has no idea where I live. Not that it would be a good thing for him to come here. My parents would never let him come in. Maybe I should go to the bakery to see him. But I can't imagine facing his family. I'm sure they read the articles in the paper. They probably think I am a whore. And I'm certain they blame me for what's happened to Sam. Who knows what they would do if I went there?* Not knowing what to do, Betty did nothing.

John never showed up for his weekly date with Betty. And it was almost a week later before John came to her home to talk to her. Betty was in her room when he arrived. But her mother answered the door. "John!" she said.

Betty heard her mother say John's name, and she cringed. *He's here. Oh, good heavens. He's here*, she thought. Her palms began to sweat. It was time for the confrontation with John that she had been dreading. Betty cracked the door to her room open just a little so she could hear what was being said in the living room.

"I would like to see Betty, please, Mrs. Howard," John said.

"Of course, John. It's so good to see you. Won't you please come in. Can I get you something to eat or drink?" Betty's mother's voice was overly cheery.

She sounds ridiculous, like she's pretending that everything is fine.

"No, thank you, ma'am."

"Well then, you just have a seat, and I'll go and fetch Betty for you."

Mrs. Howard knocked on the door to her daughter's room. "Betty," she said in the same cheery voice. "Honey, John is here to see you."

Fear of what John might say or do ran through Betty's veins like an electric shock. *He knows everything by now. He knows that Samuel and I are lovers. And that we've been lovers while John and I were together. I'm sure he's wondering why I would give myself to a Jew and not to him. I am sure he's very angry. And I dread the next half hour.* She hadn't washed her face or brushed her hair in days, but she forced herself to go into the living room. When she walked in, she looked up at John and instantly saw the shocked look on his face. *I can just imagine how I look*, she thought.

"I'll leave you two," Mrs. Howard said.

"Hi, John," Betty muttered softly, looking down at the floor.

"Betty," he said, "how could you do this to me? I'm a joke to all my friends. You made a real fool of me."

"I never meant to hurt you, John. Never."

"Yeah, you might not have meant to, but you sure did. Damn it, Betty, you really did. You don't know this, but I worked for a year to buy you that engagement ring. It might not be the biggest diamond, but it sure meant a lot to me. I worked hard for it. And I saved every penny. You know why? Because I was in love with you. I wanted to marry you. You were the girl who I cared for so much that I wanted you to be the mother of my children. And how did you thank me? How, Betty?"

She shook her head. "I'm sorry."

"I'll tell you how . . . you cheated on me. You not only went out with another man behind my back, but to make matters even worse, you did it with a Jew. During the two and a half years we've been dating, you never let me touch you. I wanted you so bad. Damn, I wanted you. But I respected you. And when you said you were saving yourself for our wedding night, I believed you. I trusted you. How could I know that you were letting a filthy kike put his Jew hands all over you."

"I'm sorry," she said, tears falling down her cheeks. He had never spoken to her that way, ever. She was appalled. But she knew how hurt he was, and she was afraid to say anything that might provoke his anger. Then he handed her his handkerchief. And the small, kind act hurt her even more than his cruel remarks. She burst into a fit of sobbing.

"I can't marry you now," he said, shaking his head. His eyes were sad. "I want the ring back."

Betty slid her engagement ring off her finger and handed it to him. "I don't blame you," she said. "I was wrong to do what I did. I should have been honest with you. I just couldn't . . ."

"I just have one question . . ." He took a deep breath and asked, "Tell me the truth. Just this once. Betty, did you ever love me?"

She shrugged her shoulders. "I don't know."

He shook his head. "I guess that's it, then. There's nothing left to say." He put the ring in the breast pocket of his jacket and walked toward the kitchen door.

"Are you leaving so soon, John?" Mr. Howard said.

"Yes, sir. I have to be going," John said, not looking directly at Mr. Howard. Then he wiped a tear from his cheek with the back of his hand and walked out the door.

CHAPTER THIRTY-FIVE

S amuel was admitted into the Jewish hospital with two broken
ribs. His nose was broken, but his jaw was only badly bruised.
One of his back teeth had been cracked; he wasn't sure when that
happened. He thought it might have occurred when John kicked him
in the face. There were dark purple-and-yellow bruises all over his
body, making it impossible for him to find a comfortable position. The
day-to-day healing of his body was slow and painful. But being away
from Betty was even more painful. He knew his love for her had cost
him, his family, and his people dearly. *I know I should stay away from her.
Perhaps Anschel was right all along. I should find a Jewish girl and get
married as soon as possible.* But the harder he tried to erase Betty from his
thoughts, the more he wanted her.

Sam's father came to the hospital as soon as he heard Sam had been
admitted, to see how he was doing.

"The doc says I have a broken nose and couple of broken ribs. I'll
be all right," Sam said.

"I can't say I am not worried. These boys who did this to you are
dangerous. I don't know if they left you thinking you were dead or
not. But if they want you dead, they'll come back again," his father
said.

"Yes, I am sure they will." Sam winced as he tried to sit up so he could talk to his father. "I want you to know that I'm sorry for all this, Dad."

"I know you are. When you're young, love seems like the most important thing in the world."

"I am crazy about her. I am ashamed to admit it to you, but if I had to do it all over again, I would. Even with everything that's happened."

"I know, that's why I am afraid for you. That's why I think it's best if the family leaves Medina."

"Did the rabbi talk to you too?"

"Yes, he came to the bakery to see me. I'm assuming he talked to you, too, son?"

"Yes. He thinks we should leave town."

"I know. So here's what I am going to do. I'm going to make arrangements. Then I'll come back."

He returned three days later to tell Sam he was planning to sell the bakery to Shlomie and move to Manhattan.

"I already put money down on an apartment," his father said, trying to smile.

But Samuel knew how much that little bakery meant to his father and he felt terrible. "I don't know what to say, Dad."

"Mother, Alma, and I are packing. Alma is packing your things for you. We will make the move without you. Then I'll come back here and get you as soon as you're released from the hospital."

Sam nodded. But he thought, *If I leave Medina, how will I ever see Betty again? I can't just leave. I have to find a way to see her before I go. Perhaps she will go with me.*

For the next two weeks, Sam's father came to see him several times to give him updates. But his mother did not come at all.

"We are all packed and ready to move. I sold the bakery," Irving Schatzman said. Then he added, "I'll be a little busy this week. I am going to give Shlomie all my mama's recipes. It was part of our deal. But this should not have any impact on our new bakery because Medina is far enough away from Manhattan that we won't have the same customers." He sighed. "Anyway, so you shouldn't feel all alone here in the hospital, I'll send Alma to see you."

"Thank you, Dad . . . for everything," he said. Then he added, "I'd love to see my sister."

"Good. She misses you."

"Dad . . ."

"Yes?"

"I know I've said it before, but I have to say it again. I am so sorry. I caused you and Mother so much pain and misery. And I feel so bad for all the Jewish people here in town too. I've ruined things for them. I've really made a hell of a mess of my life. Can you ever forgive me?"

"It happens. People make mistakes. I understand. And, of course, I forgive you," Irving said.

"That means a lot to me, Dad. More than you know."

"I'll tell Alma to come tomorrow?"

"Yes, that would be wonderful," Sam replied. He was excited to see Alma because he knew if anyone would help him find a way to reach Betty, Alma would.

CHAPTER THIRTY-SIX

Alma arrived at the hospital just after breakfast the following day. She wore a beige dress with a small floral print that was too big for her tiny frame, and so were her thick black-rimmed glasses. Her shoes were tan and sensible as was her handbag. She'd pulled her hair away from her face, and a small hat perched awkwardly on her head. He looked at her and thought, My *poor sister is not a beauty. But she has so many good qualities. She has grace and kindness. But she sure doesn't have Mom's looks or her fashion sense. Little Alma is so much like our dad. I've heard Mom tell Dad that she was worried it was going to be difficult to find a husband for Alma because of her looks. But, in my opinion, even though she's not pretty, any man would be lucky to have my little sister for his wife.* He didn't say what he was thinking. Instead, he smiled as best he could with his injured jaw and said, "I'm glad to see you."

"They hurt you badly. Those fellas from the KKK did it, didn't they?" she said when she saw Samuel lying in his hospital bed.

"They did," he said, "but I'm all right."

"You look terrible."

He laughed. "Nice thing to say."

"Well, it's true. You're all black and blue, and your nose is twisted and still crusted with dried blood. And . . ." Tears began to fall from her eyes. She took a handkerchief out of her handbag and blotted them.

"What's wrong with you? Why are you crying?"

"Because this is all my fault. I blame myself. I told you to go back with Betty when you two broke up. Instead of supporting your relationship, I should have discouraged you. None of this would have happened if I had done that. But I thought the love you two felt for each other would conquer all. It didn't."

"No, I suppose not. There is too much hatred in the world. I guess it's going to take a stronger warrior to conquer it." He tried to smile. "But don't lose heart, Alma. I'm still a warrior for love."

"Stop teasing me. I can't bear to see you this way. You're all beaten up and . . ."

"Listen to me; it's important. I don't want you to blame yourself. I chose to go back to Betty because I love her. And I don't regret my decision. Even if you had tried to discourage me, I would have done it anyway."

Betty sat down on the edge of his bed.

"What's with this outfit of yours? You're dressed like someone's bubbie," he said. "That dress is too big for you."

"I guess it's all part of the guilt I've been feeling. You know how I always argued with Mom and Dad that the Jews were Americans like everyone else. And you know how I secretly flirted with non-Jewish boys? Well, I've stopped all of that. I'm looking for a husband. A good Jewish match. So I've started dressing very modest so I can attract the right kind of man."

"And this is because of me?" he said, drawing his eyebrows together in spite of the pain that shot through his face due to his broken nose.

"Yes."

"Please, don't do that. Don't change yourself and get married just because I made a mess of my life."

"I have to. Dad think's it's best. And I agree. He says he'll get in touch with a matchmaker as soon as we move to the city."

His jaw had begun to ache from talking so much. But he had to find a way to ask her to go and tell Betty to come to see him at the hospital. It was apparent to him that it was not going to be easy to convince Alma to go to Betty for him. She was making it clear that she no longer approved of their relationship. "When are we leaving Medina?" he asked.

"A few more days. Dad already moved most of the furniture."

"How's Mom taking it?"

"She's Mom. You know how she is. She blames Dad for everything. She always has in her own strange way."

It hurt his ribs to move, but he put a second pillow behind his head to prop him up so he could look into Alma's eyes. Then he reached for her hand. Puzzled, she gave it to him. "Alma," he said, "I know you feel that you made a mistake by encouraging my love for Betty. But I need your help. I need you to go and find Betty and to tell her that I am here in the hospital. Tell her that she can come and see me here. And you must also tell her that we are leaving Medina and where we are moving. I really need you to do this for me. Please, Alma."

Alma pulled her hand away and turned to look out the window. "I can't. I'm sorry. When you get out of the hospital, have Dad contact a matchmaker for you too. You need a wife. A Jewish girl. Someone who is one of us. Someone who shares our way of life."

"You can't be serious. Not you, Alma. You are too American for this. Don't do this to me."

"I have to go. Is there anything else you want or need? I can bring you some strudel."

"Alma . . . please, I'm begging you. Please."

"I can't, Samuel. I can't." She picked up her handbag and walked out of the room.

He felt as if his entire world had collapsed. Not only was he physically weak and in pain, but he had no money, no way to stay in Medina until he could reach Betty, and no way to come back and find Betty once he and his family had moved. *Betty is probably thinking I've abandoned her. And I'm sure her family and friends have turned on her too. She probably thinks that all of this is too much for me, and I've given up on her, on us. I know she is hurt that I haven't returned.* The very idea that he'd hurt her gave him the strength to force himself to get out of the bed. He walked slowly to the nurses' station. "I need to see my doctor," he said.

"What are you doing out of bed?" a heavyset nurse, with light brown hair in finger waves peeking out from her nurse's cap, asked him.

"My doctor said I am to be discharged in a couple of days. I need an earlier discharge. I need to get out of here."

"I see," she said. "Why don't you go back to bed, and I'll let the doctor know you want to see him as soon as he comes into the hospital."

"Thank you. Thank you so much."

Samuel tried to appear pain free as he walked back to his room, but he knew he was leaning and limping.

A bowl of soup and a heel of bread arrived at eleven thirty that morning brought into Samuel's room by a young pretty girl with dark hair in long spiral curls. "Your lunch is here," she said, smiling.

"Thank you." Samuel tried to return the smile. He watched the girl place the tray on his table. He knew she was Jewish because only Jews worked at the Jewish hospital. She was certainly pretty. And if he had not already given his heart to Betty, he would have found her beguiling. Her dark eyes sparkled when she looked at him.

"Can I get you anything else? Some water, perhaps?"

"Yes, that would be nice," he said.

Then she added in a whisper, "I know who you are. And I know that the whole town is furious with you. They think you brought all of this on them. But I don't believe it was your fault. My father doesn't either. He says the goyim just needed an excuse to go after the Jews. My father is from Hungary, and he says that it happened like this all the time in Europe. You were not at fault. You were just the excuse."

"All of what? What did I bring on them?" he asked.

"The goyim are boycotting all of our Jewish businesses. The mayor put out an order telling them not to shop at any Jewish stores. People are suffering."

"Oh." He sighed. "I never meant for this to happen. I feel terrible."

Alma walked into the room. She looked at her brother and then at the pretty young girl. "Am I interrupting something?" she said. There was a lilt of hope in her voice.

"No, not at all," Samuel said. "I was just going to have lunch. But it can wait."

"Please, eat," Alma said. "I wouldn't want your soup to get cold."

"Well." The young girl smiled. "It looks like you have company. So I'll leave you."

"Thank you again," Samuel said as the receptionist left. Then he turned to Alma. "How did you get in here? They've closed visiting hours until two."

"I knew the woman at the desk. She is the mother of a friend of mine. She let me in."

"Well, I'm glad you came back. Please, sit down."

Alma sat on a chair that was beside the bed. She looked at Sam and said, "I took a long walk and thought about our conversation earlier. You love Betty, and she loves you too. I don't think you two should break up just because everyone is pushing you to do so. I know I must be crazy, but I still believe in love. And I gave a lot of thought to everything we talked about. I was wrong, Sam. I was really wrong to suggest you marry a girl you don't love just because she is Jewish. If you marry someone you don't love, you're both bound to be miserable." Then she reached over and took his hand. "That's why I came back. I feel that I must help you. I'll go and see Betty and tell her that you are here in the Jewish hospital and that you want her to come to see you. How do I find her?"

"Oh, Alma, you have no idea how much this means to me." He squeezed her hand. "She works at the lingerie factory. So go there and wait behind the building at about six o'clock. That is the end of the workday. A whistle will blow, and lots of girls will come out the main door. Just stay out of sight and wait for her to come out. When you see her, call her over. Then tell her who you are. Do you know what she looks like?"

"Only from the pictures in the paper. But I have a pretty good idea. The pictures were very clear, so I think I can find her. I'll go today."

"Alma, I don't know how to thank you."

She nodded. "I know," she said, then she continued, "I'll go this afternoon."

CHAPTER THIRTY-SEVEN

Alma waited behind the large building that housed the lingerie factory. It was growing dark, and there was a chill in the air when the whistle finally blew. Women came pouring out the door like milk flowing from a large pitcher. Their clothes, hairstyles, and mannerisms made it obvious to Alma that they were different from the Jewish girls she'd known all her life. Her legs tingled. She wanted to run away, to go home to the safety of her small community. But she'd promised her brother, so she scanned the crowd of girls in an effort to find one who resembled the girl she'd seen in the newspapers. It was hard to distinguish between them. So many of them looked alike. When she saw someone who she thought looked like the pictures of Betty, she took a deep breath. The girl was walking with two other girls. It took all the courage Alma could muster to approach her.

"Hi, B-Betty Howard?"

"Who wants to know?" the girl with the honey-colored curls asked.

"I'm Alma Schatzman, Samuel's sister."

The girl stopped walking and glared at her. "I'm not Betty. But I know her. She was a friend of mine. At least she used to be. And . . . I know who Samuel Schatzman is too. He is the dirty Jew who caused Betty a lot of problems. You have a hell of a lot of nerve coming here.

Betty's been fired from the factory. She doesn't work here anymore. And if I were you, sister, I'd get out of here quick. You're a Jew, and we don't take kindly to Jews around here."

"But I must see her." Alma clenched her fists. She was terrified, but she'd made a promise to her brother and she was determined to keep it.

"Let me get this straight, you ugly little Jew broad. Are you making demands on me?" The girl's eyes were emotionless. They looked like glass. Her face was twisted up into a cruel grin.

"I'm begging you to help me. I'm not making demands at all." Alma's palms were sweaty. "Please. Help me."

"I'm telling you to get the hell out of here before I make you sorry you came," the girl said, putting her hands on her hips. She was broad shouldered and slender but bigger boned and built more solidly than Alma, who was a wisp of a girl.

One of the other girls pushed Alma, and she fell on the concrete skinning her knee. She got up. And another one punched her in the stomach. She doubled over hardly able to breathe. She'd never seen girls act in such a violent manner. "Let's kill her," one of them said. And Alma could see the bloodlust in each of their eyes. Her entire body was trembling. *Run. Get away from them before this gets uglier than it already is. Go home. Hurry and go home. They aren't going to help you find Betty. They are going to hurt you if you stay. So go, now.*

Alma turned and started to run away. The girls didn't chase her. But she could hear their laughter as she sprinted away.

When she was far enough from the factory, Alma sat down on a tree stump to steady herself and catch her breath. On a few occasions when Alma was not in school and she'd been helping out at the bakery, she had been treated poorly by one or two non-Jewish people who came in. But she'd never experienced anything nearly as horrible as the strong hatred that came at her from those girls today. It was ugly and powerful, and like a fire it started with one and then quickly ignited in the others until it was burning out of control. *If I had not gotten away when I did, I am afraid that they really would have killed me,* she thought, crossing her arms over her chest and rubbing her upper arms. *I feel so bad because I am going to have to tell Samuel what happened. He is going to be so disappointed. Maybe he will have another idea of how I can get in touch with Betty for him. I am willing to try again. I'll go to her home if need be. I'll wait for her to come outside of her house. But I can't go back to that factory. The look in the eyes of that girl will stay with me forever. I would even be willing to knock on Betty's door and beg her parents to let me speak to her. But I hope he doesn't want me to do it. I am afraid of these people. They are mean and heartless.* She shivered. *But . . . I promised Samuel . . .*

She was so lost in thought that she did not see the two boys approaching. "Hi, Alma," one of them said.

Alma stood up. A danger signal sounded in her heart and in her brain. *Who are these boys, and how do they know my name?* She didn't say a word; instead, she began to run. The boys easily caught up with her. One of them grabbed her arm and threw her on the ground. Then he held her down while the other one pulled up her skirt.

"Remember the girls you just met at the factory? They told us you'd be here. And, damn, they were right. Here you are."

Alma was crying, and she was trying to pull her skirt back down to cover herself. "Please, let me go. I won't cause any trouble. I won't go looking for Betty anymore. Just please, I am begging you to let me go home. Let me go back to my neighborhood. I'll never come here again. I promise you . . ."

"I'll bet she's a virgin," one of the boys said, licking his lips.

"All the sweeter," the other one growled.

It was almost night. A wicked cold wind rushed by making the hair on Alma's arms and legs stand up. She turned her head away and began to weep. *It's no use,* Alma thought. Her heart fluttering like the heart of a mouse who's been cornered by a cat. *They are going to do this to me, and I can't get away. I wish I could be stronger. I don't want them to see me crying like this. I know they are enjoying it. But I can't help myself. I am so scared. Dear God, help me, please. I am begging you. If you can hear me, please do something.*

The boys were correct when they assumed Alma was a virgin. She had spent most of her time either studying, helping at the bakery, or doing tzedakah, acts of charity. She had never been to a dance or on a date. And although she'd often dreamed of what it might be like to be kissed by a boy, she'd never been kissed. Until this moment, if anyone would have asked her, Alma would have told them there was not a single person on this earth that she hated. It was true the boys she knew from her neighborhood didn't pay her much attention. Even so, they always treated her respectfully. These boys, who were holding her down and doing unspeakable things to her, were unlike any boys she'd ever known. And for the first time in her life, she felt hatred in her heart. And it felt dark and ugly like a hideous mold growing larger by the minute. "Please, won't you please stop," Alma cried out in horror. But she knew that they would not stop. She felt like an animal cornered by a hunter knowing that it was doomed. "Please, please, please, please," she repeated under her breath over and over like a chant.

But they ignored her begging, and instead, one at a time, they took what they wanted from her. She had never felt such pain or humiliation. Blood ran down her thighs, and tears spilled down her cheeks. When the boys had finished, one of the boys put his face right up to hers, his nose almost touching hers. "And . . . Alma. Your name is Alma. I'm not going to kill you. You know why? Because I want you to go home and tell that Jew brother of yours that John Anderson took his revenge out on you. You tell him that in the Bible it says an eye for an eye. Well, he took what he wanted from my girl. HE soiled her good. I can't even look at her now. And so, in turn, I ruined his baby sister."

CHAPTER THIRTY-EIGHT

Two days passed. Samuel waited in his hospital bed for either Alma or Betty to come see him. Neither of them came. Another day passed. Then Irving Schatzman, having spoken with Samuel's doctor, who assured him that Samuel was ready to leave, came to the hospital to take him to his new home, the apartment his parents rented in Manhattan.

Still weak, Samuel, accompanied by his father, boarded the train into the city. He wished he could ask his father to allow him to go and see Betty at the factory at the end of the day. But he dared not even ask. They rode the train in silence. His father did not hold this against him. Samuel knew that. Irving wasn't that kind of man. He'd always been easy to forgive, kind and willing to listen to reason. But even so, Samuel didn't dare tell him that he still loved Betty, the shiksha who, his parents believed, had caused all this mess.

When they arrived in New York City, Sam was overwhelmed by the sights, the sounds, and the smells. Manhattan seemed to be a living, breathing entity. There were people everywhere. There were buyers and sellers of goods. There were students carrying books. The Hasidic Jews with their long black coats and curled payots walked through the streets, their hands gesturing wildly as they spoke to each other in

Yiddish. They passed taverns where men of working age sat drinking. And on the corners, prostitutes in flimsy dresses winked at Samuel and his father, calling out, "Hey, handsome, how about a date?"

Sam had never been anywhere that was half as exciting as New York City. He loved the city already and he'd only just arrived. They passed two scrappy-looking young boys. One of them whistled and said, "Hey mister, wanna buy a watch? Real good quality."

Irving shook his head.

"Real cheap too," the boy said.

Again, Irving shook his head and he and Samuel kept walking. "Probably stolen goods," Irving said to his son.

"Those boys were so young to be thieves. How old do you think they were?"

"My guess is ten or eleven. But this is the city. It's a lot different than Medina. There are all kinds of people here," Irving said.

They arrived at the building where Irving had rented the apartment. "Well, this is it. I know it doesn't look like much. But I am going to do my best to buy us a house as soon as I can. Anyway, your mother and sister are up on the third floor," Irving said. "Do you need some help climbing the stairs?"

"No, I'm a little winded from the walk, but I'll be all right," Samuel said.

CHAPTER THIRTY-NINE

G oldie had done her best to make the apartment livable. But her face looked like she'd just sucked on a lemon even as she forced herself to smile at Sam. "I'm glad you are home." Samuel knew his mother, and he was certain by the look on her face that she blamed him for everything. And she resented him because they'd had to move to this apartment she hated.

"I'm glad to be home, Mom."

"Well, good," she said, then she added, "You'll be sharing a room with your father. Your sister and I will share the other room. Since there are only two bedrooms, your father and I agreed that this is best."

Samuel bit his lower lip. *My parents are not sleeping in the same room anymore. The mess I've made of our lives has destroyed their marriage too.*

"Come, follow me, Samuel. Here is our room." His father opened the door to a small space with two twin beds squashed inside.

"It looks just fine, Dad," Sam said, trying to smile. Then he added, "Is Alma home?"

"No, she went to register for school," his mother answered. "She shouldn't be too long. I expect her to be home later this afternoon."

Alma came in less than an hour later. She wore a simple gray dress that hung like a sack on her and black low-heeled sensible shoes. Sam couldn't help but think she looked like a child dressed up in her mother's clothes.

He took her arm and gently pulled her to the far corner of the living room. Then he whispered, "Alma, you never came back to the hospital to tell me what happened with Betty. I've been on shpilkes, pins and needles, waiting to hear from either you or Betty. My nerves are shot. Can we go somewhere to talk where we're sure no one can hear us."

She didn't look at him. "Yes. You're right. We do need to talk." Then in a louder voice, a voice loud enough for her parents to hear, she said, "Come with me. I have to put these schoolbooks away in my room. I'd love for you to see it. Mom did a beautiful job of decorating it."

He followed her to the room she shared with their mother.

"Sit down," she ordered.

There was no chair or desk. There was no room for either. He sat on the bed. Alma took a deep breath and turned away so he could not see her face. "I saw Betty," she lied. "And I'm sorry, Sam. But she said that she wants no part of you. She wants nothing more to do with you. She asks that you please leave her alone. She said that the relationship between the two of you has caused everyone enough heartache. She says that she is going to marry someone who is like her and that you should find someone who is Jewish."

Samuel felt his throat go dry. Was this really possible that Betty wanted him to leave her alone? He could hardly speak. "Alma, are you sure? Did she mean it, or was she just angry at me for not coming around? Did you tell her I was in the hospital and I couldn't come?"

"I told her you were in the hospital. I told her what happened," Alma said. Then she turned to look at Sam, her face clearly filled with anguish. "I'm sure she meant what she said. She was firm. She begged me to tell you to please leave her alone. I didn't come to the hospital to tell you because I was afraid you were too weak to hear what she said. I knew it would hurt you. But Betty is right. This for the best, Sam. It really is."

"I'll go to the factory and wait for her. If I can just speak to her . . ."

CHAPTER 39 | 157

"Please don't do that, Sam. Betty told me to please ask you to respect her wishes. She doesn't want to see you." Then Alma added, "I'm sorry."

"Well, if she said that, and she really doesn't want me anymore, I have to respect her wishes. But I love her. I really love her, and I believe if we try, she and I could find a way to make it work."

"I know you love her. But this is what she wants, and believe me, this is best. Look at you. You just got out of the hospital. Who knows? Next time you are caught with Betty those terrible shaygets might just kill you."

"I don't care. I could take the beatings from those KKK boys. I would be willing to endure whatever terrible things that people decided to throw at us. But I won't try and change her mind. Not if this is what she wants. If this is what she really wants . . . then I will leave her alone."

CHAPTER FORTY

Manhattan, January 1929

It was just before dawn. Goldie and Irving were in the kitchen of their small apartment. Samuel had just returned from the bathroom and was about to get dressed for work when he heard his parents arguing.

"This apartment has no heat," Goldie complained. "I am freezing in here. And look at this peeling paint. I've never seen such a terrible place. How could you bring us here? What were you thinking? We had a home in Medina. Damn the rabbi to hell for telling you to get out of town. Our children will surely catch their death this winter in this place. It's not fit for the rats that live here, let alone for human beings. Can't you do something, Irving?"

"Don't you think I would love to get us out of here. I am working twelve hours a day. But still, there is not enough money to move. We are a new business. We are going to have to prove ourselves. There is a lot of competition for Jewish bakeries in Manhattan. It's going to take time to get word-of-mouth business."

"So until then, you expect us to live like animals." She glared at him. "I hate it here. And I hate you for thinking that this place is good enough for your family. It's a real reminder of the low-class people that you came from." Goldie wrapped her arms around her chest. "I should have stayed in Medina until I got the money from my father."

"We couldn't stay there. You know that."

"I didn't say us. I said I should have stayed. Alone, without the burden of you." She stood up to pour herself a cup of coffee.

"And where would I have stayed?"

"I have no idea. With friends. With anyone. Anywhere but here."

He went over to her and put his arms around her. "I'm sorry. I'm so sorry, Goldie. You deserve so much better. But as much as I would have liked to stay in Medina, we couldn't. Not safely."

"We should have tried. This place is horrible. I hate it! Hate it! Hate it!" She stomped her foot. Then she sunk down into a chair and started to cry.

"I know, Goldie. Believe me, I am trying."

She snorted.

"Do you want to take the day off, maybe get some rest? Samuel and I can handle the bakery."

"I would prefer to, but at least at the bakery the ovens are going and it's warm. Here, it's freezing. Oh, Irving, I just can't bear this anymore. I haven't purchased anything pretty for myself in months. I feel sad and depleted. And the way things are going, I don't know how we are ever going to move out of this place."

He shrugged his shoulders just as Samuel came into the kitchen. "I will just keep working. I will work as hard as I can. And one day . . . soon."

"Good morning, Dad. Good morning, Mom," Sam said.

"There's coffee," Irving said to his son. "Take if you want."

"Thanks, Dad," Samuel said, pouring himself a cup of the steaming black liquid. *Mom is right. It's damn cold in this apartment*, Sam thought. He tried to hide the fact that he was shivering. He didn't want to make his father feel worse. So he just sipped the coffee.

"I'm going to get dressed and wake Alma up for school," Goldie said.

"Here, have some bread. We have a little butter in the icebox. Are you hungry?" Irving asked Sam.

"Not too," Samuel said. "Maybe I'll eat at the bakery."

"A growing boy should eat," Irving said, taking a bite of a slice of bread.

"I don't like to eat this early in the morning."

"Lately, you don't eat much at all. Are you sick? Do your ribs bother you?"

"No. I must be going through a stage or something. I'll have breakfast at work, Dad. I promise you."

"All right. Whatever you want," Irving said. "But I know you've been going through a lot. So if you need to talk, I'm here, and I will be happy to listen."

CHAPTER FORTY-ONE

Medina, February 1929

B etty found a job at a small restaurant called Luca's Restaurant. The owners were an old couple who were immigrants from somewhere in Eastern Europe. They didn't speak much English, and they didn't have many friends. So they had never heard about the scandal that surrounded Betty and her Jewish boyfriend. Betty did not have a specific job at the restaurant; she was their all-around helper. She cleaned the kitchen and mopped the floors. She waited tables and cashed people out when they paid their checks. For all the work she did, she hardly made any money. The pay was far less than she'd earned at the factory.

The old couple tried to offer her a free meal when she worked, but she found the food to be either bland and tasteless or overly seasoned, and she wondered how they stayed open. However, because of what had happened between her and Samuel, no one else in town was willing to hire her. So this job was the best she could hope for. It wasn't a terrible job. The old couple appreciated her, and the customers, who were mostly immigrants, didn't ask her any personal questions.

Every Wednesday night she met with Joan, her childhood girlfriend, in secret. Joan's parents had forbidden the friendship between their daughter and the notorious Betty Howard. But the girls had known each other since their mothers had walked them in buggies together, and neither of them wanted to let the other go. Still, they were careful not to be seen together because Joan had recently been promoted at the factory, and she couldn't afford to lose her job. So, during the summer and fall, they met each Wednesday night at a clearing in the woods to talk over their respective weeks. Unfortunately, the weather from December through early March made it impossible to meet outside. So, Joan would go to the restaurant where Betty worked and sit in the back while Betty cleaned up on Wednesday nights. Then they would have a quick dinner together. Most of the time Betty prepared something edible for them because they both agreed the food was terrible. The owners of the restaurant didn't mind at all. They welcomed Betty's friend and didn't charge the girls for their dinners.

"I met a boy at a party last week," Joan said excitedly when Betty sat down carrying two plates of noodles with butter.

"Tell me," Betty said, smiling. Then she picked up her fork. "Tell me all about him."

"There's not much to tell yet. He's very handsome. At least I think he is." She smiled. "And he asked me out to the picture show this weekend. We'll see what happens. He's new in town. His family just moved here from England."

"Does he have that sexy accent that all the English people have?"

"Yep."

"Is he in the KKK?"

"Nope. He works at the factory but he's a loner. Doesn't get involved with all that stuff."

He's very independent.

"What's his name?"

"George Washburn."

"Joan Washburn. It has a nice ring to it," Betty said, smiling.

"Not so fast." Joan laughed. "It's only our first date."

Betty's shoulders slumped, and tears burned the backs of her eyes. "I miss Samuel."

"I know, honey. But it's best this way. You thought that he would come back for you and he didn't. I know it hurts. But in the end, you will be better off."

"How could he just stop coming to see me? What did I do? He promised he would come back, and he never did. I don't know why. I guess what bothers me most is that I don't know why."

Joan stood up and put her arm around Betty's shoulder. Then she looked into her friend's eyes. "He probably gave it a lot of thought and decided it was best for both of you."

"And he just never came to talk it over with me? How could he do that?" Betty said, taking a towel off the counter and wiping her tears. "He knows how much I love him."

"Maybe he knew that if he saw you it would only be worse for both of you. Maybe he felt that he wasn't strong enough to resist you if he saw you."

"Yes, maybe."

"You really should start to think about dating again."

"Who? Who would date me now anyway? I have such a black mark on my forehead," Betty said as tears slid down her cheeks. "I have the mark of Cain."

Joan got up and slid into the booth beside Betty. Then she put her arms around her friend and hugged her tightly. "Pray. Ask God to help you," she whispered into Betty's ear.

CHAPTER FORTY-TWO

March 1929

P erhaps it was because Betty took Joan's advice that she was open to the possibility of a new romance, and even a little flirtatious when Roland came into the restaurant. Roland was tall and handsome with light brown hair and a strong jaw. His Eastern European accent was heavy, but he spoke and understood English perfectly. He had been delivering a foal at a farm that was located very close to the restaurant where she worked, which was known to have some Hungarian food on the menu. He and Betty bantered back and forth while Roland's friend ate his soup, and by the time he'd finished, Roland had asked Betty out for dinner. She knew she should go. However, Medina is a small town, and she was afraid he would find out about her and Samuel before she had an opportunity to tell him herself. So she suggested that he come to her home for dinner instead. Betty knew her parents would be happy that she was dating again. They would have preferred she date an American, but at least they could say Roland wasn't a Jew. And at this point, her chances of ever marrying someone as desirable as John Anderson were slim. At least they were in Medina.

"I'd be honored to come to your home," Roland said.

"Sunday afternoon after church? My mother makes a big Sunday dinner. I think you would enjoy it. Would Sunday be all right for you?"

"Yes, that would be lovely," he said, smiling.

"Then I'll give you my address." As she wrote her address on a small piece of paper, she wondered if he was able to read English.

He looked at the paper. "1217 North Ridgefield Road," he said, reading it aloud.

"Yes. It's not too far away from here. It takes me about fifteen minutes to walk home."

"What time shall I arrive?"

"Two p.m."

"I'll be there. I'm looking forward to it," he said, tucking the address into the breast pocket of his jacket.

CHAPTER FORTY-THREE

Betty's parents reacted just as she thought they would when she told them she'd invited Roland to dinner. They weren't pleased she was dating a foreigner, but they were glad, at least, he wasn't Jewish.

When John first broke up with Betty, her parents were very disappointed but not shocked. They were angry at Betty for her reckless behavior. "You've lost a good man," her father had said, shaking his head. "And after the shenanigans you pulled, you will be lucky to find any husband. No decent boy will want anything to do with you."

"I don't care what people think of me, Dad. It's for the best that John called off the engagement. I love Sam. He is the man I want to marry," she had declared.

Her father turned around and slapped her hard across the face. She turned red with indignation. Then she got up and ran to her room slamming the door behind her.

But that was months ago. As time passed, and her parents realized Samuel had somehow disappeared from their lives, they began to relax. Betty never mentioned Sam, so they thought she had forgotten him. But she didn't date anyone either. Just as her father had predicted, none of the local boys were interested. The young people who lived in town and worked with Betty's father talked about the parties, picnics, and dances they attended. Betty was never invited. And even though Betty's mother thought Betty had caused her own misery, she felt sorry for their daughter. So when Betty told her she was bringing a man home for dinner, although Roland wasn't her ideal choice, she convinced her husband that they must give him a chance.

Roland arrived on Sunday at a quarter to two in the afternoon carrying a bunch of flowers for Betty's mother and a bottle of fine whiskey for her father. He also brought a box of chocolate candy for Betty and her sisters.

"This is Roland, Father," Betty said.

Her father nodded but didn't shake Roland's hand even when Roland gave him the whiskey. "Thank you," he said in a quiet voice.

Betty's mother was more willing to accept Roland than her husband was. She was impressed by the thoughtfulness of the lovely bouquet he'd brought her. And even though he was clearly foreign, Roland was handsome.

After Mr. Howard said grace they began to eat. Betty's two younger sisters cast glances at Roland then broke into giggles. Roland smiled at them. He had an easy way about him. When Mr. Howard asked him what his intentions were concerning his daughter Roland answered, "It's not my intentions that are in question, sir. I like her very much. I'd ask her to marry me right now, but it is only our first date." He hesitated then smiled at Betty but continued speaking to her father. "Now, I would really appreciate it if you asked her what her intentions are with me. That way I won't have to wonder."

Again, the girls giggled. Mrs. Howard laughed a little too.

Even Mr. Howard had to smile.

After they finished eating Betty and Roland went for a walk. They walked until they found a tree stump to sit on. "Thank you for inviting me. I enjoyed it very much. And your family is charming," he said.

She smiled at him. Then her face grew serious. "I have something to tell you, Roland. I don't know what you are going to think of me after I tell you this. But you are going to find out sooner or later, so I think it's best if you hear it from me."

"What is this?" he said. "Are you really a princess, and once we kiss are you going to turn into a frog?"

She let out a laugh. "That is not how the story goes. Actually, the fairy tale goes the other way. The frog is really a prince, and once he kisses the girl he turns into a human prince."

"I see." He smiled and then took her hand between both of his. "Tell me, Betty Howard. What is it that is so terrible that it has wiped the pretty smile from your face and made you as serious as an old librarian?"

She took a deep breath and looked down at the ground. "There is something that I did in my recent past that gave me a bad reputation in this town. Once you hear the story, I am afraid you won't want to be associated with me anymore."

He pursed his lips and nodded his head. Then he said with a bit of sarcasm in his voice "Well, it sounds serious. So let me guess . . . you were married, and you killed your former husband?"

"No." She had to laugh. "It's not that bad."

"All right. So then at least I don't have to fear for my life."

"No."

"All right then, just tell me what the great mystery is. I can handle anything else." He smiled at her. "Really, don't be afraid to talk to me." He squeezed her hand slightly.

"I was engaged to a local boy. But something happened, and I fell in love with another boy who . . . who was a Jew. Did you hear about the case with a Jewish boy who was supposed to have kidnapped that little girl?"

"I think I remember hearing something about it. I don't pay much attention to the newspapers. I'm too busy with livestock." He smiled at her.

"Livestock?"

"I'm a veterinarian," he said.

"I see," she said. "Anyway, this Jewish boy I was in love with was the one who was accused of stealing that child. He needed an alibi or they were going to prosecute him for kidnapping. He didn't want to tell them that the night the child was taken, he was with me. But he was with me. He was just protecting my reputation. So even though I knew it was going to be bad for me, I had to go to the police and tell them the truth."

"So you told the police that you were with him."

"Yes. And once I did that, the whole town knew about Sam and me. They knew he was Jewish. There were terrible newspaper articles written implying that I was not the kind of girl a decent man would have anything to do with. Then I lost my job at the factory. I was shunned by all of our neighbors and almost all of my former friends."

"So what happened to the boy?"

"He was released. He said he loved me. He said he was going to come for me and take me away with him. But he never came. He didn't know where I lived, so I waited outside the factory every day at closing time because that was the only place he knew of to find me. I did it for a whole week." She sighed. "But he never came. Then, a few weeks later, I went to the bakery where he and I used to meet. It had been his parents' bakery, and it was located in the Jewish neighborhood. I was really nervous about going back into the Jewish sector of town after what happened between Samuel and me. I had this terrible feeling that I would be unwelcome. And I was right. But I found out some very important information. I learned that Samuel's family had sold the bakery and they had moved. Just like that, Samuel left me and moved away. I never saw him again."

"I see," Roland said as he smoothed his hair back from his forehead. "So you are concerned that people will tell me this story and I will not want to see you anymore. You think that I will believe those newspaper articles that say you are a fallen woman?" He looked into her eyes.

"Yes, I am very worried that you will feel that way. Most men wouldn't want a girl who had once cheated on her boyfriend especially with a Jew."

"I don't like it that you cheated. Now, I will admit, that worries me a bit."

"You're right. It was wrong. I shouldn't have cheated. Everything just happened so fast between Samuel and me. And I was afraid to tell John that I wanted to break up with him. I was afraid of what he would do. I wanted to tell him; so many times I wanted to tell him. But I couldn't bring myself to do it." She was trembling.

"Would you promise me that if we were seeing each other and you met someone else who you cared for more than me that you would give me the courtesy of telling me rather than cheating on me?"

"I promise. And I know that most men would be upset because the boy I was in love with was Jewish."

"Well, you're in luck, young lady, because I am not most men. I don't give a shoeshine who you dated before me. I don't care that he was a Jew. I like you, and the fact that the Jewish fellow didn't return for you is his loss and my gain. I don't care what people say about us. If you want to go out with me, I'd like to take you to dinner. Then who knows? Perhaps we'll paint the town . . . and then maybe . . . we'll get married."

She giggled. "Married? We hardly know each other."

"Stranger things have happened. So what do you say? How about dinner tomorrow night? Will you go out with me?"

"Yes," she said, smiling as she looked into his eyes and squeezed his hand.

Then he kissed her softly on the lips. "You're trembling," he said as he took off his coat and lay it gently across her shoulders.

CHAPTER FORTY-FOUR

The following evening, Roland took Betty to a small Hungarian restaurant on the outskirts of town. They were seated at a corner table with a white tablecloth and a single lit candle.

A waiter with thick, straight auburn hair and a matching mustache set a plate filled with food down between them. Then he set down two small plates, silverware, and handed each of them a menu and walked away.

"What is that?" Betty asked, eyeing the plate of food the waiter had left behind.

"Ahh, so you are a lángos virgin."

"What?" She tilted her head.

He laughed. "That is lángos. It's fried dough with a little sour cream and cheese. Try some. I think you'll enjoy it."

She looked at him skeptically, but she cut off a small piece and put it on her plate. He did the same. But he didn't eat. Instead, he watched her take her first bite.

"This is so delicious," she said, smiling at him.

"I knew it. Now you, too, will become an addict of lángos! Just like me."

She laughed.

"I can't wait until you've had some of the other food. You will say, American food, eh. Hungarian food . . . divine."

The menu was not extensive, but it claimed that all the food was prepared according to the owner's grandmother's recipes which came directly from Hungary.

"Would you like me to order for you?" he asked.

She nodded, but she was not looking at him.

"Betty, is something wrong? I thought you liked the lángos."

She put the piece of fried dough down on her plate and looked directly at him. Then she said, "You brought me to this out-of-the-way place because you are ashamed of me, didn't you?"

"I brought you to this out-of-the-way place because they have the best Hungarian food I've had since I left my home in Hungary. I am not ashamed of you. I could never be ashamed of you. You are bright and beautiful. Please don't think that," he said.

She nodded.

"You don't believe me?"

"I don't."

"I will do my best to convince you. But for right now, let's order our dinner and have a nice evening. Then after tonight, if you'd still like to go out with me, I would like to take you to one of the popular restaurants in town. Perhaps if you are free this weekend. All you have to do is tell me which restaurant is popular because, frankly, I don't know. I'm not crazy for American food. Even so, if you like it, I'll learn to like it. But I do have one request."

She looked at him not sure what to make of this strange but handsome man. "What's your request?" she asked.

"Just make sure that the restaurant you choose is a supper club that has dancing. I am one hell of a good dancer!" he said, winking at her.

She shook her head. *He makes me laugh*, she thought. *He is charming. And kind . . .*

"You like noodles?" he asked.

"Yes."

"Good."

When the waiter arrived, Roland ordered túrós csusza. "Is it enough for two?" he asked the waiter.

"Plenty." The waiter smiled.

A few minutes later, a heaping plate of hot noodles arrived. It was covered in a soft cheese and sprinkled with crispy bacon. The waiter filled Betty's plate first and then Roland's. "Enjoy," he said in heavily accented English.

Betty took a forkful.

"What do you think?"

"I think I like Hungarian food," she said.

"How about Hungarian men?"

"You're the only one I know."

"So? Do you like me?"

She let out a laugh. "You know I do."

After they finished a dessert of rétes, a thick pastry stuffed with fresh cherry filling, and thick Hungarian coffee, Roland paid the bill, and they went outside to walk toward the streetcar, which would take them to her home. It was still a little chilly, but the fresh air was a nice complement to the heavy-but-delicious meal.

"Where do you live?" she asked.

"Out here," he said. "I have a small farm, and I work my veterinary practice from home."

"A veterinarian is an animal doctor. So I assume you have lots of animals?"

"Of course. In fact, on our next date, if you'd like, I'll pick you up with my horse and cart. Elsie is a fine old horse, and I think you will like it better than taking the streetcar or walking."

She smiled at him. "What exactly is the job of an animal doctor?"

"I help the big ones, like the horses, when they are having trouble giving birth. I take care of them when they are sick. I love animals. Sometimes I like them better than people."

"Really? Do you?"

"I do."

"Why?"

"Animals don't hurt you intentionally. You know how you are scared that people are talking badly about you? Well, animals don't do that."

"But they will eat you or kill you, won't they? I mean wild ones, for sure."

"Yes, they will eat you if they are hungry. And they will kill you if they feel threatened. But there is nothing in this world like the love of a good dog."

"You have a dog?"

"I have three. But I must admit, Jenny is my favorite. She's a German shepherd mix. I got her as payment for delivering a calf for a farmer who couldn't afford my help when his milk cow was in distress. But I also have Sam and Buddy. And a barn cat, who I swear is a wise old man in a cat's body. His name is Max. He's supposed to live in the barn and catch mice. But most of the time he's in the house eating from my plate." He laughed. "They all have their own very distinct personalities."

"I've never had a pet. My father would never want to spend money on feeding animals, and my mother would say that they are too dirty to be in the house."

"Well, maybe when you get to know me better, you can come to my house and meet all of my furry friends. I think you will like them. And I know they'll love you."

"I've always been afraid of dogs."

"I promise you will be safe. And I promise by the time you leave my house you won't be afraid of dogs anymore."

CHAPTER FORTY-FIVE

That Saturday night, Roland arrived at Betty's home fifteen minutes early for their date. He wore a suit that seemed to be slightly small and a tie. In his hand he carried a dozen red roses wrapped with a gold ribbon, which he handed to Betty when she opened the door. She was wearing the best dress she owned. It was a navy-blue wool dress that brought out the blue in her eyes. "These are for you," he said, smiling. "And may I say you look absolutely beautiful."

"Th-thank you. Th-this is so sweet of you," she said. *He brought me flowers again,* she thought. *How sweet is he? John and I dated for over a year, and he never brought me flowers. Not on birthdays, not for Christmas. Not even once. He always said they were a waste of money because they died within a few days. But the thought is what counts. And this man is charming. My Roland, this very unusual foreign man.*

"So where are you taking me?" he asked as he helped her up into the cab of the cart. Then he walked around to the front and took a carrot out of his pocket. He popped it into the grateful horse's mouth and then climbed into the cab on the other side of Betty. He patted Betty's hand and smiled. Next, he snapped the whip in the air as he gently held on to the reins. The old horse began to walk slowly.

"I am a little nervous about going to a popular restaurant. But if you insist, there is a very nice supper club about three blocks from here."

"Nervous . . . you shouldn't be. I don't insist on anything. I want you to feel comfortable. However, I think it's necessary that you and I go somewhere together where we will be seen by your friends and neighbors. That way we can dispel any fears you might have about my reactions."

"I'm almost sorry I ever said anything about you being ashamed of me. Our last date was so lovely, the food, the conversation. I don't know why I felt compelled to go to one of the popular places in town. Would you be upset if I changed my mind and we went back to the Hungarian restaurant?"

"I would. Not because I wouldn't prefer the food. But because I want you to know that nothing anyone can do or say will sway how I feel about you. So please, don't be afraid. Just put your trust in me, huh?"

She shrugged. "I can't help it. I am afraid. I am afraid that someone will say something terrible, and this magical bubble you've created around me will burst. Then you'll realize that I am not the prize catch you think I am."

He laughed. "I can't imagine anyone ever having such a strong effect on me. Except for maybe . . . you."

"You say such sweet things."

"And I mean them," he said, "but I find it hard to believe that you think I would turn on you just because you dated a Jewish man."

"Around here it's a crime. I mean, not a legal crime but a crime against society."

"You think it's any different in Hungary? It's not. It's not Hungary or America that are different. It's me that's different. I just don't believe in all that nonsense. I have learned that people hate and fear anyone who is different than they are. The Jews have suffered for many thousands of years for just that reason. But I don't hate them. I don't hate anyone. There is usually no good reason for hatred. Like I said, sometimes I just prefer to be around animals to being around humans. They make more sense."

"You're an interesting man. I don't think I've ever met anyone like you."

He turned to look at her and smiled. "You haven't! And I plan to prove to you what a catch I am by showing you how well I can dance! Now, where is this place that is the most popular supper club in Medina?"

"It's called Forester's Prime Steaks. You turn right at the next corner, and it's one block up the street."

At the corner he pulled the horses' reins, and they went right then north until he saw a large black-and-white sign that said Forester's.

"It's a little expensive. I don't know if that is all right with you . . ."

"It's fine. Please don't worry about that. In fact, Betty Howard, don't you worry about a thing. Come on, let's go. Let's eat, and then, my girl, let's dance!"

She hesitated. But he took her arm and helped her down from the wagon. Then he looked into her eyes and saw she was still worried. So in a serious tone, and still holding her hand in his, he said, "The best thing for us to do is to start going out to places where we will be seen together. It's important that we break through this barrier of fear that you are trapped in. We'll face it head-on and accept whatever happens. And we'll do it together. If people make comments, then they do. And once we have conquered all of your fears, our relationship will be able to grow. And then our feelings for each other can become whatever they are destined to become."

He took her arm and led her inside the crowded restaurant. She tensed up as she glanced around the room. He put his arm around her shoulder and squeezed reassuringly. There were plenty of familiar faces. Betty felt her stomach turn as they were seated at a table beside a young couple who looked familiar to her. The woman glared at Betty, then she put her hand over her mouth and whispered something to her partner. He shook his head. None of this was lost on Roland. But he said nothing. Instead, he picked up the menu and turned to Betty. "So last week I ordered for you because I know Hungarian food. This week it's your turn. You order for us."

"What do you like to eat?" she said, but she was watching the couple as they stared at her.

"Something very American. Pot roast and potatoes? That's very American, isn't it? What do you think?"

"Yes, it is." Her voice was shaky.

The couple was still staring at Betty. Roland turned to the man and said, "I know that the young lady I am with is the most beautiful girl in this restaurant. But with all due respect, sir, do you think you should be insulting your date by staring at mine?"

The man's face turned scarlet. And the woman bit her lower lip. When the other couple's food arrived a few minutes later, the man said to the waiter, "Can you pack this up and bring the check? We'd like to leave now."

After they were gone, Roland smiled and winked at Betty. She smiled back and took his hand.

"You handled that so well," she said.

"I only told the truth. You are the prettiest girl in the restaurant. And he couldn't take his eyes off you," he said.

"His girlfriend was appalled. Then he was so embarrassed." She let out a laugh.

Roland laughed too. "See, I told you I would take care of anyone who was rude."

As they rode back toward Betty's home, she turned to Roland and said, "I have something to tell you."

"Another surprise?" he said.

"Don't be like that . . . please."

"I'm sorry. I didn't mean to be rude. Forgive me. I was just kidding. Please tell me."

"Well," she said, "I didn't tell you when we were seated, but I got nervous because I knew the girl who was sitting next to us. I didn't recognize the boy, but I went to school with her. She was very popular. I think she had a lot of friends and boyfriends because she is so pretty, but sometimes she's also very mean."

"Not as pretty as you," he said and winked at Betty.

CHAPTER FORTY-SIX

The following weekend, Roland picked Betty up and brought her back to his farm. As they rode up the winding path to the front of the house, Betty saw a sign that said, "Roland Horvath, Doctor of Veterinary Medicine. Clinic to the Right."

Roland noticed Betty was watching him as he turned to the left, so he said, "The clinic is on the right; my home is on the left."

They drove up to a large white building made of wood that had been freshly painted. He helped her down from the cart, and then he took her inside.

"Let me put Elsie up. You just go ahead and make yourself comfortable. I'll be right back."

"Elsie?"

"The horse, my dear. Have you forgotten her name already?" Roland said, taking a carrot out of a bowl on the kitchen table.

But just as he was about to walk out the door, they were greeted by a big-boned, long-haired German shepherd. "Jenny!" he cried, and she put her paws on his shoulders and began kissing his face. "You have no manners. We have company. Come on now, get down, and act like a lady. Sit."

The dog sat down. Roland turned to Betty. "Don't be afraid. She is just overly friendly. She won't jump on you. She only does that to me."

Roland was right. Jenny never jumped on Betty. She sat quietly at her feet and put her head on Betty's lap. At first Betty was afraid of her but the old dog was patient. And with soft nuzzles, old Jenny won Betty over. Next, Max the tomcat came over and wanted to know more about his master's guest. So he climbed the sofa and sat above Betty's head, purring. She found the rhythmic sound comforting.

Roland walked back in after putting Elsie up for the night. When he saw Betty and Max he let out a short laugh. "Looks like you've made friends with my brood. At least some of them. You'll meet the rest soon."

"I like them. I was afraid at first, but they are so sweet."

"Just like their daddy," he said. "So are you hungry yet?"

"I am."

"I'm glad to hear it because I have a special dinner planned for you."

"You cooked?"

"I can't lie. I didn't. I carried it out from the Hungarian restaurant. But I think you are going to really enjoy it. "

"What is it?"

"It's called toitott kaposzta."

"And what exactly does that mean?"

"Stuffed cabbage. It's cabbage stuffed with meat and rice and other good things."

She shrugged. "I'll try it."

He got up and began warming the food. Jenny followed him hoping he would drop a delicious morsel for her. And as soon as Jenny's large paws had vacated Betty's lap, Max climbed on and stretched out.

"It looks like my animals have taken a liking to you. That's a good sign. My father always said to be cautious when one of your pets didn't like a particular person. He said that animals know things we don't. And when your pets dislike someone, it means that person is not a true friend."

"So I guess this means you and I are real friends," Betty said.

"I would certainly like to think so." He smiled.

"Is your father here in the US or is he still in Hungary?"

"He passed away several years ago. He was still in Hungary. Kept promising me he would come here even for a visit, but he never did. He always said that too many people depended upon him back home. And he just couldn't leave them."

"Was he an animal doctor too?"

"He was, but he never went to school for it the way I did. He was a natural. My father grew up on a farm as did I. And you know what still haunts me to this day?"

"Tell me," she said.

"Well, he had this jar on a shelf in the kitchen with all the money he'd saved from his entire life's work. When I was old enough, he took that jar down and counted out the cash. 'This here,' he said to me, 'this is for you to go to school.' I told him I wanted to be a veterinarian just like him. And his answer was that he wanted me to be a better doctor than he was. He felt that if I went to school, I would be able combine all that he had taught me with all the modern medicine I would learn."

"He saved everything he could to make you what you are today. That's a wonderful story."

"Yes, it is. He was a wonderful man. So I went to London, and that's where I earned my degree. And you know what? I still use a lot of the old folk methods my father used. The ones he taught me. May he rest in peace."

"You still miss him. I can tell."

"Every day. Sometimes, I have a particularly difficult case, and I go outside, and I talk to him. I say, 'Dad, what would you do?'"

"And does he answer?"

"Not in words. But quite often, if I sit outside for a while and let my mind work, the answer will come to me. I believe it comes from my father."

She smiled at him and took his hand in hers. Several moments passed. Then she said, "I've never been to Europe, but I would love to go some day. I would love to see where you grew up."

"Oh yes, Hungary is a beautiful country."

What about your mother? Did she want you to go to London?"

"She died giving birth to me. I was an only child. My father and I were very close. Not only were we father and son, but we were best friends."

"So how did you ever end up here in Medina?"

"A friend of my father's moved here to America. He settled in Medina. A few years later, the same fellow sent my dad a letter saying that the Medina farmers needed a good animal doctor to help them with their livestock. I had already finished school. My father thought it would be a good opportunity for me to come to America. So here I am."

"Did you ever go back and see him before he died?"

"Many times. I even considered moving back home because I missed my dad so much. But I had already established myself here in America. I came to understand why my father couldn't leave Hungary. I couldn't just leave my patients here in America either. As a doctor you become attached to the animals that depend on you. Does this make any sense to you?"

"It does," she said. "How long have you been in the United States?"

"About ten years."

"And you've never been married?"

"I didn't say that."

"You were married?"

"I was married for two years. My wife passed away."

"I'm sorry."

"Yes, me too. But it was a long time ago. She was from Hungary. She died of the Spanish flu a year after we arrived in Medina."

"I don't know what to say."

He smiled at her. "It's all right. It's been a long time. I get lonely sometimes. And at first, I raged against God. I was so angry. She was so young and beautiful. I couldn't understand why she was taken from me. But time passed, and I learned to live with the loss. What else could I do."

She nodded. Then a few minutes later, she asked, "I don't want to be rude, but how old are you?"

"It's not rude. I'm not ashamed of my age. Although I am much older than you. I hope this doesn't make a difference in our relationship. But I'm forty-two."

"You look young. I thought you were in your late twenties."

He laughed. "Nope. I guess you could say I'm an old man." Then he hesitated. "I hope you haven't lost interest?"

"I haven't." She smiled.

Once the food was ready, Roland set the table. Gently, Roland coaxed Max off Betty's lap so she could get up and come to the table. She stood and stretched her legs. Then they sat down to dinner.

"It's awkward being here alone with you," she said. "Except for Sam, I've never been alone like this with a man."

"Not even your fiancé?"

"Never. We always went to dinner or to see a movie. John was nice to me, at least until the end. But somehow, I never felt close to him. I was always a little afraid of him. I don't know why. He never did anything to cause me to feel that way. And yet I think I sensed that he had a cruel streak."

"You're not afraid of me, are you?"

"No, never. "

"I'm glad. I would never want you to fear me."

"I don't. In fact, I feel closer to you than I ever felt to John. You're easy to talk to."

"So why is it awkward to be here with me?" he asked.

"I don't know. I guess I just don't want to say or do anything that would make you stop liking me."

He laughed a little. "No need to worry about that, sweet Betty."

After they finished eating, Roland started a fire in the fireplace, and they sat in front of it hand in hand.

"I want to tell you that what you did for me last week at the restaurant meant a lot to me," Betty said.

"I will always stand up for you. I guess you don't realize how I feel about you. I like you a lot. I might even be falling in love with you."

She touched his face, but the mention of love sobered her up. "I like you very much, Roland. But I can't lie to you, my heart is still with Samuel. I am still in love with him. Perhaps that's why I feel a little awkward."

There was a long silence. Then Roland said, "Maybe . . . maybe"—
he took her hand in his—"if we just continue seeing each other . . . you
will start to have feelings for me."

"I do have feelings for you, and they are growing. And . . . I know
that Samuel is gone. I have no plans of putting my life on the shelf
while I wait for him to return. Because I know he will never return. But
I must be honest. A small part of me will always love him. I will work
on making that part of me smaller and smaller as time passes." She
took a deep breath then continued, "I am ready to start a new life. And
I would like very much for you to be a part of that new life."

"I would like that," he said, then he kissed her. She felt her body
respond. It wasn't frantic and passionate the way it had been when
Samuel kissed her. She would never forget that heady feeling she felt
when Sam touched her. It was as if nothing in the world mattered
except the moment. Sam's touch was like magic to her. It made her so
hungry to feel him inside her that she lost all sense of right and wrong.
It was not at all like this with Roland. But it was very pleasant. He
smelled good, fresh like parsley, and his hair was clean. His kiss was
gentle and warm. And she found she was very happy when he kissed
her again.

The following Wednesday evening, Roland and Betty went to the
cinema where they saw *Sadie Thompson* starring Gloria Swanson and
Lionel Barrymore. As they left the theater, Roland asked, "Would you
like to go somewhere and have coffee and some cake?"

She nodded but didn't speak.

"What's wrong?" he asked.

"That movie was about a fallen woman. Sometimes I feel like a
fallen woman."

He put his arm around her. "Well, you won't fall too far because I'll
always be there to catch you." Then he winked. And she had to laugh
in spite of herself.

CHAPTER FORTY-SEVEN

April 1929

O ne evening Betty and Roland were sitting by the fireplace at Roland's farm. They were surrounded by his pets, animals that Betty had come to love. Jenny, the dog, had her head on Betty's lap, and Max, the cat, was sitting on top of the sofa with his head on Betty's shoulder. Roland hummed an old Hungarian folk song as he softly petted the head of a new puppy who had wandered onto the farm the previous day. Roland found that lots of stray animals appeared on his property. He assumed they had been dropped there by people who didn't want them. But he didn't care. He adored every one of them.

"What are you going to name him?" Betty asked.

"I haven't thought about it. Any ideas?"

She shrugged.

"I just got an idea," he said. "How about little blessing? We could call him Little One for short?"

"He is a blessing," Betty agreed. "I can't believe I was ever afraid of dogs. Now I love them."

"He's just a baby, so he's the littlest blessing in my life right now,"

Roland said. Then he took her hand in his and added, "You know what's been the biggest blessing in my life?"

"Your career?"

"Yes . . . that's been a big one."

"Jenny? Max?"

"Yes, all of them have been blessings. But the biggest blessing in my life has been you, Betty. You've filled my loneliness with joy. You've put new life into my days. I so look forward to our time together."

"So do I, Roland," she said. "I must admit that before I met you, I was afraid that the scandal about me and Sam had ruined my chances of ever dating anyone again."

He kissed her hand then gently turned her face so he could look into her eyes. "Have you ever thought of what life might be like if we got married?"

Betty felt her heart leap. She would love to be married, to be settled down in a home of her own. Maybe even to have a child of her own. These were dreams she thought she would have to abandon when Samuel didn't return. She had resigned herself to being an old spinster who worked at a restaurant forever. *How lucky I was that day Roland came in for lunch. Talk about blessings*, she thought. *Roland has turned out to be as much a blessing to me as I am to him.* As she gazed at him, with his golden-brown hair illuminated by the firelight, she thought, *He truly is a wonderful man.*

"Sit right here," he said, standing up. Jenny stood up to follow him. "Keep her company, Max." He put the cat on Betty's lap. Then he left the room. She waited, wondering where he'd gone. When he returned, he knelt before her and presented her with a small open box. Inside the box was a bright blue-white diamond on a simple gold band. Clearing his throat, he said, "I know I'm twice your age. But I promise you, if you'll have me, I'll be good to you. I'll do whatever I can to make you happy. What I am trying to say is, Betty Howard, will you marry me?"

For a moment she was stunned. Over the past few weeks Roland had given Betty every indication that he planned to propose. She should have been expecting this, but now that it was actually happening it felt unreal and a little scary. But she was also excited . . . and happy. "I am speechless," she mumbled as she looked at him on his knee holding a beautiful diamond ring that caught the light from the fireplace.

"Do you like me?" he asked.

She nodded. "Very much."

"Well"—he took her hand in his trembling one—"I love you."

"I think I love you too. And my answer is yes. I would love to be your wife."

CHAPTER FORTY-EIGHT

B etty and Roland were married in a small civil ceremony three weeks later. Only their immediate family and closest friends were present. Joan attended, against her parents' wishes, but she was the only friend of Betty's who did. No one else had stayed in contact with Betty after the scandal with Sam. They were afraid to tarnish their own reputations and ruin their chances to marry someone who was respected in town. A few Hungarian couples whom Roland had known since his arrival in America attended. Betty wore a simple blush-colored dress that had been her mother's. Roland wore the same suit he'd worn when they went out on dates. This was the not the wedding Betty had dreamed of as a child. There were no flowers, and it did not take place in a big beautiful church. But she was happy and excited. Her eyes sparkled, and her skin glowed, and she was beautiful in that special way that a girl can only be on her wedding day.

After Betty and Roland said their vows, everyone went to an American steakhouse that Betty's father chose. They had a nice, quiet dinner, although several of the townspeople still stared at Betty from across the room. Joan did not acknowledge them, but she left the restaurant early. She did not even wait for the cake to be served. Joan claimed she had to be at work early the following morning. Betty knew better. She understood Joan's concern about bringing down the wrath of the townspeople on herself. So she kissed her friend and thanked her for coming.

The wedding cake was served. And once they'd finished, Betty and Roland left the restaurant. They rode in Roland's horse and cart back to the farm where they planned to spend their honeymoon. They had talked about getting away, taking a week or so to celebrate their marriage but decided against it because they had no one to care for the animals. Roland and Betty both agreed that Roland could not leave his practice unmanned for any length of time. Betty didn't mind. She found she liked the animals, and since they'd become engaged, she had quit her job at the restaurant and started helping Roland at the clinic by working the front desk. The people who brought their pets in to see Roland didn't seem to care much about her past. Their only concerns were helping their beloved cat or dog in the animal's time of need. And because Betty treated the animals with gentle kindness and was sensitive to the fears and pain of their owners, they often brought her gifts. She received bushels of oranges and apples. Sometimes she received fresh eggs and milk.

Quite often, Roland would have to leave the clinic and go to a neighboring farm to help a horse who had colic or a cow with a breach birth. He would sometimes be gone overnight. Before Betty started working at the clinic, Roland would simply leave a note on the door. But now, Betty was able to stay at the house alone. And when the pet owners came in, she would comfort them then carefully write down the patients' symptoms and promise that Roland would be in touch as soon as he returned.

But after tonight everything would be different. Roland was no longer just her fiancé; he was Betty's husband. Her heart beat with excitement. *I am someone's wife. Someone wonderful and kind.* She smiled at him as he opened the door to the house. Then he easily lifted her in his arms and carried her over the threshold. Closing the door behind them with his foot he walked into the bedroom and gently placed her on the bed. Even though Betty often had stayed at Roland's house, it had happened only when he was forced to go out of town. So they'd never slept in the same bed, and they had never made love to each other before. Roland had always been respectful of Betty. She often wondered if he was that way because he was so much older than she. He'd said he felt privileged to have such a young fiancée, and he never wanted to do anything that would make Betty uncomfortable. There had been times when Betty wanted him to be more forward. She would have gladly gone to his bed. A sweet smile came over her face when she remembered him saying he wanted their wedding night to be memorable. *Roland is so smart because he was willing to wait; tonight is going to be very special for both of us.*

She lay on the bed and waited, listening while he washed up. Once he returned to their room, Betty got undressed. She overhead him talking to Jenny the dog, who was laying on the floor at the foot of the bed. "I hope I can make her happy. I will certainly try." Betty felt warm and loved as she washed her face and hung up her dress.

Roland lay on the bed. Max, the cat had jumped up beside him. As he was petting the soft fur, he thought of his previous wife, Maria. The young, vivacious girl who had died, leaving a hole in his heart and a brand on his memory. Maria was frozen in time. She would never grow old. In his mind and heart, she would always remain young and beautiful. He thought of her running up the hill with Sully, the golden retriever, who had been her dog, racing behind her. That dog had loved Maria so much that the poor thing died two weeks after Maria passed. There had been no medical explanation for the dog's death. It had never been sick. The poor thing died of a broken heart. After Maria died, he'd spoken to her often. He would tell her about his day, about the animals, and even about Betty. Now, as he waited for Betty, he spoke to his former wife in a soft whisper. "Maria, since the day you left me to go to heaven, I have lain in this bed and talked to you every night before I went to sleep. But tonight, my dear Maria, tonight . . . is different. In a way I feel as if I must ask for your forgiveness for my being unfaithful to our love, to what we once shared. But in my heart I truly believe that wherever you are, you understand that I need someone in my life. Betty is a good girl. She is kind, and in many ways she reminds me of you. Please be assured that no one will ever take your place in my heart. Even so, tonight will be the last time I will speak to you before I sleep. The time has come, and I must say goodbye because tonight my new life with Betty begins. I know you, and you would want me to be happy. And wherever you are, you realize that I have come to love Betty very much. I pray that she and I will have a long and happy life together. I feel in my heart that you are looking down and smiling. You know how lonely I have been. It's been a long, hard, and painful journey since I lost you, but I have finally found happiness again. So after ten long years I am finally able to say goodbye."

Betty walked into the bedroom wearing a white satin negligee with a lace overlay that she had made. Her golden hair hung loose. She smiled at Roland. He pulled back the covers and patted the bed. Betty turned out the lights and got in beside him.

Roland took her into his arms and held her there for a long time. He kissed her slowly and gently, caressing and kissing every inch of her body from her eyelids to her to toes. Unlike the wild and blinding passion she'd shared with Samuel, making love with Roland was a gradual, slow build of sweet tender passion that culminated in a warm and satisfying climax. Once they'd finished, she lay in his arms contented. And for the first time since she'd met Samuel, Betty fell into a deep and restful slumber without thinking of Samuel.

Living with Roland was always an adventure. There were dogs having puppies, kittens in need of bottle feeding, who'd been abandoned in front of the clinic overnight. Betty held frightened animals while they were examined. She even cleaned cages. And strangely enough, she would not have traded her life as the wife of a veterinarian for anything.

One Sunday, Roland decided Betty should learn to ride a horse. At first, she was reluctant. She was afraid she would fall. But Roland coaxed her into getting behind him onto the horse. "Put your arms around my waist. I won't go too fast. I promise. At least not the first time." He laughed.

"Don't laugh at me, Roland. I'm scared," she said, holding him tightly.

"I'm sorry for laughing. Are you comfortable?"

"No, I'm not," she said.

"Well, I must admit that I love it when you hold me like you want to squeeze the life out of me."

She laughed. "I'm holding you so tight because I'm scared out of my mind. It looks like a long way to the ground."

"You won't fall. Do you trust me?"

"I do."

"Then just relax."

Betty found she enjoyed the gentle rhythm as the old horse walked slowly through the farm.

Another day, Roland taught his young wife how to maintain their vegetable garden. "I find gardening peaceful. It feels good to get your hands dirty with the earth."

"It is peaceful," she said, the sun shining on her hair and warming her back.

"And you must agree that the fresh produce from our garden is far better than the stuff you buy at the store." He picked a cucumber and took a bite. Then he held the cucumber in front of Betty's lips, and she took a bite too.

"I do agree with you on that. The vegetables are so crunchy and fresh," she said.

One night a week they went to their favorite Hungarian restaurant for dinner, but most of the time they were content to stay at home. They prepared their meals together, and after they finished their dinner, they played cards, or Roland read to her from his favorite book of poems. And they made love. A sweet gentle expression of the gratitude they both felt for one another. Theirs was a quiet existence that Betty came to love.

CHAPTER FORTY-NINE

May 10, 1929

On the tenth of May in the year 1929, Lady Liberty trembled as the stock market plummeted, crashing like an unmanned airplane out of control. This created a new and troubling time in American history. People who had once been rich lost their investments and were now poor and destitute. The working class lost their jobs. Small family businesses closed because no one had any money to purchase their goods or services. People were unable to pay their rents or mortgages and were evicted, and many of them had little children. Almost overnight, bread and soup lines formed outside churches and the Salvation Army to offer a small meal to those who were starving. Tent cities of homeless and destitute people appeared in the parks. Americans were frightened and desperate for help. They needed a president who could take charge and save them from what seemed like the end of the world.

Across the sea in Germany, the German people faced horrors of their own. After losing the First World War, the morale of the German people was low. Unemployment soared. Even those who had a little money found that the money they had became worth less and less as hyperinflation threatened to destroy the country. Yet even in the face of all this uncertainty, artists, musicians, and writers from all over the world flocked to Berlin for inspiration. In Berlin, it was a time of wild abandonment. Sex, drugs, and perversions of all kinds became the norm. Germany, too, was desperate, lost, and seeking a leader, a leader who could restore their economy and their pride. A führer who could make sense of their troubled world and tell them who and what had caused such a dark cloud to descend over their cultured land. A land which had been home to such great artists as Beethoven and Brahms. The German people were begging for a leader who would find and rid them of whatever dark menace was strangling their country.

There was a man. A little man with a comical mustache. This comical little man had been a failure all his life. When he was a child, his father had abused him. Then he'd been rejected by the art school that he'd dreamed of attending. For several years he'd wandered living the life of a homeless vagabond until he served as a soldier for Germany in WW1. Once the war ended, this little man, who had been laughed at all his life, joined a radical political party. He was arrested and served time in prison for rioting in the streets. And . . . it was prison that he found his dark calling. It was here that he wrote a book. A book about his struggles. In this book he gave the German people hope for a better future by revealing his dark and ominous plans. Oh yes, this man had plans to save Germany from the danger of the Jews who he blamed for all the country's problems. This book was just another form of blood libel. Another accusation. But few ever read the book. No one took this silly little man seriously. And that . . . was a deadly mistake.

CHAPTER FIFTY

Manhattan, May 1929

Goldie Schatzman had almost lost hope that she would ever receive the money from her father that she needed for passage back to Germany. Since the stock market crash, sales at the bakery were dropping rapidly. People couldn't afford the luxury of buying baked bread. What little money they had was used to buy flour.

Alma had started school, and she was there all day, but Goldie, Samuel, and Irving spent many frightened hours in the empty bakery waiting and hoping they would have customers. Very few came in. And the occasional ones who did never spent much. Goldie was in charge of keeping the books for the bakery, and although Irving was in charge of keeping track of their personal finances, she knew the family had almost depleted all their savings just to keep the doors of the business open. Soon they would be unable to afford to keep the bakery. Each of them, Goldie included, would be forced to find work in order to put food on the table and to continue to pay the rent on the rundown apartment where they lived.

At least the long, frigid winter in that horrible flat is finally over, she thought. When she'd first moved to Manhattan, she'd found the hustle and bustle of the city somewhat exciting. But that was only because she had so many wonderful memories from her childhood growing up in a big metropolitan city. How she had loved living in Berlin with her parents. But growing up under the wing of a rich patriarch was a lot different than living as the wife of an unsuccessful baker. Her father's money had enabled her to live a life most people only dreamed of. She was able to shop for pretty clothes and go to fancy restaurants with her many friends. Every day she had somewhere to go and something to do. There were parties and picnics. There were book signings by famous authors, and art shows at the galleries. On Sunday her father took the family for carriage rides through the park. Once a year her parents took her traveling, sometimes to London, sometimes to France. She'd loved those cities, but she never tired of her life in Berlin. And at first, she had foolishly let herself believe that Manhattan would hold some of the same delicious wonderment that Berlin held for her. However, Goldie quickly discovered that living in Manhattan without her father's money was a miserable existence. It was a far cry from her youth. Sometimes she would take a bus up to town where she would see the rich people enjoying their lives the way she'd once enjoyed hers. All the glitter and glitz of city life was right there only inches from her fingertips. But try as she might, she could never grasp it. After a day of watching the rich women on the Upper East Side, Goldie felt like a small child looking through a window at toys she would never own.

The lack of heat in the winter, the foul smells that wafted through the halls of her apartment building when her neighbors were cooking, the constant noise, the beggars, and the prostitutes on the streets made her feel like she was being dragged under water and drowning in a sea of unhappiness. Sometimes she was so hungry for her old life that she was paralyzed by depression and unable to get out of bed. On those days Samuel and Irving worked at the bakery without her. On those days she lay in bed contemplating suicide. *I would rather be dead than go on like this. If my father doesn't send us money for passage out of here, I am going to do it. I am going to end my life,* she thought, wondering how much longer she should wait before resigning herself to the fact that her father was not going to send the money.

Then on a rainy morning on the first of May, she had received a letter from her parents. Her hands trembled when she saw her mother's neat handwriting. Quickly, she opened the envelope. When a check fell to the ground, she let out a small cry. She picked up the check. It was enough money for passage for her and the two children. And it had been signed by her father.

When she'd written to her parents, she'd lied to them. She'd told them she wanted to bring Samuel and Alma to Berlin just for a visit with them and that was why she needed the money. Goldie never told them she planned to stay in Germany and never return to America and to her husband. She decided it was best to save that information until she was safe on German soil. If her father had known her plan, she was certain he would have denied her the money and told her that her place was in America with Irving. So she'd enticed him by promising him a wonderful visit with his two grandchildren. Both of whom he'd never met. She'd dangled the bait. And for a while she thought he might be wise to her. Or he was going to ignore her request altogether. However, he'd finally responded, and she would soon be on her way back to Germany. Once Goldie was at home, she would tell her parents how poorly Irving was doing. She would tell them about the apartment where she was living. And, of course, her parents would have to allow her and the children to stay.

CHAPTER FIFTY-ONE

As soon as Goldie received the money, she ran to the bank and cashed the check. Then she returned home with the money safely in her pocketbook and sat down to write a letter to Leni.

Dear Leni,

The money arrived! My father, the honorable Joseph Birnbaum, finally found a soft spot in his frozen heart and sent a check. I shall be returning to Germany soon. I will be bringing my two children with me. Irving refuses to come. He is failing miserably since we've moved to Manhattan. He took all the money we had from the sale of our business and home in Medina and used it to open a new bakery in New York City, but the business was unsuccessful. I have mixed feelings about Irving. I spent nineteen years of my life with him, so I know that to some degree, I will miss him. Even so, if I am honest with myself, I am glad to finally be free of this marriage. I've felt like I have been drowning since the day I married Irving. So, although goodbye will be painful, the pain won't last long. If you understand my meaning. The economy here in America has taken a real downturn. The stock market crashed, and it has sent waves of despair through a newly unemployed population. The newspapers I've read say that the economy is bad in

Germany too. But don't you worry, my friend, my father has plenty. No matter what happens to the economy, Birnbaum's ready-to-wear factory will always make plenty of money. My father will see to that! So, once I am home, I will help you financially if you need it. I send you love, and I look forward to seeing you soon.

Your friend, always,
Goldie

CHAPTER FIFTY-TWO

The day after she received the check, Irving was running low on sugar at the bakery. So he sent Samuel to the general store to buy some. As soon as they were alone, Goldie turned to her husband. "I got the money from my father yesterday."

"Money? To help us?" Irving had somehow forgotten about her wanting to return to Germany.

"No, Irving. Money for passage for the children and I to go back to Germany."

"Ah, yes, I remember now," he said, his shoulders slumping. "I'm sorry. I'm forgetful these days. I think it is because I'm so tired."

"It's all right," she said, feeling compassion for him. Goldie accepted that she wasn't in love with Irving, but she had spent the greater part of her life with him. And in her own way, she cared for him, not like a husband, but almost like a brother. She studied him for a moment. *Poor Irving, with his thick spectacles, his once heavy dark hair starting to thin and to gray. That serious expression he always wore as if he was in pain, not necessarily physical pain, but the pain of a man who was always just a step behind his dreams. Only a man like Irving would have willingly taken on a child who was fathered by another man and been so kind to that child. I am grateful to him for that kindness toward Sam. But now, I must go. The children must go too. It is no longer safe here for us. And my heart cries out for Berlin, for the wonderful, magical, cultured city of my birth.* Sadness came over her. It felt so final, knowing that once she left for Germany, she would probably never see Irving again. This was the end of a chapter in the book of her life. It was painful and terrifying, but it was also wildly exciting. *Irving could have come with us. I gave him the option. But he didn't want to, and now it's too late for him to change his mind. My father only sent enough money for me and the children. In a way, I am really glad he isn't coming. And in another way, I am not. How can I be happy and sad at the same time?*

"I know how fond the children are of you," she said, "I am too, Irving."

"I would like to believe that." He smiled wryly.

"It doesn't matter anymore, I suppose," she said, looking away from him. She added, "The children don't want to go. So I've decided to tell them that I have changed my mind about moving and that we are only going to Germany for a visit and are going to return here in a few months."

"But it's not true, is it?" he asked with a note of hope in his voice.

"No, Irving, it's not true. I want to go home. I never want to see this place again," she said. "But I am afraid that they won't get on the boat if they know we aren't coming back to America."

He bit his lip. His face was red, and his voice was deliberate and controlled. "I know you want to go," he said, "and I won't keep you here in America against your will. Especially with what is going on here with the economy." He turned and walked away from her to look out the window, across the street where he saw two men begging. Then he turned back to look at her. "Perhaps you are right; it might be better in Germany for you and the children. After all, at least your family is wealthy. Every day is a struggle for us here. I don't mind working hard. But if your parents can give the children a better life, I will not stand in your way. Nevertheless, I will not allow you lie to them. They need to know the truth about what you plan to do."

She glared at him. She wanted to remind him that Samuel was not even his biological child and that he had no right to tell her what to say to him. But she knew that Irving had raised him, and he did have a right. So she just nodded. "You win. I'll tell them the truth."

That night after dinner, Goldie gathered everyone into the living room. Irving sat in his easy chair. Sam and Alma sat on the sofa. Goldie smiled at them all, then she stood up in the center of the room as if she were going to give an acceptance speech for some kind of an award. "I have good news," she said cheerfully. "We are going to Germany. And as you know, your grandfather who lives there is rich. We won't have to worry about money anymore. You can buy pretty dresses, Alma, and study wherever you'd like. And you, Sam, you will find a huge array of beautiful Jewish girls who will be interested in making a match with you. Not only will they be unaware of this messy incident in Medina, but they will be very impressed with your grandfather's status. All in all, things will be much better for us there. Unfortunately, your father has the bakery to run, so he won't be joining us . . ."

"I don't care about pretty dresses, Mother. I don't want to leave here. What about Father? I don't want to leave Father."

"He might join us later," Goldie said, touching her daughter's arm. "And you can certainly return to America to visit him. Your grandfather will give you the money."

Samuel looked at his father, who nodded as if he agreed. But looking closer, Samuel could see the hurt in Irving's eyes, and there were a thousand questions he wanted to ask him, but he didn't. All he said was, "Dad, do you think this is best?"

"I do, son," Irving said, his voice cracking.

"But who will help you in the bakery if I leave with Mom?"

"I don't know. But there is a very good possibility that we won't have the bakery much longer. We don't have enough customers to pay our bills, and our savings are running out. I will get a job and save money. Once I can afford to open another bakery, I will send for you, your sister, and your mother. Once I have reestablished myself, I will be able to provide for you if any of you want to come home. Right now, I can't afford to take care of you." He hung his head.

Samuel looked at Alma, who got up and knelt beside Irving's chair. Then she leaned over and embraced her father. "I don't care if we lose the business. I want to stay with you and help you, Dad."

"No, a young girl needs a home. You need nice clothes. You are sixteen. Soon you'll be getting ready to get married. And if you are ever going to make a good match with a nice Jewish boy, who has a good job and comes from a decent family, you will need money for your dowry. Your grandfather can provide that. I can't. Your grandfather is an asset to your future."

Alma lay her head on her father's shoulder. "Dad, I don't want to live in Germany without you. Once I marry, I will have to stay in Berlin if my husband insists."

"I know. Maybe God will bless me, and I will be able to send for you and provide for you before you are ready to make a match. But for now, I think your mother is right. This is best."

CHAPTER FIFTY-THREE

Alma was very superstitious, although she never told anyone. When she walked to school, she was careful not to step on cracks in the street. She believed some days were auspicious, and others were dangerous times, and the best thing to do on those days was to stay close to home and take care. She tried to do good things, making time to help out at the shul and make mitzvahs where and whenever she was able. Her hope was that if she did good things, God would look kindly upon her and her family. And because of her superstitious fears, she was convinced she had caused her father's business to fail when she'd deliberately lied to Samuel about what happened when she went to speak to Betty.

Sometimes she watched Samuel when he didn't know she was watching him, and she felt so sad because she could see the loss of joy and hope in his eyes, and she was overcome with guilt. But how could she ever tell him what really had happened that day? How the events that had unfolded had changed her life. Before those two boys raped her, Alma had been a happy and normal fifteen-year-old girl. She'd had a healthy interest in boys and was excited to find her future husband and build a home. Not anymore. She cringed at the idea of a man touching her in those very private places that had been violated by those horrible boys. And since that day, when those boys had branded pain into her soul, she refused to go to the parties at the synagogue with her girlfriends. In fact, she had not been back to visit with her friends in Medina since they moved to Manhattan. It was as if the girls she grew up with remained pure, sweet, and innocent. But she? She was scared and could never be the naïve girl who she'd been before that day. Alma was damaged forever.

There were nights she couldn't fall asleep because each time she closed her eyes she saw the monstrous faces of those boys hovering over her as they invaded the most sacred part of her young body. The memory of the pain was so real and so close to the surface that it rose, and she felt it again. Tears would stain her pillow as she wept for her lost innocence and for the children she would never bear. How could she tell her father she wasn't interested in a finding a good match? How could she ever explain that she hoped never to marry. If she'd been a Catholic, she would have joined a convent and closed the door to marriage forever. But, of course, that was not an option to her. So she decided that once her parents or grandparents started bringing men home who were to be potential husbands, she would make sure to do things to discourage them and ensure they disliked her.

Her grades suffered, too, since that fateful day. Sometimes she was unable to concentrate during her classes. She was easily distracted by anything, a loud noise, the sound of a man's voice that reminded her of the voice of one of her attackers, or even something as simple as a memory of the way things were before she was so brutally attacked. There were days Alma rode the streetcar all the way to school only to walk away without ever entering the classroom. On those days she would wander the congested streets of Manhattan. And before the stock market crash, she felt safer in crowds. But since the market crashed and so many people appeared to have not only lost their jobs and their homes but also their minds.

She had begun to feel a chill of fear whenever she walked past the tent cities. No one had bothered her, but the vacant looks in their eyes were horrifying. And so lately she was not wandering the streets. Instead, she would dress and leave for school. Then she would wait and watch from across the street until her parents and brother left for work. Then she would return home and lie in bed all day with an empty, lonely feeling buried deep in her belly. Alma hardly spoke to her brother anymore. Looking at him only made her feel worse as she was haunted by her lies. So she avoided him whenever possible. There were times when she was so angry that she felt like she might explode, and she wished she could talk to someone about what she was feeling. But there was no one to talk to. It was all my own fault, she told herself over and over. I should never have agreed to go and talk to Betty for Sam. I should have refused. I know that the goyim hate us. I've always known it. If I had refused to go to their goyisha neighborhood, those boys would never have gotten their filthy hands on me. And now I am going to pay the price for the rest of my days.

CHAPTER FIFTY-FOUR

G oldie noticed her daughter hardly ate and that she'd lost a great deal of weight. But instead of being concerned, she assumed it was because Alma was a teenager. Soon she would be presented to potential husbands, and she wanted to look her best. *After all, it's so unfortunate, but my daughter is just not a very pretty girl. I am sure she realizes it. And she probably figures that if she were fat, it would be even harder for her to find a decent man. Poor thing, it's such a shame she turned out to look like Irving instead of me. And she is so withdrawn, not at all fun or carefree like I was. Alma is so much like her father. But perhaps she will grow out of her introverted ways. She is a teenager after all.* Goldie never suspected what happened to her daughter, and Alma never said a word.

Samuel, too, had become withdrawn and irritable. But as far as Goldie was concerned that was to be expected. Her handsome son had been through so much. Once they arrived in Berlin, Goldie was sure things would be much better for all of them. Her father would help her children make good matches. And as far as Goldie was concerned . . . she would be home and back in the lap of luxury living the life she missed. In order to keep down the gossip that she knew would circulate about her among the other rich Jewish families in her neighborhood, she'd made up a story. She planned to lie and tell them that

Irving had been very successful in America. She would say they'd had a wonderful marriage. And then with crocodile tears she would explain that he had recently become ill and passed away. "I could not bear to be in America without my beloved husband, so I was driven to return home to Germany, to the comfort of my family." She practiced these words and her fake tears until she felt her performance was thoroughly convincing. Goldie knew that if she told her parents Irving had been a terrible husband, that he'd been physically violent toward her, she could convince them to go along with this story. She would file for divorce. Her father would pay for it. And as for her children? They would want to tell their grandparents the truth. But if they enjoyed the luxurious lifestyle her family provided, they'd better go along with her story too. Because if they didn't, they might just find themselves back in that cold-water flat in Manhattan.

Goldie was in a wonderful mood as she packed to leave. She averted her eyes from Irving's because his sadness was so great that it usurped her joy. Finally, she was returning to the life she loved, and she was exhilarated. She was leaving him, his poverty, his promises, his clutching love, and everything he stood for, behind. At first, she thought she would miss him, but as the sailing date grew closer, she was too excited to think about anything but home. And the last thing she wanted was to face his pain. Dutifully, Alma and Samuel packed their things. Neither of them complained. But she overheard Samuel talking to Irving in the back of the bakery one afternoon in the last days before she and the children were to leave and the Schatzman's bakery was set to close.

"I'll stay here with you, Dad. I'll get a job, and together we can save up money and start a new business."

"I don't want that. If you stay, I'll be responsible for taking care of you. And quite frankly, I don't even know how I am going to take care of myself. I've been looking for a job. I can't find one. Our rent at the apartment is paid up until the end of July. For that I am grateful. You and your mother and sister sail out July twenty-second. At least you'll have a place to stay until you leave."

"And then what will happen to you?"

"I don't know, son. All I know is I have failed as a father and husband. It was my job to provide for you and I am not able to do that. So, please, go live with your grandfather. He can take good care of you and your sister. I will find comfort in knowing that my children have a safe place to sleep and plenty to eat."

"But Dad . . ."

"Please, Samuel. Don't ask me any more questions. I don't want to talk about this. Just go with your mother."

"If I write to you, will you write back to me?"

"Of course I will. You are my son. You will always be my son," Irving said, and he thought, *I raised you. It was me who was there on the day you were born. I don't care whose sperm fathered you. I am your father. I held you and walked the floor with you when you had measles. I will always love you.*

Hearing this conversation made Goldie feel guilty. She was ready to say goodbye to her marriage. But thinking of Irving alone and penniless in Manhattan made her sad. She knew her children would want her to ask him again if he would join them in returning home. But if he said yes, she would have to wait until her father sent her more money for his passage. Something she didn't want to do. Not only that, if he returned with her to Germany, then she would still be married to him. Irving Schatzman, the baker. But . . . if he stayed here in America, and everyone thought he was dead, she would be free to pursue other relationships. Relationships with exciting men, artists, wealthy men, any man but Irving Schatzman, the baker. *And . . . he did say he wanted to stay here. He said he loved America, didn't he? That was what he said. The truth is I don't want him to come back to Germany with me. The truth is that I want to leave this miserable marriage behind me. I won't ask him. I won't let guilt get in the way of my dream of going home without him.*

CHAPTER FIFTY-FIVE

After Alma told Samuel that Betty did not want to hear from him anymore, Sam was miserable. He could not rest so he put all his energy into working. He worked at the bakery during the day. And he secretly searched for a second job. If he had found one, he would have told his mother that he was going to stay in America and help his father get back on his feet. But Sam didn't find any work. There were no jobs to be had. He had very little formal education, and the only work experience he had was the bakery.

One night after work, Goldie asked Sam to stop and buy some carrots and potatoes on his way home. As he walked through the menagerie of outside vendors, who hawked their wares on the streets, he began to think. *Perhaps my mother is right,* he thought. *Maybe it is best that I, too, go to live with my grandparents. I'll miss Dad, but at least there is a good chance that Grandpa will pay for me to go to school. I've never had that opportunity before. And once I graduate, and I have a degree, I'll return to America, and then I would really be able to help Dad. Except for my father, I have nothing left here in America. The girl I love is gone. The bakery is closing. We've lost our home because of me. I have no friends. The entire Jewish community in Medina hates me. They blame me for their loss of income during the boycott and for putting them all in danger. I wonder if they believe me that I never had anything to do with that little girl. I think some of them do, but some probably don't. And the worst part of it all is that if Betty would have me, I would risk everything to go back with her. Even my life.* He kicked a half-eaten apple into the street where a waiting horse gratefully received it. *Losing Betty has been the worst part of all of this. Worse than being ostracized, worse than the beating from those hoodlums, more painful than the broken ribs, the broken jaw, and all the rest of it. If she were still by my side, I could endure everything. I'd stay here in the US. I'd beg her to marry me, and I'd search until I found some kind of work. Any kind of work. I wouldn't care if I spent all day scrubbing floors. I'd do whatever needed to be done to support my wife.*

"I'll take these," he said, handing five potatoes and a bunch of carrots to the man who ran the vegetable cart. But when Samuel went into his pocket to pay, he found that his wallet had been stolen. Frantically, he searched for it. But it was gone. He'd been pickpocketed. He apologized to the vendor. And turned to walk away.

"Here." The vendor threw him an apple.

"Thanks," Samuel said as he caught it. But he was miserable. All of his money was gone. Everything he'd earned that entire week. And now he'd have to go home and tell his mother what happened and ask her for money so he could go back out and buy vegetables for dinner. His memory went back to a night not long ago when they'd still lived in Medina. On that night his family had eaten chicken for dinner with mashed potatoes. His mouth watered at the memory. *What have I done to my family? What I have I done to myself?* He walked home dejected.

CHAPTER FIFTY-SIX

M *anhattan,* **July 1929**
The ship was soon leaving for Germany. Samuel and Alma were completely packed and ready to leave.

"You might as well ship all this furniture to your parents' house," Irving had said a month earlier. "I'm going to lose the apartment at the end of July, and I'll have no place to put it."

Goldie nodded. "No use leaving all of these things here in this place. You're right; it's best to ship them to my parents."

Samuel thought it was heartless when his mother took the last of the family's savings to ship her precious furniture back to Germany. Even though Irving suggested she take the stuff, Sam thought she should have left it behind so his father might try to sell it. *Damn it, Mom, couldn't you even leave Dad with a little dignity.* She took everything. *When the bakery closes, and he loses this apartment, my father will be destitute.* Samuel felt guilty about leaving. But when he spoke to his father once more offering to stay and help him, Irving refused again.

"Let me get on my feet. Then you and your sister can come back here to visit with me," Irving said, forcing a smile.

Every time Alma passed her father in the house, she ran into his arms and hugged him. "Please come with us, Dad. Please," she begged him every time.

"I can't. You three have already booked your passage. There is no money left for me to join you."

"Mother will write to Grandpa and ask him to help. We can wait and take another ship when your passage money arrives."

"No, you're already scheduled to leave," he insisted. "It's best this way."

CHAPTER FIFTY-SEVEN

G oldie received a letter from Leni the day before she and her children were to board the ship that would take them to Germany. She clutched it tightly and ran into her room to read it.

Dear Goldie,
I count the days until your return. I can imagine that it must be some-
what difficult for you to leave behind two decades of your life.
However, I am confident that once you have returned home, you will
be certain that you have made the right decision.

I was not surprised when I read about the treatment of the Jewish
people living in Medina after that incident with Sam. For some reason
it seems that non-Jews are always blaming us for everything. My
latest boyfriend, who is a historian, dashingly handsome, and ten years
older than I, says that it's been this way throughout history. They feel
the same way here in Germany toward the Jews. And lately it's been
getting worse. There is a lot of hatred toward the Jewish people. Some-
times there are even demonstrations in the streets where people are
complaining about the Jews causing Germany's economic problems.
But I don't let all of that nonsense bother me. My boyfriend is quite

sure it is only temporary. And he is absolutely brilliant. Not to mention wildly sexy. I can't wait for you to meet him. Of course, you know me; if you don't hurry I might be with someone new by the time you arrive!

Unfortunately, the newspaper articles you read are correct. Our economy here is very bad. Nonetheless, I know that because of your father's business savvy, you won't need to worry about money.

I am so excited! I can't wait to see you again! You are my oldest and dearest friend, Goldie. Safe travels to you!
Leni

CHAPTER FIFTY-EIGHT

New York Harbor, July 22, 1929

Goldie looked stunning in her black-and-white drop-waist dress. It was the finest dress she owned. Every man at the harbor turned around to cast an admiring glance her way. Looking ten years younger, vivacious, hopeful, and beautiful, Goldie was on her way back to the life she adored, and her skin was glowing as she stood at the dock ready to board the ship. The dress was not new. It was one she'd bought before she'd left Germany. But it was very good quality, and it fit her curvy figure like a glove. Her golden hair curled around her head in perfect finger waves imitating the styles the movie stars wore. A slight hint of rouge accented her high cheekbones. Blood-red lipstick, and dark lines around her eyes gave her an alluring air of mystery. Irving stared at her and thought, *I can't believe that our marriage is over. Just like that—it's the end. But I always knew in my heart that she was too good for me. She is so beautiful, and her family is rich. Never in my wildest dreams would I have thought that I would marry someone of her class. Well, she did the best she could during our marriage. I always knew that she wasn't happy with me, but I made myself believe that she would learn to love me, though things never got better even after nineteen years. But she worked with me in the bakery. I wonder if she knew how often I wished I could give her more. I don't know if she had any idea how hard I tried. And I did try. I wanted her to be happy. I wanted her to love me. But it never worked. I could never give her enough. It doesn't matter anymore. My whole family will soon be on their way to Europe, and I know it's the best thing because I have nothing to offer them. Still, I know in my heart that I was lucky to have nineteen years with the beautiful Goldie illuminating my home. She gave me two perfect children. So even though my future is uncertain, and I may very well end up living in a tent city, I can't complain because, up until now, I've had a good life. Whatever comes next is in God's hands.*

Goldie walked over to her husband and took his hands in hers. A single tear fell down her cheek. "I'm sorry, Irving," she said. "I'm sorry it ended this way."

"I know."

"Can you forgive me?"

"I already have," he said. Then he gently kissed her.

Alma ran over and put her arms around her father. "I will miss you so much."

"You will go to school in Europe and become a fine lady. Then you'll come back and visit me, right?"

"Yes, I will. I promise you." She was weeping. Irving handed her his handkerchief.

"Shh, don't cry. It's going to be a wonderful adventure for you. You are going to live with the Birnbaum's, your mother's parents. They will give you a good life. You'll have every comfort a young girl should have." He smiled at her wistfully. "Now, stop crying. Write to me? Yes?" He had a quick moment of regret. *Maybe I should have gone with them. But how could I? How could I ever face my father-in-law knowing I'd failed his daughter as a husband and provider? No, it's best that I stay here.*

"I will. I will write all the time."

Samuel extended his hand to his father who caught him in an embrace. "Be a good boy," Irving said to his son.

"Dad, I blame myself for all of this."

"It's not your fault."

"Yes, it is. If all of that stuff had not happened with me and Betty and that kid, and the Klan, you would still own the bakery in Medina.

We might not be rich, but we wouldn't have lost everything. We would have gotten by even in this bad economy because our friends and neighbors in the Jewish community would have continued to buy from us."

"If they had the money they would have. But I think that the economy has hit them just as hard as it hit here in Manhattan. The little town of Medina is no exception. After all, who is buying bread these days when it's much cheaper to buy flour? We are in a Jewish community in Manhattan, and very few people here are buying from a bakery. Times are hard for everyone. Jewish or not. Anyway, don't blame yourself for anything. You never touched that child. I know that. I've always known it. What happened was a witch hunt for Jews. It's the same old story, the blood libel. You were just a scapegoat. I know that. You fell in love with the wrong girl. Believe me, I understand. It can happen to anyone." He sighed wistfully as he glanced over at Goldie. "Anyway, son, I want this. It's a good thing for you to go with your mother to Germany. Your grandfather will pay for you to go to school. You can make a good career for yourself. You won't have to get up before sunrise to stand over a hot oven and make bread."

"But what about you, Dad? What is going to happen to you after you close the bakery?"

"I have a couple of job interviews on the line." Irving smiled. But he was lying. He had no interviews. Every time he applied for work he was told there were no openings. He'd applied at a couple of the local Jewish bakeries. He told them how much experience he had. But they were not interested. Both of them explained they didn't need any extra help right now. So he went to non-Jewish bakeries. They wouldn't even give him an interview when they heard his name was Irving Schatzman. It could have been the economy. It probably was. But he couldn't escape a nagging thought that it might just be because he was Jewish.

Irving felt a veil of loneliness wash over him as he watched his family board the ship. His stomach was in knots. He felt like he might just double over and vomit. First, Goldie walked onto the ship. Irving noticed all the men were watching her. Once on board, she turned back to look at Irving. *This is probably the last time I will ever see her*, he thought. She smiled and waved. Then she turned and walked inside the massive ocean liner and was gone. Next, Alma climbed the gangplank. She turned back to look at her father. Then she blew him a kiss. He could see her face was wet. She blotted her nose with his handkerchief then she turned and disappeared into the belly of the big ship. And finally, Samuel boarded the ship. He stood at the rail for a few seconds and looked down at his father on land. Their eyes met. They held each other's gaze for several seconds. Irving could see the guilt in Sam's eyes. He knew that no matter what he said, Samuel would still blame himself. Irving managed to give his son a smile and a nod of encouragement. With Sam still standing on the deck, Irving turned and walked away from the boat. Then with his shoulders slumped, he headed back toward Delancey Street.

CHAPTER FIFTY-NINE

S amuel entered the ship's cabin, where he and his family were scheduled to stay during their passage back to Europe. It was very small and cramped. And in the middle of the cabin stood his mother with her hands on her hips. She was engaged in a heated argument with a young man who was a member of the ship's crew.

"These accommodations are simply unsuitable," she said.

"I'm sorry. This is all that we have available. You are welcome to leave the ship if you so choose. But I am sorry, madam, I don't have any place to move you."

"For goodness' sake. Where is the captain? I have to speak with someone who has some authority. Not an idiot child like you. I spent a fortune to be on this boat, and you mean to tell me that this is the best you can do? This cabin is small and dirty. And these bunk beds . . ."

Samuel had never seen his mother behave so forcefully. She'd always been demanding and strong. But not to this degree. She seemed like a spoiled, arrogant child. And it made him wonder if this was the way she had been when she lived with her wealthy family in Berlin. The way she'd been before she'd married his father.

"I am truly sorry, but you can't see the captain right now, madam. He's very busy."

"Well, we will see about that now, won't we?" Goldie turned to Samuel and Alma. "Wait here. Don't move. I'll be right back. But don't unpack a single thing. Because we are not staying in this filthy cabin. I am going to demand that they move us." Then she stormed out.

"I'm sorry for her behavior," Alma said, looking down at the floor as she addressed the ship's employee.

He shrugged and left.

Once they were alone, Alma glanced over at her brother. He shook his head. "You know Mom," he said. "She just wants everything to be right."

Alma nodded. "Yes, I know," she said. She had not slept at all for the last two nights. Every time she closed her eyes, she thought of her father destitute in New York. She wished he'd agreed to come with them. He claimed he had job opportunities. But Alma wasn't stupid. She knew how difficult it was to find work. Every day on her way home from school, she passed the long lines of people who gathered twice a day outside the church for a bowl of soup because they could not afford to eat. She'd overheard her mother call them lazy, good-for-nothing degenerates, but Alma knew they were not lazy people. They were poor souls, just working folks who'd lost their jobs or businesses. *In fact, they are just like my father*, she thought.

"Here, let me get that for you," Samuel said as he hoisted her heavy trunk onto the small cot where she would sleep.

"Thanks, but Mom said to wait before we start unpacking. I don't know if she'll be able to get our stateroom changed. The young man said they don't have anything available. But then again, you know Mom. She just might be able to do something."

"I'll move your suitcase for you again if we get a room change." He smiled at her. "Don't you worry."

Alma studied her brother. She'd agonized over whether to talk to him, to tell him the truth. He might be angry with her for lying to him. But at least she would not have to carry the burden of this lie anymore. And she knew that once this boat left the dock, taking them far away from Betty, if Sam ever found out what she did, there was a good chance he would never forgive her. A long, loud horn blared making her jump. *How long before we set sail?*

"Stay here. I'm going to check and make sure Mom is all right," Samuel said.

"Samuel," Alma said, her voice filled with more urgency than she'd intended.

He stopped in his tracks then whipped around startled by her tone. "Are you all right?"

"Yes." She whimpered then continued. "Please sit," she commanded, patting the other bunk. He sat down beside her.

"Samuel, I've done something terrible. Something very terrible to you. And I know you didn't deserve it . . ."

He took her hand. "Alma, you're rambling. Please, just tell me."

"I am so afraid because I know you are going to be angry with me. I know you will." She struggled with the words.

"Alma, come on, now. Just tell me."

"I did something terrible."

"You said that already. Now, please, just tell me what it is that you did. Tell me before Mom returns."

The horn blasted again. Soon it would be too late. Alma felt like she might cry or faint. She looked into her brother's eyes and saw that he was concerned about her.

"Alma . . . please . . . what is it? Tell me what you did," he said, his eyes glued to hers, searching her face for clues. "Are you pregnant?" he asked boldly.

"No. No, thank God," she said.

"Then what is it?"

Alma made a hissing sound as she sucked in her breath. Her hands were trembling and cold, although the ship's cabin was nauseatingly hot. "Well, like I said, it's about you."

"All right. Go on . . ."

"When you were in the hospital and you sent me to tell Betty that you wanted her to come and see you. Do you remember?"

"Of course."

"And . . . I went to find her at the factory . . ."

He tilted his head to the side. She could see he was puzzled. "Yes, I remember everything. I don't know what you are trying to say."

She threw her hands up. She couldn't tell him. Samuel took her shoulders and gently shook her. "Talk to me, Alma."

"Yes. I must tell you. I must," she said then continued. "Well, I went to the factory. But I lied to you. I never saw Betty. I asked several girls as they were leaving if they knew her; none of them did. But then I found one who said she knew her. She was mean. She told me that Betty had been fired from her job. I asked her if she knew anything else, like where I could find Betty so I could talk to her. But the girl wouldn't give me any more information."

"So you never saw Betty? You lied and told me that you saw her, and she said she wanted me to leave her alone. Why would you do that, Alma? Why?"

"You could never have found her anyway. What difference does it make? The love between the two of you was cursed from the beginning. You are from different worlds."

"How dare you make that decision for me. You kept the truth from me. Alma, how could you?" His face was red. His fists were clenched. "I've based every decision I've made since that day on your lie . . ." The loud foghorn sounded again. The boat started to rock; it was getting ready to leave the United States for Germany.

Samuel glared at his sister with hatred.

"Please forgive me, Samuel. I've suffered too."

"Not like I have. I love Betty. She loves me. You stood in our way. I will never forgive you." Then he turned to leave the cabin. "I have to hurry. I have to get off this ship."

"Samuel . . . they raped me," Alma blurted. Then she looked down at the ground and covered her eyes with her hands.

He stopped cold in his tracks and turned to look at Alma. "Who?" he said. "Who raped you?"

"Betty's ex-fiancé and a bunch of his KKK friends. I was on the way home after I talked to the girl at the factory. He and his friends attacked me. They hurt me." She gagged but forced herself to go on and tell him everything. "That horrible boy who was engaged to your Betty? Well, he said to tell you that you took his girl, so he was going to ruin your little sister." She was weeping now. Her hands covered her face. "Forgive me; I was angry. I wanted us, our whole family to stay as far away from the goyim as possible. Sam, I was hurt . . . Samuel, please."

He grabbed her, taking her into his arms and holding her close to him, squeezing her tightly. "Alma, I'm so sorry that happened to you. Another thing that was my fault. I want you to know I forgive you for lying to me. I love you. You are my sister, my blood. I will always love you. But I can't go to Germany. I have to get off this boat before it leaves the dock. I have to go and find Betty."

"I understand," Alma said, squeezing Samuel tighter. "Please be careful. Those boys will kill you if they find you. They are horrible boys."

"Don't worry about me. I'll be all right. I'll write to you at Grandpa's house." He kissed her forehead and ran out the door of the cabin leaving his trunk and everything he owned behind. Several men were pulling up the gangway when he got to the front of the ship.

"Hold the gangway. I have to get off."

"Too late to get off now," one of the men said.

"I must. Let me off."

The men stopped pulling the gangway. "I suppose you can get off if you hurry. But if you leave the ship, we won't wait for you to come back. We're getting ready to set sail."

Samuel nodded. "Thank you," he said and climbed quickly down the gangway and back on land. Then he stood for several moments dumbstruck and watching as the boat set sail.

CHAPTER SIXTY

After Sam's bar mitzvah at thirteen years old, he started working for his father at the bakery. His father encouraged him to save as much as he could for his future. "Someday you will marry, and you'll want to purchase a home for your family. If you save, you will have a good start," his father told him. And he'd listened. But before he left for Germany, he'd offered to give his father his savings.

"Please take it," Sam said. "You'll need it here in America. I am going to live with Mom's family. They have money. I won't need it."

"You can't go there without a little kinipple. A little bit of savings of your own. You don't want to be asking your grandfather every time you want to buy an ice cream, do you?"

"Dad, please. This is serious. Take the money. There isn't much. But it might help you until you can find work."

"I absolutely refuse. The day I take your savings is the day I bury myself six feet under."

"Dad! Why do you say things like that?"

"Nu? A father should take everything from his son? What kind of father is that? I won't do it, Sammy. Go to Germany. But have a little kinipple on the side. You'll see, you'll be glad you have it."

"Dad," Sam said, shaking his head. *You are always thinking of everyone but yourself.*

There wasn't much money. But every penny Sam had saved was tucked away in the lining of that suitcase that he had left on board the ship. That money was on the way to Germany, and in order for his sister to find it, he'd have to write and tell her where he'd hidden it. Sam sighed. *I wasn't thinking straight after Alma told me about Betty. All I wanted to do was make sure I didn't leave America. I have to see Betty. I have to find a way to marry her. But now I haven't got a penny to my name. All I have are the clothes on my back and the gold Star of David Dad gave me, which I wear around my neck.* Slowly he walked back toward Delancey Street. *How am I going to find Betty if she no longer works at the factory? I don't know where she lives.* He'd acted in haste, and now he wondered if he'd responded too rashly. *I know it was pure madness to get off that ship. I can just imagine my mother's reaction when she got back to the cabin and found me gone. She is probably driving herself nuts with worry because she can't get off the ship and shake me until I can't breathe. Poor Mom. She's always trying to control everything. I will miss her.* He felt the pain of loss fall upon him like a dark cloud. *I have to admit, Mom is probably right, that our lives would be better in Germany. Her father is rich; we would always have a roof over our heads and food in our stomachs. And although my mother never knew it, I was going to speak to my grandfather about sending for my father. As soon as my dad wrote to me in Germany and told me where he was living and how I could reach him, I was planning to write to him and beg him to join us. I believe, with enough coaxing from me and Alma, he would have. If my grandfather was willing to give me the money, I would have arranged everything. But then, of course, that was before Alma told me about Betty. And once Alma gave me the smallest glimmer of hope that Betty might still be waiting for me, I had to come back. Nothing else means as much to me as that girl. If there is any chance I could find her and explain. If there is any chance she and I could hold each other again and laugh about this all being nothing more than a misunderstanding. But how can I go to Medina with no money, no job, no bakery, and nothing to offer the girl I love but life in a tent city. I am a good-for-nothing fool.*

He was walking through Delancey Street toward his family's bakery. The smell of garlic salami made his stomach growl. He was hungry. He began salivating and could taste the salami. But he had no money, and even if he did, he would not have wasted it on a salami sandwich. Besides, he had other things on his mind.

"Fresh ripe red strawberries and healthy green asparagus. All picked today. Cheap. Very cheap," one of the vendors said, holding up a handful of blood-colored berries.

"No, thanks," Samuel said.

"Hello, Samuel." It was Chana, the girl who worked for the shoe-maker next door to the bakery. For some reason he could never remember her name. She was a redhead, short and curvy with slender, delicate hands and feet. Her skin was like cream, and there was a sprinkle of freckles across her nose. "Samuel." She said his name again a little louder this time. "Don't you say hello?"

He nodded. "Hello."

On several occasions in the past, when Sam had finished working, he had gone to the park to play baseball with some of the young men who lived in the same apartment building. And a few of them mentioned this redheaded girl. One of those boys stood out as having been almost obsessed with talking about the redhead. His name was Avi. He was a tall, lanky boy with a bad complexion who worked for the tailor a few doors down from the bakery. "Do you know the girl who works for the cobbler next door to you? The redhead? She's a real looker."

"I've seen her. She talks to me sometimes."

"What a beauty, huh? She's got those big breasts and curvy hips. I hear she's fast too."

"Fast?" Sam asked. "Like she runs fast?"

"No, dummy. Like, she's easy. I've heard that she's given in to lots of guys."

"I wouldn't know," Samuel said, not wanting to hear this testos-terone-filled teen talk about his lurid fantasies.

Just then the redhead called Chana walked over and pulled on Sam's sleeve. "Are you all right?" She interrupted his thoughts bringing him back to the present. "You seem distracted."

"I'm sorry, but I don't feel much like talking."

"Chana, come back in here and do some work. Why are you

standing outside talking to the neighborhood boys again? Oy, I work hard all day. I sweat and I slave in this place just to make a meager living. Just to make a few pennies. And will you just look at me? I'm getting so old. So what do I do because I am old and feeble? I hire a girl to help me. I give a girl from the neighborhood a job so she can help put food on the table for her parents. And this is how she thanks me? This talking to the boys all day like a kurve, a whore, is what I have to put up with." The old cobbler, who was Chana's boss, was complaining about her, but he was not addressing her directly. Instead, he was looking up at the sky as if he were talking directly to God. This was common among the old Jewish men from Europe. And Sam didn't see anything strange about it.

"Chana, you are getting yourself a reputation," the shoemaker said, shaking his bald head, which was shining in the bright rays of the sun, like it had been polished.

Then the shoemaker noticed Sam. "Oh, it's you, Samuel. I heard bad news. Nu, so your parents are closing the bakery? Is it true?"

"Yes, I am afraid it's true," Sam said, wanting to get away from this man. He didn't want to explain that his parents had split up, and his mother was on her way back to her rich parents in Berlin leaving his father penniless.

He looked at the girl. *Chana. I don't know why I always have trouble remembering her name,* he mused, then he was taken back to the first day he'd met her. It was early in the afternoon just a few weeks after the bakery had first opened. She'd come in to buy some cookies and bread. He waited on her and found her to be not only pretty, but bold and outspoken. She told him her name, which he promptly forgot. All he remembered about her was that she had a body like Mae West, and that she had a lot to say and asked a lot of questions. "What's your name? These cookies look wonderful. What's in them? Have you read any books by Victor Hugo? What was the last movie you saw?" He knew she was only trying to be friendly and make conversation, but he was not in the mood to make friends, especially female friends. He was still heartbroken over Betty. But he had to admit, Chana was funny, and she made him laugh. When a woman walked by with a giant hat, she'd made a joke about how strong the woman's neck had to be to carry a hat that was so absurd.

The next day when she returned to buy a coffee cake, she waited until they were alone in the store. After the few customers were gone, she turned to him conspiratorially and whispered that she thought he should know that everyone in their small Jewish community in Manhattan knew all about him and Betty and what had happened in Medina. "It's not a secret. But I don't care what people say about you or your family. I like you, and I like your parents."

"I'm glad." Samuel sighed. He tried to be kind to her. "Thank you for letting me know," he said, wishing she hadn't told him.

Then he even gave her an extra black-and-white cookie. But after she left, he sat down in the back of the bakery and put his head in his hands. *My family left everything behind in order to escape the shame I brought down on them. But somehow it followed us here, and even though this is a big city, there is no escaping it.* He thought about Chana. It was obvious she liked him, and that was why she felt the need to tell him. He felt certain that if he asked, she would accept a date with him regardless of the scandal that surrounded him. Sam shook his head. *She's pretty, no doubt about it. But I can't go out with someone else. I am just not ready. Not yet anyway. I have to have time to get over my feelings for Betty before I can even think about another girl.* He recalled how the skinny pockmarked boy, who worked at the tailor shop, said Chana was fast. And he couldn't help but think of how sexy and curvy Chana was. It had been quite a while since the last time he and Betty had been intimate. Samuel felt an ache, a strong need that throbbed in his loins. He was ashamed of his weakness, of the desire that rose within him. His heart yearned for Betty, but his body hungered for sexual release.

I'll admit Chana is very pretty. And the thought of her being fast excites me. But my heart belongs to one woman, Betty. I wish I didn't want to sleep with Chana so badly.

The cobbler patted Samuel's shoulder bringing Sam out of his thoughts and back to the present moment. "Oy, I'm so sorry to hear you are closing the store. I really am. When I heard about it, I was so upset. I hoped it wasn't true. You and your family have been good neighbors. I was afraid that with a bakery next door there would be problems with lots of insects. But you must keep the place spotless because I haven't had any trouble."

"Yes, we keep it very clean," Sam said. He was itching to get away from this conversation. But the cobbler wanted to talk.

"And I also heard from someone, I couldn't tell you who, of course, because that wouldn't be right, that your mother went home on a boat back to Germany leaving your poor father here all alone. Oy vey, the poor man. But I thought you and your sister were going with your mother. So I was surprised when I saw you . . ." The old man was still rambling.

Samuel didn't speak. He couldn't. He was unnerved by the old cobbler's mindless chatter about his family. The redhead was watching his eyes. Any small twinkle of attraction that had surfaced for the girl had faded away due to the shoemaker's incessant chatter. "I'm sorry, but I have to go," Samuel said, and without waiting for a goodbye, he turned away and walked toward the door to the bakery. *What an annoying yenta. The old bastard should mind his own business,* he thought as he walked inside his father's broken dream.

As he entered the bakery, Samuel heard his father's voice coming from the back room. Someone else was there with him. They were negotiating for the sale of equipment, which would be delivered upon the closing of the bakery. Samuel's shoulders slumped. His heart was heavy. In a couple of months, the bakery would be gone. He didn't want to go back there and be a part of the death of his father's business, so he walked back outside and turned the opposite direction from the cobbler's shop. Then he began to walk. *I need to move my body. I'll keep walking until I can calm down. If I don't, I just might explode.* He thought the sounds of the city were like sad refrains of music in the background of his thoughts. *Betty, where are you? How can I find you?* Then a girl with raven-black hair walked by him and he remembered Joan. Joan, Betty's friend, who also worked at the factory. *If I can find her, she might know how I can locate Betty. I don't have anything to offer her in exchange for the information. I wish I could give her some money, but I don't have a cent. All I can do is beg her to tell me anything she knows about Betty. When we met, Joan seemed to know how Betty and I felt about each other. I would assume Betty told her how in love we were. I don't know if she'll help me, but I must try.*

"Excuse me. What time do you have?" Samuel asked one of the vendors along the street. Sam didn't have a watch. He'd packed it in his suitcase that morning, and now it was sailing off to Europe.

The man looked up into the sky. "I think it's about four o'clock, maybe five," he said.

"Thanks." Samuel gave him a quick smile. Then he began walking quickly toward the train. But he remembered he didn't have the money for the fare. *I'll have to go back to the bakery and ask my father for some money,* he thought. *But I doubt he will give me any to take a train back to Medina. First of all, he is going be angry that I got off that ship. Then he'll want to know why I need money. If I tell him that I am going back to Medina to try and find Betty, he'll be more than angry; he'll be furious. And I really doubt he would give me a penny. Not that he has much. I'm going to have to find a way to get my hands on some cash without his help. It might take me a week to get enough to get back to Medina, but I'll find a way.*

Samuel walked the street for the remainder of the day clenching and unclenching his fists. As he walked, he saw the homeless and hungry lining up in the soup lines. *The whole country has gone to hell,* he thought. *There are so many people out of jobs, starving, and desperate. So many poor, disconsolate folks who would put in a full day's work in exchange for a meal. What special skills do I have? None. What could I do that might bring some cash?* Samuel leaned up against a building and let his mind wander. He'd always had a beautiful tenor voice. In fact, as a boy he'd considered becoming a cantor in the synagogue. He was ashamed of what he was about to do, but he had no other option. So he took off his hat and laid it down on the ground and began to sing. He felt ridiculous, but he sang. People stopped to listen as he crooned Yiddish songs that reminded them of their mothers, of their families, of their homelands. Soon a crowd gathered around him. As his confidence grew stronger, he sang louder. People dabbed their eyes as tears fell to their cheeks. And they were so moved that they dropped nickels, dimes, and quarters into his hat. All day Samuel continued to sing. By the end of the afternoon he had one dollar. He returned to the apartment where his father was still living. At least he would be living there for the next week.

"What are you doing here?" his father said, shaking his head. "Why are you not on the boat with your mother and sister?"

Samuel shrugged. "I'm sorry. I'll leave if you want me to, Dad. But I'm here. I jumped ship."

"I can see that. Jumped ship, oy vey, Sam, what were you thinking? Don't you realize that we have very little time left in this apartment that is paid for. I've talked to the landlord and she is willing to work with me. She says I can stay here for a few months if I promise to pay. But I don't know how I can make that promise. I feel bad to lie to her. But what else can I do? I have been looking for work, but so far I've found nothing. And soon the bakery will be closed . . ."

"I know. I know everything you are telling me, Dad. But I am here, and I am going to help you. You shouldn't have to face this alone. We'll find the money to live here. We'll do it together."

"Oh, Samuel, I wanted better for you."

Samuel wished he could tell his father the truth. He wished he could tell him about Betty. But he couldn't. Not yet. Not until he found her again. And once he did, he would know where he stood.

"I don't know what to say. All I can say is, do you want me to leave?" Samuel asked again.

"No, of course not. I would never want you to leave. I only wanted you to go to Germany because I wanted a better life for you. But you are here now, and I will do what I can to make life as good as possible for us. Anyway, sit down. Let's eat. I have a little bit of soup. Mrs. Silverman, you know her; the woman who lives upstairs brought me a small pot of the soup she made for her dinner. She knows your mother left today. I don't know how she knows, but she does."

"Yes, well, in this neighborhood, everyone knows everything about everyone else."

Irving Schatzman laughed. "Now, that's true. So we can be upset about it, or we can enjoy the soup. I say we enjoy the soup," he said as he ladled out a bowl for each of them.

CHAPTER SIXTY-ONE

For the rest of the week, Samuel stood on the corner in front of Joseph Fine's Jewish Deli and sang his heart out. Sometimes the crowds sang along with him. They recognized the Yiddish tunes, and the memories warmed their hearts, so they thanked him by dropping a coin or two in his hat. But by the beginning of the following week he still didn't have enough money for a round trip train fare to Medina and back for himself and Betty, should she choose to come with him. Samuel stared into the mirror in his room. He hated himself. He blamed himself for everything that had happened to destroy his family and himself.

And now that there might be a chance for him with Betty, he realized that even if he went to Medina and found her, he had nothing to offer her. *I don't even have a job. What am I going to do? Am I going to go to her home and say, Betty, come and live with me and my father on the street? I'll sing and beg for money, and if we're lucky, there will be enough for us to eat that night,* he thought as the anger he felt toward himself mounted. *Damn it all. I have to find work. I must find some kind of job that pays me enough to make a living. A few coins from begging might help me and Dad to get something warm in our guts, but it's not enough to support a wife.* Samuel's fingers moved through his pocket jingling the coins he'd earned that day. He fished them out and counted. *A half dollar. Fifty cents*, he thought, and his mind started racing.

Since he'd moved to Manhattan, he'd seen men around town who were rumored to belong to the Jewish syndicate. Everyone, especially his customers at the bakery, told tales about these fellows with their fancy suits and shiny automobiles. One day, one of the old men who came in every morning to buy fresh challah for his grandchildren was there when several members of the Jewish underworld walked by. The old man told Samuel and his father who they were.

"They are very rich, and very powerful. They can be found at the speakeasies and sometimes having breakfast at one of the delis," the old man said. "You ever been to a speakeasy, Samuel?"

"Not me," Samuel said.

"No?"

"No," Samuel said, then he added, "that's not exactly true. I had some wine on Passover one year when one of our customers gave Dad a bottle. We knew it was bootlegged. But it was good."

"Yes, I'll bet," the old man said. "I buy bootlegged wine for Shabbat every week. If you want some, just let me know. I'll get it for you."

Then another time, about a month later, Samuel had been working the front of the bakery while his father was in the back. He was packing up an order for Mrs. Glassman, a regular customer, when a middle-aged, well-dressed gentleman walked in. Sam handed Mrs. Glassman her order then turned to the man and said, "How can I help you?"

"A dozen apricot rugelach," the man said in a soft voice. He wore a dark gray finely tailored suit. His nails were manicured. It was easy to see he was someone important. Samuel thought he might be a doctor or a politician.

"Right away, sir." Samuel bagged up the cookies. The man thanked him and left.

Samuel was wiping down the counter when Mrs. Glassman returned. "I forgot. I need an extra challah. My sister and her husband are coming to eat by us today," she said.

"Of course." Samuel put the bread into a bag.

"Do you know who that man was?" Mrs. Glassman whispered as if she were about to share a secret with him.

"What man?" Samuel asked, not knowing who she was talking about.

"The man who was here before. The one in the gray suit. The older handsome man."

"Nope, he's not a regular. I don't think I've ever seen him before. He might have come in; I just don't remember."

Mrs. Glassman told Samuel the man's name was Morton Laevsky, and he was the head of the Jewish organized crime in New York. Samuel had not paid much attention at the time. But from then on Sam was aware when Laevsky came into the bakery. Sam realized he did come in once in a while, and he watched Laevsky, fascinated, wondering what his life was like. Having grown up in a law-abiding and very protective home, Sam had never met anyone like Laevsky. But he knew these men dealt in alcohol. And he knew there was a lot of money in it because it was illegal.

It had been quite a while since the last time Sam saw Laevsky. At that time, he had not even considered working for him. But now he was in desperate need of a job. And he was willing to take whatever risks were necessary to earn a decent living. But he had no idea how to find Laevsky. He'd heard that the man went to speakeasies. *But where does one find a speakeasy? They are hidden. Of course they are; they are illegal.* Sam was racking his brain. Then he realized, *Chana knows everyone and everything going on in this neighborhood. She'll know how I can find Laevsky,* Samuel thought as he headed to the cobbler's shop.

Chana was sitting on a bench working on the sole of a leather shoe when he walked in. She looked up and smiled at him. "Samuel, what can I do for you?" she asked.

"I need to talk to you," he said. "Are we alone?"

"My boss is in the back room," she whispered. "Why, what is it?"

"I need to talk to you alone."

"Nu?" She smiled. "So maybe we'll have a date?" Then joking, she said, "I thought you'd never ask."

He nodded, figuring she would be more likely to help him if he showed her some interest.

"Really, so this must be important. Yes? So when do you want to take me out?" She giggled a little. But the serious look on his face stopped her laughter. She studied him.

"Are you free tonight?" he asked.

"For you? Of course?" she said, then she added, "I really have been waiting for you to ask, Samuel Schatzman."

He smiled at her. She returned his smile.

"Is eight o'clock all right?"

"Sure. Let me give you my address," she said, taking a pencil and paper out of the drawer.

As soon as Sam left the store, Mr. Goldsmith, the cobbler, came out of the back room. "Chana, you are too good to be throwing yourself at all of these boys. You should have more self-respect. You're beautiful, and you're pretty smart. If you ask me, you should go to the shul and see if the rabbi can find you a nice boy, a gute neshome, a boy with a good soul."

Chana didn't answer. She just nodded and went back to work.

The cobbler shook his head.

CHAPTER SIXTY-TWO

S amuel was getting ready to go to Chana's home to pick her up
when his father walked into the room.

"Nu? So where are you going?"

"I have a date."

"A date? With who?"

"Chana, the girl who works for the cobbler next door to the
bakery."

"Oh yes, Chana Rubinstein. She's a pretty one. Spunky too."

"Yes," Samuel said, "she is pretty." *But not my type,* he thought, and
he suddenly felt guilty. He wasn't exactly lying to his father, but he
wasn't exactly telling him the truth either.

"Do you need money for tonight? I don't have much though."

"No, Dad. I have some money. Don't worry about it."

"Are you sure?"

Samuel nodded, then he left the apartment. The address Chana had
given him was in his pocket. He had not yet looked at it, so he took it
out, and in his mind he plotted out the route he would take to her
home. Once he knew where he was headed, Samuel walked through
the city. Even though it was eight o'clock and starting to get dark, the
streets were still filled with people. Manhattan was so different from

Medina. And in many ways, he liked it better. He enjoyed the hustle and bustle here. He loved meeting people from so many different places in the world. *I could be happy here. I don't miss the small-town pettiness of Medina*, he thought. *All I need is plenty of money and Betty, and New York would be a great place to live.*

Chana was waiting outside for him when he arrived. Her fiery locks were pulled back from her face with clips. She wore a faint stain of red lipstick and rouge. Her black dress was tight and low cut just enough to show the slightest hint of cleavage. She smiled and waved when she saw him turn the corner and head toward her.

"Hi, Chana," he said, realizing he probably should have brought her flowers or candy or something. But she didn't seem to care. She walked over to him and hooked her arm in his.

"Where are we going?" she asked, looking up into his eyes. He was at least a full head taller than she, and her petite frame made him feel strong and masculine.

"I don't know," he said. "Where do you like to eat?"

"How about Chinese food?"

He figured Chana had suggested Chinese food because it was the least expensive food available. *She is a good person. She doesn't want me to feel pressed for money.* "Sounds good."

"I know a cute little place right over on Canal Street," she said, squeezing his arm as she walked beside him.

The restaurant was nothing fancy. But it was clean. A pretty Chinese girl seated them at a cozy table in the back. Sam had not eaten Chinese food before, and he was unsure of what to order. Without embarrassing him, Chana said, "I love the vegetable egg foo yong here. Do you like omelets?"

"Sure."

"Then you'll love the egg foo yong. Can I order for us?"

Samuel was relieved. "Yes, sure, that would be great." He smiled.

After Chana placed the order, there were a few moments of silence. Then he bit his lower lip and said, "Chana . . . do you happen to know who Morton Laevsky is?"

"You mean Morty Laevsky? Why do you want to know?" she said as the waiter placed a plate of two steaming egg rolls on the table.

"Do you know where I can find him?"

"Why would you want to find him? He's dangerous. You can get into a lot of trouble dealing with him. Everyone knows that."

"I need a job, Chana," he said sincerely. "I have to earn money. The bakery will be gone. My dad and I are going to be on the street."

She sat back in her chair and was silent for several seconds. Then she said, "That's why you asked me out, isn't it?"

"Part of it, yes," he said.

"And what's the other part?"

"I like you. I'd like to get to know you better," he lied.

She looked down at the table. "I'd really like to believe you. But I don't. It doesn't matter anyway. I'll help you find Laevsky."

"Do you have any idea where he goes or what he does? I heard he goes to speakeasies."

"Yes, that's right. Have you ever been to Mike's speakeasy?"

"Me? No," Sam said.

"We'll go there tonight after dinner. I don't know Laevsky personally, but I know some of the boys that work at Mike's. I'm sure they know him. If not, they'll know where you can find him."

"Thanks. You don't know how much this means to me," he said.

"I hope nothing bad happens to you because of this, or I'll regret it for the rest of my days," she said just as another steaming plate of food arrived at the table.

Sam was too nervous to eat.

After they finished and Sam paid the check, they walked for six blocks to a small opening between buildings. Chana led Samuel through an alleyway to a door that blended in with the building and had no handle. She knocked. They waited. Finally, someone came. "Who is it?" the voice said.

"Hi, Lenny, it's me, Chana."

He opened the door. "Get in here, you hot tomato." He smiled, pulling her arm gently.

She giggled and pulled Samuel inside.

"Who's the lucky fella?"

"Schatzman, Samuel Schatzman. His folks own the bakery on Delancey."

"Oh yeah. I heard that they were closing. It's a real shame. But nobody could compete with Fanny's around the corner. Sorry to say it, but she's got the best bakery in town. And she's been there forever."

"Yeah, Fanny's bakery is still doing well even in this terrible economy," Sam said.

"Lenny, you know lots of people, right?" Chana said.

"Sure, doll. Lots, why?"

"You know a fella by the name of Morty Laevsky?"

Lenny grew quiet. "Maybe. Who wants to know?"

A heavyset black man took the stage and began playing a trumpet.

"I do," Samuel said. "I want to meet him."

Lenny let out a laugh. "You think it's just like that? You ask, you meet? Nu? Are you meshuga? Laevsky doesn't make nice like that."

"I'll bet he might want to meet me. What do you think?" Chana said, pushing her chest out.

Lenny looked her over slowly from the top of her head to her feet, his eyes gliding slowly over her ample bosom. "Now, there's a good chance that you're right. He just might want to meet you," he said, his eyes twinkling with mischief. "Now, what man wouldn't want to meet a zoftik girl like you, Chana?"

"Yeah, and I'll wager that you like zoftik girls, too, don't you Len?"

"You know it, doll," he said, winking at her.

"There just might be something in it for you if you arrange a meeting for my friend Sam with Laevsky," Chana said, touching the lapel on Lenny's jacket.

"For you, doll . . . I'll do my best," Lenny said.

She let out a laugh. "Big titties get 'em every time," she said to no one in particular. Then she turned to Samuel and giggled. "You're blushing, aren't you?"

He nodded his head in embarrassment.

Chana waved her hand and continued. "Well, don't you worry. I am fairly certain that Lenny will find a way for us to have a meeting with Morty Laevsky."

Lenny walked over to Chana and said, "Why don't you two take a seat? Have a drink and enjoy the music. Let me see what I can do."

Chana nodded. Then she hooked her arm in Sam's and led him to a table in the back away from the stage.

She ordered two whiskeys. When the drinks were set down in front of Sam, he took a big gulp and immediately spit it out on the table.

Chana laughed. "Too strong, bubbelah?" she said, reaching over and patting his hand.

"Tastes like turpentine."

"You ever drank turpentine?"

"Nope, but I would imagine that this is what it would taste like." Samuel wiped his mouth with the back of his hand.

"It's panther piss," she said.

He looked at her not understanding.

"You know, bathtub booze," she whispered. Then a pretty girl in a sparkling silver dress got on stage and began to croon a love song. Chana forgot her conversation with Samuel and began to sing along softly. The girl sang three more songs before Lenny returned accompanied by another young man wearing a well-made suit.

"This beauty over here is Chana Rubinstein," Lenny said, then he turned to Chana and said, "This not-so-handsome fella is my friend Izadore, but we call him Izzy." He patted Izzy's back.

"Chana and I have met before," Izzy said, then he added, "It's good to see you again."

Chana smiled at Izzy and nodded. Then she took a sip of her drink.

"Izzy knows Laevsky real well. He can introduce you."

"When?" Chana said.

"How about now," Izzy said, winking at Chana. "Follow me."

"Thanks, Lenny. I owe you," she said. Then she and Samuel followed Izzy toward the back of the bar.

"I still expect payment, Chana," Lenny called out loudly as they passed him.

"Don't I know it," Chana said. Then she turned to whisper in Samuel's ear, "Big tits work on these kinds of fellas every time. They get mesmerized so they can't see straight. Then they give me whatever I want." Sam looked at Chana with shock in his eyes. Samuel had never heard a woman speak this way. He was flabbergasted. He said nothing because he didn't know how to answer.

There was a short, narrow hallway behind the bar that led to an office. It was small but furnished comfortably, with a nice sofa, a cherrywood desk, and three chairs. There was a wool rug on the floor. On the wall overhead was a painting of a bunch of Irish setters laying in the sun in a green valley.

"Sit down," Izzy said. "Mr. Laevsky has agreed to meet with you."

They waited for almost a full half hour before the man, who had come into the bakery in the recent past, walked in through a back door. He wore a gray suit similar to the one he'd worn when he bought the apricot rugelach. Without saying a word, the man sat down. He glanced from Chana to Samuel, then he said in the same soft voice, "Nu? So you wanted to meet me? Why?"

Samuel cleared his throat and forced himself to speak. "I need a job. I was hoping you could help me. I will do anything. Anything at all."

"Aren't you the baker's son? Schatzman, right?" Laevsky said, studying Sam.

"Yes. You remember me?"

"Of course. I make it my business never to forget a face. So why do you want to work for me?"

"The bakery is closing. I am desperate for a job."

"I'm not surprised. Lousy rugelach. Worst I ever had. Rubbery," Laevsky said, sucking air through his teeth.

"But you came back more than once. Why would you do that if you didn't like it?" Sam said. Chana gave him a reproachful glance. But for a moment Sam forgot who he was talking to. He forgot how important and dangerous this man could be. He was offended by what Laevsky said about the bakery.

Chana shook her head at Sam. He could see the fear in her eyes, and he knew he'd overstepped his boundaries. He'd probably just lost any opportunity of working for Laevsky, and he might have even endangered himself.

There was a long pregnant moment of silence. Then Laevsky let out a belly laugh. "I went to the bakery several times because I was observing you. I knew you were made to work for me. You have the hunger that I look for in a man. And here you are, asking me for a job. I didn't know how long it would take before you got tired of baking breads. But I am glad to see you, Schatzman. Welcome."

Sam cocked his head and looked at Chana, who shrugged her shoulders. "Thank you, sir," Sam whispered, not sure of what else to say.

"So you need a job, and you will do anything? Is that what you are saying?" Laevsky said.

"Yes, sir."

Just then a handsome young man wearing a flashy suit entered the room.

"Hey, Screwy, haven't I told you to knock?"

"Sorry, I didn't realize you had company. I just wanted to let you know that I got a craps game going upstairs."

"Good," Morty said, then he turned to Sam. "You play craps?" he asked.

"No," Sam answered.

"Good for you. A man who doesn't drink and doesn't gamble has a better a chance of survival, don't you think, Screwy?"

"Sure, why not," Screwy said.

"And, by the way, this is my partner, Screwy. We call him Screwy 'cause he's a little nuts. But he's a good fella." Then he added, "Screwy, this is Sam."

"A pleasure to meet you," Sam said.

Screwy nodded. Then he winked at Chana.

"Anyway, I'm interviewing Sam here for a job. So get out of here, and I'll see you later."

Screwy nodded. Then he took another long look at Chana and smiled before he left.

Once Screwy was gone, Laevsky turned back to Sam and sighed. "Sounds like you're desperate. You should never show another man when you are desperate. It's always a mistake. Life is a game, kid. And when you let a man know that you really need him, then he knows he can do whatever he wants with you. Do you understand me?"

This was not a game for Samuel. He was, in fact, desperate and wringing his hands. Within weeks he and his father would be home-less. They had no money and soon would have no food. The girl he was in love with was miles away in Medina, but he could not go to her until he was earning a living. His whole life depended on this man. No, this certainly was no game. "I need this job. I need it. I am not playing any game. I don't have the luxury of playing a game."

Laevsky sat back in his chair and reached under his desk. He pulled out a bottle of brandy. "Would you like a drink?" he asked.

"No, thank you."

"I would," Chana said.

"Is she your girl?" Laevsky asked, indicating Chana.

"No, but she is my good friend."

"She likes you a lot. I can tell." He poured the brandy into a glass for Chana, and then he poured one for himself. "I'd grab her if I were you," Laevsky said, then he drank the entire glass in one swig. "Good?" he asked Chana.

"Very," she said, still sipping the brandy.

Then Laevsky turned to Samuel and said, "All right, down to business. You need a job. I can help you. Can you drive?'

"I can learn."

"Can you shoot a gun?"

"I can learn."

"You have two days to become an expert at both. I'll have Izzy teach you everything you need to know. But you've got to be sharp, or you won't get it. But if I were going to bet, I'd bet you'll come out just fine," he said, then he turned to Chana. "And as for you, young lady, you're far too pretty and far too good for a fella like him."

"I like him, Mr. Laevsky."

"I know. I can see that. I'm getting old. I know I'm an alter cocker. It's a shame because if I were twenty years younger, I'd go after you myself. But you could do better than this guy over here. Take it from me, kid; this young punk is going to break your heart if you stick with him."

"I'll take my chances," Chana said.

Laevsky shook his head, let out a small laugh, and said, "Women, all of you got long hair and short brains." Then he knocked on his desk and Izzy came in. "Izzy, I need you to teach this fella how to drive and how to shoot a gun. You got two days to teach him, and he better be good. You'll be traveling with him, so your life depends on it. Like I said, you got two days. Let me know if he can make the cut or not."

"Will do, boss."

Samuel cleared his throat and sat up straight. Then he mustered up all the courage he could manage. "How much does this pay?" he said.

"It pays by the job. But I can promise it's more than you'd get anywhere else. A hell of a lot more than you'd make baking bread. And you'll find that if you can do this job and do it well, money won't be a problem for you anymore," Laevsky said.

"I'll do it and I'll do it well," Samuel said.

"Good. Now, get out of here and stop taking up my time. I expect you to show me what you can do. "

"Yes, sir."

"All right, follow Izzy. He'll take you out the back door. And, Schatzman, if I were you, I'd get plenty of sleep. You have a big day ahead of you tomorrow. You've got a lot to prove. It's not as easy as you think to learn to drive a car and shoot a gun. But if you have the chutzpa and the talent to match, then you've got a job. If not, you're on your own. That's the best I can do for you, Samuel Schatzman."

"Thank you, sir. I'll learn what you want me to learn. You'll see. You won't be sorry you gave me this chance."

"Yeah, we'll see. Anyway, *zie gezunt*, kids," Laevsky said, lighting a cigar. Then he added, as he let his eyes scan Chana's body, "My *zayde* used to say youth is wasted on the young. Boy oh boy, was he ever right."

CHAPTER SIXTY-THREE

Chana took Samuel's hand as they walked back to the apartment Chana shared with her middle-aged parents. Even though it was after midnight, the streets were far from empty. They passed couples who walked arm in arm and couples smooching in the dark alleyways. Prostitutes beckoned, and groups of drunken men lay sprawled out on the sidewalks. In the park, the tent cities were filled with the unfortunates who had lost everything. Some were hobos, men who were traveling alone from town to town in search of day jobs. It was a dangerous life—freight trains that could easily have sucked them beneath their mighty wheels, ripping off their arms or legs, or killing them instantly. They faced the dangers of other desperate men who would easily stab them for a quarter. And in the middle of these dirty and desperate men, there were also families bunched together frightened and hungry. Mothers holding fast to little children with empty stomachs and frightened eyes.

"You sure you want to do this with Laevsky? I've heard that once you get involved with him, you can't quit the job."

"It doesn't matter. I need to make money. I have no choice. Look around you. I don't want to be one of these poor souls waiting in line for some charity soup. What's going to happen to them once winter comes? They'll freeze out here. I am too young and too strong not to find a way to earn a living. And right now, Laevsky is the way."

"Do you want me to come to your training with you? I'll tell my boss I'm sick and that I need the day off."

"No, you need to keep your job too. You'd be quite a distraction." He smiled then added, "It's best if you go to work."

"Maybe we can have dinner tomorrow night? You can come to my apartment after your training is over."

"Your parents won't mind?"

"A nice Jewish boy? They'll be thrilled. My mother will cook all day."

He shook his head. "I don't know if I'm such a good catch. I don't have much to offer."

"You see that Star of David around your neck? Well, my mother will be glad that I am finally bringing home a Jewish fellow. The last two fellas I brought home were goyim, and she threatened to commit suicide if I even entertained the idea of marriage."

"Yes, our people like to stick together, don't they?" he said with a sad wry smile. He thought of Betty.

"It's not so much that we like to stick together, it's more that the goyim never really accept us. I dated those two boys, but when it came to marriage, neither one of them wanted to bring me home to meet their families. The bottom line is we are Jews and they are goyim. They might do business with us, but they don't really like us."

"I don't think that's true of everyone who isn't Jewish," he said, thinking of Betty.

"Believe me, it is," she said as they stopped in front of the building where she lived. "See you tomorrow night?"

"Yes. What time?"

"Whenever your training is over. We'll hold dinner for you."

"But I don't have any idea how long this training will last."

"It's all right. Just come after you're done. I'll tell my mom that you have to work, and you'll be here as soon as you can. She'll be glad to hold dinner for you."

"Oh, Chana, I don't want you to do that."

"It's my pleasure." She smiled at him warmly. And he thought she was very pretty.

CHAPTER SIXTY-FOUR

The following morning, Izzy drove Samuel out to an old farmhouse. When they arrived, he told Samuel to follow him to the backyard. The idea of shooting a gun was unnerving for Sam. He wasn't sure what to do. But Izzy assured him that he was capable of learning.

"We always use this place for target practice. It belongs to Laevsky," Izzy said, leading Sam to a wooden block with the picture of the shadow of a man. "That's your target," he told Samuel, indicating the picture. Then he gave Samuel a gun and showed him how to shoot. Samuel felt the sweat forming on his brow as he aimed and then pulled the trigger. The sound was deafening as a rain of bullets roared out of the tommy gun. When he rubbed his ear, Izzy smiled at him, then he asked, "You all right?"

"I think I might have broken my eardrum," Sam replied.

"Nahh, you're fine. It's just loud. You'll get used to it."

"And what's that smell? It smells like my hair is on fire."

"It's the gunpowder. The more you practice, the more you'll get used to that too," Izzy said. "You don't want to give up, do you? You want this job, right?"

"Yes," Samuel said, but he already knew he hated guns.

By midafternoon he could hold the gun steady. By evening he could take aim and hit his mark.

"Tomorrow I'm going to teach you to drive," Izzy said.

"I thought Mr. Laevsky wanted me to learn everything in two days. He said I needed to be ready to work in a day."

"Yep, he sure did. You'll be going on a run with me tomorrow. You'll learn to drive while we are on the job."

"What's a run?"

"You'll see. Be ready at eight in the morning. I'll pick you up. And pack a small bag with a change of clothes."

"For what? Where are we going?"

"Don't you worry about that. Just do what I tell you. That is, of course, if you are still interested. If not, just say the word."

"I'll be ready."

Samuel thanked Izzy for his full day of instruction. Then he left and walked a mile back to Delancey Street, where he turned off the busy thoroughfare and onto a side street. Then he walked past three tenement houses until he arrived at Chana's apartment building. It was almost eight o'clock, and even though she'd told him to come whenever he got off work, he felt funny ringing the bell so late. He was just about to leave when Chana came bouncing down the stairs.

"Come on up," she said. "Sometimes our bell doesn't work."

I didn't ring the bell, he thought. *How could she know I was here?*

"You look exhausted," Chana said. "I'll bet today was hard on you."

"It was."

"After today, do you still want to work with Laevsky?"

"I have no choice. I told you that already." The irritation he felt was apparent in his voice, and he immediately regretted how ungrateful he sounded. "I'm sorry," he added. "But you're right: I'm tired and irritable."

"Well, if you would rather have a job in a bakery, I saw Fanny today, and she said she'll hire you. You know Fanny's bakery."

"Fanny's?" he said. "I know of Fanny's, and I'm pretty sure that is the biggest Jewish bakery on the Lower East Side, isn't it?"

"Yes. Actually, her family has owned the bakery since the late

1800s. Her zede built it for her bubbie when they first came here from Europe. She's named for her bubbie. They are pretty big, Sam; they have ten employees."

"And you're friends with her?"

"We grew up together, went to school together, that's why she's willing to give you a job. She said she'd do it for me."

"Did she say what the pay is?"

"Two dollars a week."

He smiled at her and ruffled her hair. "Two dollars? I need more than that."

"Two dollars isn't bad. We can make it on two dollars a week, especially if we add my salary."

She thinks we are a couple. How am I ever going to make it clear that I don't want anything more than friendship? I should tell her about me and Betty. But if I do, I am afraid she will be mad at me. And women when they're mad can be a holy terror. I'd better wait until I'm in good with Laevsky, or she could say or do something to put a kibosh on the whole deal. "Thanks for trying, kid. But I'm going to take my chances with Laevsky."

"Well, I'll tell Fanny that you aren't sure yet. There's no reason to close the door. We don't have to give her a yes or no right now . . ."

"Fair enough." He smiled. "But I am hoping that this job with Laevsky works out."

Chana put her arm through Samuel's, then she led him up three flights of stairs. Two twelve-year-old girls who were playing with jacks and a ball on the second floor giggled when they saw Chana, who winked at them.

"The kids are out late, huh?" Sam said.

"Yeah, they always are around here," Chana answered him as she opened the door to her apartment. Then she called out, "Mom, Samuel is here."

An older version of Chana came out of the kitchen wearing a pale pink apron. She had Chana's bright red hair, but her hair was sprinkled with gray and pulled into a bun, and there were lines around her mouth and eyes. "Samuel, come in. It's so nice to meet you," Mrs. Rubinstein said. Looking at Chana's mother, one could see she had once been as beautiful as her daughter. "Sit, please. My husband is a cripple. He is in bed. He and I already ate. This is a dinner for two, just you and my Chana."

"I'll serve us, Mom," Chana said.

"All right. If you need anything, let me know," Mrs Rubinstein said, and then she left the room.

Chana served Sam and herself heaping bowls of steaming chicken soup with thick slices of hearty bread.

"This is real good," Samuel said.

"Thanks. I wish I could claim I made it. But that would be a lie. I worked all day. My mother is the cook. But I agree with you, my mom makes great soup." Chana smiled at him. "Want some more?"

"Yes, I'd love some."

She ladled him another bowl of soup. "So how did it go today with your training?"

"I learned to shoot a gun."

"Mazel tov," she scoffed. Then she added, "What are you going to do when you have to kill a man? You think you can do it?"

"I don't know. I have to tell you the truth. I liked being a baker and working for my dad. I hate to admit it, but I'm really just a simple fella. When I was young my plans were to take over the bakery and get married and raise a family. Then life interfered."

"You mean that bad business in Medina?"

"Yeah, that's when everything changed. The Schatzmans were an established family in Medina. Now here in Manhattan we are nobodies. Nobody knows us. They don't come to our bakery, not to buy challah or rugelach or even to say hello or good Shabbos."

"There's lots of competition here in the city. But if you wouldn't have come to the city, you would never have met me. And . . . Samuel Schatzman, I am going to be the best thing that ever happened to you."

He tried to smile. *I should tell her the truth,* he thought. *I am a real jerk for leading her on. She thinks there is a chance for her and me, but the truth is I am still in love with Betty.* "Chana, listen to me," he said, trying to find the right words to tell her. "I like you. I like you a lot, but . . ."

She put her hand over his mouth to silence him. "Follow me," she whispered. He followed her to her bedroom. Chana closed the door behind him. Then she unbuttoned her blouse. His heart skipped a beat.

She removed her blouse and he thought, *She is breathtakingly beautiful.* He remembered one of the boys he knew brought a deck of cards with naked girls on them to the synagogue when he was only twelve. A group of boys, Sam included, snuck upstairs into a loft where they slowly went through the cards until the rabbi caught them and took the cards away. But he still remembered the pictures. The girls were big breasted and wide hipped. And they had long hair like Chana's. Until tonight, he was convinced women like this only existed in movies. That was until he saw Chana's clothes drop to the floor.

"What about your parents?" he said, breathless, feeling his manhood hardening.

"It's all right." Chana smiled. Then she came very close to him and whispered in his ear, "Don't worry, my mother won't come in, and my father can't get out of bed."

When he felt her hot breath against his neck, Samuel lost sight of his resolve to tell her that he was in love with someone else. Chana's eyes were glued to his as she pulled the clip out of her hair, and her wild scarlet curls fell about her shoulders. There was no denying that she was magnificent to look at.

She put her arms around his neck. Then she pulled him onto the bed and leaned back until he was on top of her.

Making love with Chana was much different than he remembered the sweet tender fondling of his youth with Betty. He and Betty had both been virgins the first time. The first few times he and Betty were together they found their lovemaking to be clumsy and unsatisfying. Finally, after months of becoming familiar with each other they settled into a steady routine that was an expression of their innocence and love for each other. But Chana was anything but calm and settled. She was wild, and she did things to him he'd never dreamed of. By the time they'd finished, he was out of breath and not sure he was ready to break things off with Chana quite yet.

The following morning Izzy was outside Sam's apartment in the cab of a large truck.

"Hop in," Izzy said when Sam came down the walkway.

Samuel climbed up and got into the seat. Next to him was a Tommy gun just like the one he'd learned to operate the previous day.

"Ready for an adventure?" Izzy asked.

Samuel shrugged. "Sure," he said, trying to hide his fear.

"Then here we go." Izzy started up the truck, and they pulled onto the road. "When we get out of the city, I'll teach you to drive. It's too congested here," he said.

They rode in silence for a while. Then Izzy pulled a thermos out from under the seat and cracked it open. "Want a swig of coffee?"

"Sounds great."

Izzy sipped the coffee, then he handed the thermos to Sam. "Careful, it's hot."

Sam took a sip. "It's good," he said.

"It's hot anyway, right, Sammy?"

Samuel nodded. "Yep."

"Can I ask you a question?"

"Yeah, sure."

"Is Chana your girl? I mean are you two serious or anything," Izzy asked.

"No, we're just friends."

"I know it's none of my business, but I was just wondering," he said, then added, "She's a nice girl. But she's not the kind you marry if you know what I mean. She's got a real bad reputation. Lenny told me that Chana's done some prostitution to earn money to help support her folks. Her father's a lazy, good-for-nothing alcoholic, and her mother can't earn a dime. From what I hear, Chana works all day, then she takes on men at night."

"Poor kid," Samuel said more to himself than to Izzy. He was quiet for several moments thinking about how kind Chana had always been to him. Then he turned to Izzy and said, "Listen, I like you. And I sure appreciate you teaching me the ropes. But I am only gonna tell you this once. You see, Chana is my friend, and if I ever hear that you're spreading dirty gossip about her again, I'll knock you out."

"Whoa! A tough guy," Izzy said. "Don't get me wrong; I'm not scared of you. But we are going to be working together, and it's not good that we should get off on the wrong foot. So I want you to know that I didn't mean anything bad. Just thought you ought to know what people are saying."

"I don't care what they say, and if you don't mind, I am asking you to keep your mouth shut about Chana."

"I respect your wishes. Anyway, you're right. Chana's a good kid, and there's no point in spreading all that stuff."

They rode in silence for a few minutes, then Samuel said, "Thanks. I'm sorry I was so harsh with you. It's just that Chana has been a good friend to me. And I'm sure her life is pretty hard."

"Don't even think about it. I hold no grudges."

"So now that we're on the road, can you tell me where we're going?" Sam asked.

"I suppose I can. We're going up to Canada. We have a load of molasses in the back of the truck that we are going to drop off. Once we do, we'll load up with whiskey. Then we'll bring it back to New York."

"You've done this before?"

"Sure, I do it plenty. So will you if you stay with Laevsky. He might get you involved in gambling or dope, but for the most part he needs men to make these runs."

"How often do you have to use the gun?"

"So far, never. Laevsky pays off the cops. And for now, they leave us alone. But we can't be sure what tomorrow brings," Izzy said.

Once they had left the city and were driving through the lush green countryside, Izzy pulled the truck over and got out. "Come on and slide into the driver's seat," he told Sam.

Sam did as Izzy asked.

"Put your hand on the steering wheel, like this." Izzy placed Sam's hands. Pointing to the pedals, he said, "That's the gas; it's for when you want to go. That's the brake; it's for when you want to stop. Don't push either of them pedals too hard. Just take it easy."

"And this?" Samuel put his hand on the gearshift.

"Let me show you how that works."

Within a half hour, Samuel was driving.

"Not bad, kid," Izzy said. "You're a fast learner. I have to admit you had me scared at first when I told you to hit the brakes, and boy did you ever." He laughed. "I just about shit my pants when we almost went through the windshield."

Sam laughed too.

"But now you've got the hang of it. And I have to say, you're a pretty good driver, and you're not bad with the gun either. I think you're going to work out just fine in this job."

They drove through the day stopping by the side of the road to eat a packed lunch, and by that evening they had reached their destination. They pulled into the back of an abandoned warehouse where they switched trucks and then immediately headed back to New York.

"How often do we make these runs?" Sam asked.

"Usually about every other week."

As the sun rose, they crossed the Brooklyn Bridge back into the city. Sam yawned.

"Are you tired?" Izzy asked.

"You bet."

"You'll get used to it."

Before Izzy dropped Sam off at his apartment building, he handed him an envelope. "From the boss," he said.

Sam looked at Izzy, puzzled. "What is it?"

"Your pay. What else would it be?"

"Thanks. I thought I'd have to go the speakeasy tonight to get it. And to be frank, I was afraid I'd have trouble getting paid."

"The boss is real good about paying. You never have to worry about him when it comes to your money. You take care of him, and he will take care of you. By the way, you did a damn good job, Samuel. Welcome to our family."

Sam nodded. "I'm glad to be a part of it," he said and put the envelope in his pants pocket.

"By the way, if you're not busy, you want to come to the speakeasy tomorrow night? Drinks are on me."

"Yeah, sure. Why not?"

"You planning on bringing Chana?"

"If you want me to, I will."

"Yeah, why don't you? I think it would be fun," Izzy said.

CHAPTER SIXTY-FIVE

S am stretched as he walked into the apartment. It was quiet. *My father must be asleep in his room. It's late, but I've noticed that he has been sleeping a lot lately. Even during the day,* Sam thought. He sat down on the sofa and took the envelope out of his pocket. When he tore it open his eyes grew wide, his breathing shallow. "Well, ain't that the bee's knees," he said aloud in disbelief. His hands trembled as he lay the pile of bills on the sofa beside them and began to count. Fifty dollars. It couldn't be fifty dollars for one night's work, could it? He counted it again. It was fifty dollars. *A fortune,* he thought. Now he and his father would not have to leave the apartment. He wanted to wake his father to tell him the good news. But instead, he lay down on the sofa for a minute to relish in the excitement of the moment, and within seconds he was fast asleep, the money held tightly in his fist.

In the morning before his father awakened, Sam went downstairs to see the landlord. He paid the rent for the next two months. Then he walked outside and sang softly to himself as he made his way to the general store where he purchased flour, eggs, cheese, and coffee. When he returned to the apartment his father was awake.

"Dad, I brought home breakfast. I'm going to bake us bread, and we'll have hard-boiled eggs with chunks of cheese . . ."

"Where did you get the money for all of this?" his father asked.

"I got it." Sam smiled, setting his purchases carefully on the counter. "I have a job now. And . . . I also paid the rent for the next two months, so we won't be out on the street."

"A job? Nu, so that's plenty good. I'm glad to hear it. But what kind of job?"

"I'm driving a truck," he said. *I'm not really lying; I'm just not telling him the whole truth.*

"Who taught you how to drive?" his father asked.

"They did. It just so happens that this girl who worked next door to us on Delancey Street knew of someone who needed a driver. You know the one, the redhead; her name is Chana."

"Yes, the zoftik, pretty one. I know who she is."

"She's very nice. She helped me a lot this last week."

"Well, mazel tov. What good fortune this is, my son."

"I know, it sure is, Dad. For the first time since that incident in Medina, Samuel felt the guilt he carried being lifted. "I'll take care of you, Dad."

"Well, I would rather not be a burden, so let's hope I can find work too."

CHAPTER SIXTY-SIX

C hana was thrilled when Samuel appeared at the cobbler's shop later that day.

"How was it working for Laevsky?" she asked.

"Good. It was even better than I expected. I worked with Izzy. Nice fella."

"Yes, he is."

"Chana, remember you're here to work." It was the old cobbler yelling out from the back of the store.

"I won't keep you. And I realize it's last minute. But I was wondering if you'd like to go to the speakeasy with Izzy and me tonight."

"I'd love to," Chana said, her pretty face brightening.

"Is nine o'clock too late? Maybe we can have a quick bite and then head over and have some more of that . . . what did you call it . . . panther piss?" He laughed.

She laughed too.

"So I'll pick you up at nine? What do you say?"

"I say it sounds good." She smiled.

"See you then." He turned to leave. Then as he opened the door he whipped back around. "I was just wondering; how did you know I was at your door the other evening even before I rang the bell?"

"You really want to know?"

"Yeah, I am curious."

"It's nothing really that magical, I'm afraid. I was just watching out the window and I saw you."

"You were watching for me? I can't believe that you are so nice to a boring fella like me."

"Of course, Samuel. I was watching for you. You fool, I like you . . . a lot. In case you can't tell."

"Chaaana! Work?" Goldsmith hollered, banging something on his table to make sure he got Chana's attention. "You"—he pointed to Samuel—"you have shoes that need a new sole? You have a belt to fix? No? Then go on your way and let the girl work."

"See you tonight," Sam said to Chana.

She smiled.

CHAPTER SIXTY-SEVEN

That night Izzy picked Samuel up in his automobile, and then together they picked up Chana who looked ravishing in a tight red dress. They went to a small Italian café for a quick spaghetti dinner, then they drove to the speakeasy. Lenny was at the door. He shook Izzy's hand then turned to Samuel. "Welcome to the family, Sam. I heard the news. I heard you are one of us now. Laevsky hired you."

"Yes, it's true."

"How do you like it?"

"I do."

"Well, good." Then he turned to Chana. "You look beautiful as always," he said, grabbing Chana's backside.

She removed his hand and said, "Kiss mer in tuchas, kiss my ass." But her tone of voice was flirty, and Lenny just laughed.

Izzy introduced Samuel to several other members of the gang. They were all Jewish New York street boys, most of them under forty.

"This is Mel, and this is Mike. This is Joe and Rob, Ben and Jake." Some of them were with girls who wore low-cut dresses; others were alone or in pairs.

"Nice to meet you," Samuel said to each of them as he was introduced. But as the evening wore on, he met so many of Laevsky's employees that he was having a hard time remembering their names.

A jazz band played. And Samuel, Izzy, and Chana drank until they were so drunk that Chana got up on the stage and began to sing off-key with the band until Lenny gently helped her back to her seat.

Izzy was so drunk that he came within feet of hitting a tree on the way home.

And as for Samuel, he used the alcohol to convince himself that it was all right to spend the night making love to Chana even though Betty was in the back of his mind.

CHAPTER SIXTY-EIGHT

S am could see that each day his father was falling deeper and deeper into depression as the months passed. With Irving's wife and daughter gone, the bakery closed, and because of his inability to find work, he began to let himself go. He stayed in bed all day without washing and sometimes refused to get up when Sam tried to coax him to eat. He'd grown thin and quiet, and Samuel was worried. His father had always been a vibrant man, working long hours. But recently he told Sam that he felt worthless, like a failure. Sam felt that if he didn't do something to help him, his father might commit suicide. So not knowing what else to do, he asked Chana if she could ask Fanny to hire his father at her bakery.

"I don't know if she will do it, Sammy," Chana said, stroking Sam's hair. "When she offered you a job, she was doing it as a favor to me."

"I really need your help with this, Chana. Please, will you just try?"

"For you? Of course, I'll try." She kissed his cheek.

Sam's relationship with Chana was special to him. She always looked in his eyes when he spoke and made him feel like every word he said was important. Her hands caressed his face; her lips brought comfort to his hot brow after a long day at work. When he was tired, she rubbed his back; when he was upset, she listened. He found she was unlike any girl he'd ever known. There was no subject he could not discuss with her. Sam didn't have to censor his words. Chana never judged him. She was his friend, his confidant, and his lover. Sam and Chana dined together at least three times a week and afterward he always spent the night. Sometimes they went to the speakeasy with Izzy, where Sam slowly acquired a taste for alcohol. And Chana wore her heart on her sleeve, leaving no doubt in Sam's mind that she was in love with him. And he found he cared deeply for her, but at night Betty still haunted his dreams.

One afternoon when Samuel and Izzy were on their way back from Canada with a truck full of whiskey, he told Izzy all about Betty. He told him everything that happened in Medina and how he felt he had to find Betty again if he was ever going to be happy.

"It's hard between a Jew and a shiksa. I stay away from them. Too much bullshit. Their families look down on you; their brothers want to kick you in the tuchas. Kick you in the ass. Eh, my bubbie always said that it's just as easy to fall in love with a Jewish girl as it is with a shiksa."

"Yeah, I know. I've heard the saying. But I never planned to fall for Betty. It just happened. We were both young. She was pretty and blonde and different. And before I knew it, I was involved."

"You still love her after all this time?"

"Yes. I think about her all the time. I want to marry her."

"And what happens to Chana when you and Betty get back together?"

"I don't know. I wish I had an answer. I've tried to break off my relationship with Chana because I know it's wrong to lead her on. But every time I try, she draws me in. I mean, I've never told her about Betty. But . . . I guess it's the sex that pulls me back to Chana. I can't seem to give her up."

Just then they heard the sound of a police car following them.

"Hide the gun," Izzy warned. "And be calm. Let me do the talking," he warned as he slowly pulled the truck to the side of the road.

Izzy rolled down the window. "Afternoon, Officer," he said, holding a one-hundred-dollar bill in his hand where the police officer could see it.

"Good afternoon," the policeman answered. "Where are you two headed, and what is in the back of your truck?"

"We're headed to New York City. We're carrying a load of cucumbers."

"Cucumbers, huh?" The cop shook his head.

"Yes, sir," Izzy said, laying the bill across the steering wheel to be sure the police officer saw it.

Samuel's heart was racing. Izzy was trying to bribe this cop. If the cop refused and decided to check the back of the truck they'd both be arrested. And from there? Jail time?

The police officer eyed the bill, then he said, "We've had a lot of trouble with bootleggers bringing whiskey into the States from Canada."

"Well, Officer, you wouldn't have to worry about that with us." Izzy flashed him a smile as the cop took the bill.

"Good to know that," the policeman said. "Now, you boys drive carefully."

"Yes, Officer," Izzy said.

As they drove away, Samuel glanced at Izzy. "A hundred dollars?"

"Yep. It's a hell of a lot of money. You have any idea what a cop earns. It ain't much. So the hundred-dollar bill gets 'em every time."

"Is it your money?"

"Hell, no! Laevsky pays it."

Then they both started laughing out of relief.

CHAPTER SIXTY-NINE

The day after Samuel returned to New York following his run to Canada, he went to see Chana.

"I have good news," she said. "Fanny said she would give your father a chance. She said if he's a good baker, she'll keep him on."

"Really! That is good news," Sam said.

"Why don't I come over and make dinner for you and your father tonight? That way I can tell him myself," Chana suggested.

"Sounds great. Here, let me give you some money so you can buy the food." Samuel pulled a few dollars out of his pocket.

"That's a lot," Chana said.

"Keep the change." Samuel winked at her.

"By the way, I don't have your address," she said.

"You mean to tell me that you, Chana, who knows everything about everyone on the Lower East Side, doesn't know where I live?"

"You never told me."

"We'll have to fix that," he said and wrote down his address and handed it to her.

CHANA ARRIVED, with a basket filled with food, at six o'clock.

"Sorry I am so late. I got off work a half hour ago, and then I went shopping for all this stuff for dinner. I got here as soon as I could. I hope a late dinner is all right with you."

"It's fine," Sam said. "Let me introduce you to my dad."

Irving whispered to Sam that he liked Chana as soon as he met her. Then after they'd finished the delicious dinner Chana had prepared, she surprised Irving with the news about the job she'd gotten for him.

"Fanny is a friend of mine, and she would love to have you come and bake for her bakery if you are interested," Chana said to Irving.

"Interested! Of course I am," Irving said, then he turned to look at Sam. Pointing at Chana, he added, "I love this girl. She's a good one, Samelah. Don't let her slip away."

Sam smiled at his father. "I'm glad you're happy, Dad."

"I am. Thank you, Chana."

"Of course, Mr. Schatzman. Anything for Sammy's dad," she said.

"I'm going to walk Chana home, Dad. I'll be back," Sam said.

"I know you won't be back tonight. So I'll see you in the morning," Irving said, giving them a wink.

Both Sam and Chana giggled as they left the house.

"I like your dad," she said as she put her arm through Sam's.

"He really likes you too. And I want you to know I appreciate you going out of your way to get him a job. He needs to work. Not for the money. I am earning good money now. But he needs a purpose; you know what I mean?"

"Of course I know what you mean. And I am glad I could help."

They walked quietly for a while.

"I have some things I must tell you," Chana said.

"I already know. I don't care," Samuel said.

Chana stopped walking and turned to look directly at him. "What do you know?"

"About the prostitution. Is that what you wanted to tell me?"

"Not all of it," she said. But then she added, "I want you to know that I don't do it anymore. I don't do it because of you. Because of how I feel about you. But like I said, that's not all I have to tell you. I have a dark secret that I have never told anyone."

"What is it? You can tell me."

"I know I can. And . . . I do trust you . . ."

He stopped, turned her to face him, and took her hands in his. "Tell me," he said.

She opened her mouth to speak. But just as she was about to speak, Izzy came sauntering around the corner and walked up to them. "Hello, where are you two crazy kids headed?"

"I'm walking Chana home."

"How about you join me for a drink first?" he said.

Chana shrugged. "Whatever you want," she said to Samuel.

"Sure. Why not?" Sam said, and the three of them went to the speakeasy where they drank until almost two in the morning. Then they parted. Izzy watched his two friends as they headed toward Chana's apartment with their arms wrapped around each other.

CHAPTER SEVENTY

I zzy couldn't sleep that night. He saw the way Chana looked at Samuel. She loved him. It was all over her face. But Izzy knew the truth. Samuel was not in love with Chana. He was in love with some shiksa he'd left behind in Upstate New York. And Izzy . . . Izzy had never told anyone, but he was in love with Chana. He knew her past. He knew what people said about her being loose and fast, but he didn't care. They were kids together, grew up in the same neighborhood. He'd watched her turn from a chubby little redheaded girl, whom everyone called fatty, into a gorgeous vixen. But the funny thing was, he was crazy about her even when she was the fat little quiet girl in the back of his history class. And because his family lived so close to hers, just one tenement to the right, he often heard her mother calling for Chana from her kitchen window. "Chana, come in and wash the clothes. Or Chana, come in and make something for dinner."

Later when Chana was older, there was gossip about the heavy burden her parents put on her. People talked in this little Jewish neighborhood. They said Chana was forced to support her parents, or they would have perished long ago. But they didn't forgive her for selling her body. She was looked down upon. But Izzy forgave her. He knew that poor Chana had been doing whatever she could to earn extra money from the time she was eleven. And he also knew that even though life was hard for her, she was always kind to everyone, especially those who were less fortunate.

He had been in town shopping for his mother one afternoon. At the time he and Chana were both about fourteen, and Chana had already lost her childish fat and had transformed into a beauty. As Izzy was walking back home, he passed a crippled teenage boy who was struggling to get down the stairs in front of the city library. The boy's body was twisted, and each step turned him around to where he hugged the bannister so he wouldn't topple down the stairs. Several teenagers, some of whom Izzy recognized as his classmates, had gathered around. They were laughing at the boy and mocking him. But no one would help him. Izzy knew the other teens were afraid to get too close to someone who was deformed. They were afraid it might be contagious. He was afraid too. But just as all of this was happening, Chana came walking out of the library. She assessed the scene before her. Then she turned around and yelled at the other teens. "Shame on all of you."

Chana dropped her books and ran over to the crippled boy. She put her slender arm around his waist. Slowly and carefully she helped him down the stairs. It was at that moment Izzy fell in love with her. He loved her kind and gentle ways, her soft voice, her genuine smile. She was different than the other girls, and although he knew his parents would never approve, he fantasized about marrying her.

Things had changed since they'd met Samuel. Now Izzy was obsessed with the look he saw in Chana's eyes every time she looked at Samuel. *If only she would look at me that way*, he thought. *I would marry her no matter what my parents said.*

In the past Izzy had paid Chana for sex. It only happened a few times. It drove him mad with jealousy to know she sold her body. And because of this he tried to convince himself he wasn't in love with her. He told himself time and again that she was not the kind of girl a fellow would marry, and it was only sexual release he was after when he went to her bed. But deep down inside his soul, Izzy believed Chana was his bashert, the woman he was meant to share his life with.

When Chana was in his arms, he felt as if he were a puzzle that had just found its missing piece. Many times, he'd tried to tell her how he felt, but he stumbled over the words. He was certain she didn't share his feelings, and because of that, he was afraid that if he told her he loved her she might exclude him from her life altogether. So he kept his mouth shut. And he would have continued to pay her for sex if that was his only opportunity to hold her in his arms. But then Samuel came into their lives. And he saw the changes in Chana.

He was hurt by the relationship he saw developing between Sam and Chana and that was why he'd lashed out and told Samuel that Chana was a prostitute. Not only was he hurt, but he was also hoping that once Sam found out, it would end any interest Samuel had in his girl. But it didn't. Every time they went out as a group of friends, Chana took Samuel home with her at the end of the night. And then to make matters worse, the next time Izzy had offered Chana money for sex, she told him she was no longer doing that. "How are you surviving on what the old cobbler pays you?" he asked her.

"Not easily," she admitted. "But I just can't do that anymore. I'd rather do without."

"Here," he said, handing her the five dollars he would have paid her. "Take it."

"But I said I can't do that anymore." Chana shook her head.

"I know. And I'm saying take this money as a gift."

"Oh . . . I couldn't."

"Do it for me, Chana. We've known each other our whole lives. I make plenty. Just take it. In fact, here . . . " He pulled out a one-hundred-dollar bill. "Take this. It should help you and your family for a while."

She shook her head.

"I insist," he said and pushed the money into her handbag.

"Thanks Izzy. I mean, really . . . thanks."

He smiled at her and touched her cheek. "Glad I could help, kid," he said.

After that, all he could think about was convincing Sam to hurry and get back to Medina to see Betty. Sam had told him that he planned to go back as soon as he had enough money. So every time Laevsky asked Izzy how Samuel was doing, Izzy showered his coworker with praise. And because of Izzy, Laevsky gave Sam a raise. Izzy knew how generous his boss could be, and he hoped now that Sam was earning good money, he would feel confident to ask Betty to marry him. The raise was substantial. It was double what Sam was earning when he started. Laevsky was now paying Sam one hundred dollars each time he and Izzy returned from Canada with a truckful of bootlegged whiskey.

CHAPTER SEVENTY-ONE

Winter, 1930

One afternoon between runs, Sam's father was at work, and Sam was alone in the new flat he'd rented for them. It was far nicer than the previous one. They had a bathroom with a claw-foot tub and hot water, right in the apartment, not down the hall anymore. The heat in the apartment worked well and served to ward off the winter chill. Plus there were fans for the summer. Before Samuel rented the second-floor apartment on the Upper East Side, he made sure it was large enough for him and his father to have their own rooms. But most important, Betty must find it comfortable when he brought her back with him to the city. He was almost ready to go to Medina and get her; he just needed a few more things. First of all, he asked Mr. Laevsky to help him purchase his own automobile. It was a sleek black car that made Sam feel accomplished when he sat behind the wheel. Laevsky got him a good deal on it because he bought it from a friend of Laevsky's. Since Sam had been earning good money, he had been having his suits made by Laevsky's tailor, Jake Feldman. Jake was the finest tailor in all of Manhattan, and the clothes he designed for Sam made him think he looked like a movie star. He had a special silk suit made for his visit back to Medina.

At night when Sam had time to think, his thoughts were always of Betty. Over and over in his mind, he replayed his fantasy of how the day would play out when he went to see her again. He imagined how her lovely face would light up with love and admiration when she saw him and his fine clothes and fancy car. In his fantasy she would squeal with delight when he proposed. And she would cry tears of joy when he told her that he had never stopped loving her. She would fall into his arms, and they would make love when he confessed that everything he did, he did for her. Sam only had one more thing to do before he went back to Medina. He would purchase a diamond ring because he planned to get down on one knee and propose.

Whenever he had these delightful thoughts of Betty, they were overshadowed by the guilt he felt toward Chana. He liked Chana. Liked her a lot. But Betty had been in his dreams since the last time he saw her. And she was the girl he loved, the only girl he'd ever really loved.

Sam poured himself a shot of whiskey. Over the past several months since he'd had his first drink, he'd come to really appreciate and enjoy the taste of alcohol. He especially liked it on a cold winter day when it warmed him from the inside out.

There was a knock on the door to his apartment. Sam had been walking around in his underwear, so he grabbed his robe before opening the door.

It was Chana. He could see by her tear-stained face that she had been crying.

"What's the matter?" he said, gently pulling her inside.

"Do you remember I once told you that I had a secret? Do you remember I said I had something that I had to tell you?"

"Yes, but you never brought it up again."

"Well, now I have to tell you my secret because I need your help," she said.

"Sit down," he said, taking her hand and ushering her over to the sofa. "Talk to me, Chana." He sat down beside her and put his arm around her shoulder.

"I hope that what I am about to say doesn't disgust you and make you want to run away from me. I've been so afraid to tell you . . ."

"Go on. Trust me. I'll help if I can," he said.

"I have a brother. A younger brother," she blurted out. "No one knows he exists. No one. Not Izzy or Lenny or anyone. That's because my little brother's not right in the head. He's in an asylum for the insane."

"Where?"

"Bellevue."

He nodded. "Here in New York."

"Yes," she said. "I am so ashamed, so ashamed, Sam. You knew I was prostituting myself, but you never knew the real reason why. It was so I would be able to afford keep him in a private facility. I was selling my body to pay for it. Please forgive me. I'm not that kind of girl. I never wanted to do that, but I had no other way. The cobbler hardly pays a living wage. But then when I met you, I just couldn't do it anymore. I couldn't bring myself to allow anyone but you to touch me. And so I quit prostitution. But that's when I had to have my brother, Abe, transferred to Bellevue, which is a state hospital. The private facility was way too expensive. Anyway, yesterday the administrator at Bellevue contacted me. The doctor said Abe has become too difficult for them to handle. They want to give him some kind of treatment to calm him down. I don't really understand what it is that they want to do. But the doctor asked me to come to the hospital so he could explain it better. I went to that hospital once when I first had him transferred. It was horrible. I can't go there alone. I am begging you to go with me. Will you?"

"Of course I will," he said, hugging her close to him. She nuzzled her head into his neck. "You want to go right now?" he suggested.

"Can we?"

"Sure, just let me get dressed," he said.

CHAPTER SEVENTY-TWO

S am started the car, and they drove up First Street until they saw a large black wrought-iron gate on the right-hand side.

"Is this it?" he asked Chana.

She nodded. "Yeah."

He parked the car then opened her door and helped her out. She was unsteady on her feet. "It's all right. I'm here with you," he said, holding her arm tightly as they entered the large brown brick building.

"We're here to see Dr. Erickson. My name is Chana Rubinstein. My brother is Abe Rubinstein," Chana said to a large woman who was sitting as a desk in front of the door. Her hair was combed back from her face making her look severe and angry. She nodded. "Sit down. I'll go and get the doctor for you." When she stood up, Samuel noticed her legs were unshaved. They were covered in thick, dark hair.

A strong odor of urine permeated the room. Chana glanced at Samuel. "Thank you for coming with me," she said.

Sam took Chana's hand and gently squeezed. "It's going to be all right. I'm glad to be here with you. You shouldn't have to face something like this all alone."

The doctor's heels clicked on the tile floor as he walked into the room. He wore a starched white coat and crisply pressed black pants. He was an older man, slight of build, with thinning gray hair.

"I'm Dr. Erickson," he said. "You must be Chana?"

"Yes, and this is my friend Samuel Schatzman."

"Nice to meet you both. I have recently been assigned to your brother's case. As you know until last week Dr. Tam was his doctor. But your brother was giving him a lot of trouble. And I'm the fellow here at Bellevue who takes on the difficult cases." He smiled.

"Can I see my brother?" Chana said.

"Are you sure you want to? We've had to restrain him. He got into a fistfight with another patient and knocked out two of that man's teeth."

"Yes, I am sure, Doctor. I would like to see him, please," Chana said, glancing at Sam, who nodded at her.

"All right. Follow me."

They walked down a long corridor. The walls were painted white, and the floor was white tile. The heavy odor of urine still prevailed but now it was mixed with the harsh smell of rubbing alcohol that made Sam's eyes burn.

After they passed through a set of large double doors, they entered a ward with rows of beds set up along both walls. To their left there was another room. This one was set up like a large living space with patients sitting in wheelchairs playing cards.

"Hello there, Dr. Erickson," a woman with wild wiry gray hair called out in a fetching voice. "Want to fuck me?" She lifted her hospital gown to reveal a pair of dirty gray underpants and bare sagging breasts. Then the woman began to cackle loudly.

Another man was screaming, "I shit in my chair. I shit in my chair." Feces ran down the side of the wheelchair.

Chana's mouth fell open.

"I'm sorry," the doctor said. "The patients don't always know what they are saying and doing. Their disease takes hold of them. It is very sad. They are insane. But, of course, I'm sure you understand."

Chana nodded.

Then the doctor took out a key and unlocked a door at the end of the hall. He led them inside. The walls in this area were green tile that was covered in black mold. In this room the patients were strapped to their beds. They called out obscenities.

"You bastards, let me out of here," one said.

"I'm going to kill you when I get loose," another chimed in.

"Again, I apologize," Dr. Erickson said to Chana.

Then they walked past a young man with bright blue eyes and wavy brown hair. He struggled to free himself from his restraints, but they were very tight. Then he started laughing wildly. "Do you know who I am?" he said. "I'm the forest elf. I save little children." He laughed again. "I don't belong in here."

There was something about that man that made Chana shudder. The doctor saw her tremble. "That one is certainly a frightening case. He is not from New York City. They brought him here from Medina. He was convicted of raping a little girl. Apparently, he raped her and then left her for dead. Fortunately, the child survived. But he is here awaiting trial. My guess is he'll get the death penalty."

The man who called himself the forest elf pulled against his restraints. Then something caught his eye and he stopped. "I know you," he said to Sam in a singsong voice. "Aren't you Samuel Schatzman?" he said. "I remember you distinctly because I am Frank Weston. You don't know me. But I know you."

Sam and Chana stopped in their tracks and looked at each other. Sam shuddered. *How does this nut know my name?*

Sam walked over to the man. "How do you know me?" he asked suspiciously.

"Do you remember little Evelyn Wilson? Well, it was me who kidnapped her. She was playing with flowers in the forest when I took her. I told her the truth that I was the forest elf. But I lied when I told her that I protect little children. Do you know what I did next?" He let out a loud laugh. "I raped her and then I tortured her too. I would have killed her, but my folks wouldn't let me. Do you know what they did to protect me? They took that little girl, and they scared her until she peed her little white panties. They scared her into thinking we were Jews. That's how you and your Jew friends got the blame for the crime."

He's lucid. I believe him. Sam wanted to put his arms around Frank's throat and squeeze until all the life seeped out of him. "You bastard, you ruined my life. And I would bet money that you ruined the life of that poor little girl too," he said.

Frank started to cackle again.

"I heard she's dead. I heard she killed herself. Drowned in the pond just a half mile from her house. I would've liked to have see it, but I missed it. Shame, isn't it?"

"Shut up, you bastard. Shut up before I lose control and put an end to your miserable life." Sam clenched and unclenched his fists. *This pathetic excuse for a man isn't worth killing. If I really want him dead, all I have to do is talk to Laevsky. He would have one of the boys take care of it. But why use up a favor like that? The law is going to take care of it anyway. I'd like the to go to the newspapers and ask them to print a story to let all the Jews of Medina know that I never did anything wrong. But I doubt they'd ever do that for me. After all, Frank is a madman. And me . . . I'm a Jew.*

"Sam . . . Sam." Chana shook his shoulders. "Are you all right? The doctor is concerned. Hell, you're as white as a sheet. I am worried too."

"Yes, I'm sorry. I'm fine. Let's go and see your brother."

CHANA'S BROTHER lay tightly restrained on a small cot. His hair was long and wild. His face was scruffy and unshaven. But his eyes were the most telling. They seemed to be separate from the man as they darted wildly about the room, filled with anger and madness. At first, Abe didn't seem to know anyone was there, but then suddenly his eyes stopped moving, and he looked directly at Chana, his eyes burning into her soul. "So after all this time, you finally come to see me? I've been laying here suffering, Chana. Suffering, and all because of you." He spit the words out, hissing like a serpent. "You know what you are, Chana? You're nothing but a dirty whore. A dirty good-for-nothing whore who put me in this place." Then he spit at her. When she recoiled, he laughed. "But I have a something to tell you. I have a power you don't recognize. You know what it is? It's that I can see demons all around you. There they are here with you right now. And you know what they are doing? They're laughing because they know that you are about to take a fall, big sister. You are about to pay for what you have done to me."

Chana shivered. Samuel put his arm around her and drew her close to him. She was unsteady on her feet. He held her tightly hoping she could somehow draw from his strength.

"He's miserable, restless, angry, and when he's not restrained, he's violent," Dr. Erickson said as they headed toward the office where doctors did consultations with family members. Once they were in the office, Dr Erickson sat down behind a desk, then he turned to Chana and said, "Please, won't you both sit down." After they were all seated, the doctor continued, "I have a treatment option that I believe will help him. It's called electro-shock therapy. We've had a lot of success with it with other patients who were difficult to handle and acting violent and out of control."

Chana nodded. She was still trembling, and Samuel still had his arm around her.

"I don't know how much it is. But don't worry, Chana. I'll help with the cost," Samuel said.

CHAPTER SEVENTY-THREE

Before sunrise the following day, Samuel sat in the living room of his apartment. He was sipping a cup of steaming black coffee. The previous night had been difficult for him. He'd been unable to sleep. Every time he closed his eyes, Frank's face appeared in his mind. And then his thoughts turned to the poor little girl Frank raped, and he felt sick.

Sam had always wondered who had taken little Evelyn Wilson and why. He often thought it could have been a plan devised by Betty's fiancé to discredit Sam and turn his life upside down. Sometimes he wondered if it was something that had been created by the KKK to take business away from the Jewish shops and bring it back to the non-Jews. But now he knew the answer. All of the terrible things that had happened to Sam and his family in Medina were due to the horrific acts of a madman. Nothing more, nothing less. There was no well-thought-out plot. Just a crazy child killer who hunted little children. And Sam happened to get caught up in the web. The entire incident still left him unnerved. Because he realized that once again, as it had throughout history, the blame for everything had fallen upon the Jews. And he'd always grown up believing that it couldn't happen here. Not in America.

Gazing out the window at the darkness, he felt sad. Reaching up he caressed the Star of David he wore around his neck. *I am a Jew*, he thought, and tears ran down his cheeks. Not since his father had given him that necklace on the day of his bar mitzvah had he felt such great pride in his heritage.

He sat there for at least fifteen minutes before he heard his father getting up for work. Irving went into the bathroom. Sam took a deep breath as he watched the bathroom door close. *Should I tell him about Frank? Sam wondered. Hasn't Dad had enough tough luck? He wrote to Mom so many times, and she still has not answered any of his letters. Poor fella, he still loves her. When I tried to write to her and apologize for jumping ship she never even answered me either. I guess she's so angry at me that she's written both of us off.*

Since Goldie and Alma had been gone, a couple of brief letters from his sister addressed to both Sam and his father arrived. Alma told them a little about Berlin. She said she liked her grandparents and planned to meet with Irving's parents too. She told them about school and how much she missed them both, but she never mentioned their mother.

"Good morning," Sam's father said as he walked into the living room already dressed and ready to leave for work.

"Good morning, Dad," Sam said. *That job has been so good for him. It's given him a reason to get out of bed. He's half the man he was when I was younger, but at least he doesn't seem like he is ready to die. He has a purpose. A place to go. He feels like his services are needed. I'm forever grateful to Chana for this. But even so, he is still so fragile. My mom hurt him. And between her leaving and his losing the bakery, he is a broken man.*

Irving turned on the light in the kitchen. Sam could see him from his seat on the sofa in the living room. He watched his father pour himself a cup of coffee. His heart ached when he saw that his father's hands shook. Irving took his coffee and sat down beside his son. He blew on the hot liquid then began to sip slowly. "So, boychick, what do you have planned for today?" Irving asked Sam as he did every time Sam was awake early enough to see his father leave for work.

"I have to leave for a couple of days. I have to go on a trip for work," Sam lied. But it was at that moment Samuel decided two things. First, that he would never tell his father about Frank, and second, he was going to Medina today to find Betty.

CHAPTER SEVENTY-FOUR

S am put the small box with the engagement ring, he'd bought for
  Betty, into his pocket. Then he went down to his car and tucked
his gun under the seat of his automobile. *I hope I don't need to use this.
But just in case that ex-fiancé of Betty's and his KKK brothers decide they
want to beat up on me again, this time, I'll be ready. I'm not going to stand by
and let them put me in the hospital again. After all, if I learned anything from
what happened to me in Medina, it's that a Jew, like me, has only himself to
depend on. And a pogrom can happen anytime, anywhere. The rabbi at our
shul when I lived in Medina used to say, "America is a free country, and no
pogrom could ever happen here." Well, I wonder if the rabbi still believes that.
I know what I believe. I believe that even in America the Jews have to watch
their backs. And as long as the Jews have no homeland of our own, we are
defenseless against hate crimes.*

Sam had been thinking about Chana and Betty. And he decided the
only honest thing to do was to tell Chana the truth. He dreaded it, but
he knew he must tell her that he still had feelings for Betty before he
left for Medina. It was the only way he could cope with the over-
whelming guilt he was feeling. Chana deserved to know the truth. He
had to tell her before he returned with Betty. It would come as a
terrible shock if he didn't. And Sam had to make it clear that once he

and Betty were married, he and Chana could remain friends but nothing more. There would be no more nights of passionate lovemaking. A light snow began to fall, and as the tiny white flakes melted, they looked like teardrops running down the car's windshield. Sam's hands trembled as he held the steering wheel. Then as he turned the corner on Delancey Street to head to the cobbler's shop he felt sick. *Am I making a mistake? Of course not. How could this be a mistake? I've been in love with Betty since the first time I saw her. Chana has to know.* Sam tried to take a deep breath, but it caught in his throat. *I shouldn't be so nervous. Chana will understand. She has always been understanding.*

He rubbed his gloved hands together and then walked into the shoemaker's store.

Chana looked up from her worktable when the door opened. "Sam! What brings you here?" she said, her eyes sparkling with delight at having seen him.

"I have to talk to you, Chana. It's important."

"Well, you're in luck. My boss just went to Fanny's to buy a sweet roll, so we're alone. Go on, talk."

"That's good. I'll try to be as quick and to the point as I can," he said, hoping he wouldn't lose his courage.

"Is everything all right?"

Sam sighed. Then he blurted out these words, "Chana, you are beautiful. And you have been so kind to me. You helped my dad find work. You brightened my days . . ." He stopped and stared at her for a second.

Her eyes were glowing. "Go on . . ." she said.

"I don't know how to say this."

"I'll help you," she said. "If you are proposing, my answer is yes."

He reached up and squeezed his temples. How had he made such a mess of things? Sam turned away from Chana. He couldn't look her in the eye. *Say it fast,* he told himself. *Say it and get it over with.* "I . . . well . . . I am not asking you to marry me." He cleared his throat and glanced at her. *Damn, just look at her. She is so confused, and I feel like a heel.* She was squinting her eyes, and a deep line between her brows formed. He recognized that deep wrinkle; it appeared whenever she was worried about something. His heart raced. "I never wanted to hurt you. Things just got out of hand between us. I don't know how it happened. But I have a girl in Medina. I've had a girl all this time. I know it was wrong, you and me, I mean. I should never have started it. You see, this girl in Medina . . . I am in love with her. I'm going to marry her."

Chana turned away from him. She didn't holler. Her voice grew very quiet and calculating instead. "You made love to me. I thought you were different. Not a jerk like the other fellas I know. I didn't think you were the kind of man to make love to someone if you were in love with someone else," Chana said, then she turned around and looked directly at him. He couldn't meet her gaze. He knew he was wrong and had to turn away. "Don't you look away from me. Look at me, Sam. You made love to me."

"When Izzy told me about you—you know what I mean. About the things you did. I figured that sex didn't mean that much to you."

"You are a bastard. Damn you, Samuel Schatzman. How could you be so stupid. You figured that if I could sell my body then I had no feelings. You thought it was perfectly fine for you to use me until you could find a way to get your real girlfriend back." She dropped her head. For a few moments she was silent. Then she said, "When I first met you, I thought the sun rose and set on you. I thought you were the most handsome and respectable man I'd ever met. I wanted to be good enough for you. I wanted to be the kind of girl you would marry. So I quit the prostitution even though I had to have my brother transferred to the state hospital, and I could hardly afford food for my parents. But because I wanted to be the kind of girl you would be proud to be with, I did it." Her face was red with anger, and tears ran down her cheeks.

"I never meant to hurt you. Things just happened between us."

"But you did hurt me. And I truly believe that you think I am dirt beneath your feet, don't you, Sam?"

"No, no . . . I never thought that . . ."

"Didn't you? If you didn't you would not have led me on all the while knowing you planned to marry someone else. You're no good. I can honestly say that you hurt me more deeply than any man who ever paid me for sex. And I hate you." She glared at him and then continued, "And you can believe me, you don't know this because I always smile, no matter how much pain I have inside, but every time I took money for sex, it was like a knife in my heart. But I knew I had no other choice. I was saddled with a lazy, good-for-nothing father who lay in bed all day and drank and a mother who had no idea of how to earn a living. And then to add to my misery I had a crazy brother, who my parents kept as a secret. Abe was a mess from the time he was born. He needed to be institutionalized. My parents were scared of state hospitals. They didn't want him to go to one. But private care costs plenty, and somebody had to pay for it. Somebody had to pay the rent and put food on the table. So, at first, I got a job working for this damn shoemaker. He hardly paid me a living wage. Even so, my parents and I could've gotten by on what I earned had it not been for my brother. My mother cried and cried to me. She was so afraid of putting Abe in a state hospital. She got on her knees and begged me not to. So what was I going to do? You tell me?"

He shook his head and wrung his hands. "I don't know. But, Chana . . . I never held the prostitution against you."

"Oh, really? Didn't you, Sam? You thought of me as the kind of girl you play with but never marry. Well, I've got news for you, brother. I'm not a toy. I'm a human being. A person with feelings with a heart and a soul. And let me tell you, this love affair I had with you was far more devastating to me than anything else that I have had to endure in my life. You know why? Because I loved you, and you led me to believe that I could be like other girls. I used to go to sleep every night dreaming that someday you and I would get married and we would have a little place of our own, a kid or two. But that was my dream. It was never your dream."

"I'm sorry," he whispered, hanging his head.

"Did you even hear me, Sam? I said I love you. I guess that doesn't mean anything to you. I thought you knew it. But maybe you didn't. So there, I've said it."

He threw his hands up in the air. "I don't know what to do. All I can say is I'm sorry."

"I thought you loved me too."

He felt like he might vomit. *What have I done? I have really made a mess of things. I hurt someone I care for.*

She glared at him. "Never mind. This conversation is going

nowhere." She wiped the tears from her cheeks with the back of her hand. Then she managed a smile and said, "I understand; you just don't love me. You never did. I was just making believe, it was all just my own fantasy. That's all you and I ever were." Then she pointed to the door. "Get out of here and never come back. I never want to see you again."

"I'm sorry." He managed to get the words out.

"Go!" she screamed. "Just go."

He walked to the door and stood there for a few seconds. Then he turned to look at her. Her pretty face was covered with tears again. She had already sunk back into her chair and she was weeping hard. The sound of her crying reached into his chest and squeezed his heart. He felt her pain, but he had no idea of what he could do to ease it. Anything he said or did would give her false hope. So he turned and left the shop, closing the door softly behind him.

CHAPTER SEVENTY-FIVE

The ride out to Medina should have been pleasant. But Sam couldn't get Chana off his mind. As he left the busy streets of New York behind, the landscape opened into a winter wonderland of virgin snow. There were picturesque little farms with white fences, small wooden houses, and red barns. He drove for a while until he reached the familiar landscape of Medina. His home. He passed the park where he and his friends had played baseball. Then he saw the ice-cream-and-candy store where his father sometimes took him, just the two of them, to talk and bond.

Then he took the fork in the road that led to the non-Jewish section of town and turned onto the main street. It seemed to Sam that nothing had changed. At least not here. But he wondered how much had changed in the Jewish part of town since the boycott. He knew for sure one thing had changed, Schatzman's bakery, his father's dream, was gone. He drove slowly down the main road and looked at the small shops and, in the distance, the factories. In a very strange way, it was hard for him to believe he'd ever lived in this small town in the middle of a farming community. He had changed so much since he left. And even though he'd lived in Medina much longer than he'd lived in the city, the heartbeat of Manhattan had gotten under his skin: it was in his blood.

Sam drove to the lingerie factory where Betty had worked when he knew her. This was the only connection he had to her, and it was a weak connection at best. If, for some reason, Betty's friend Joan no longer worked at the factory, then Sam would have no way of finding Betty again. It suddenly dawned on him that he'd acted rashly. He'd broken Chana's heart. Then he had driven all the way to Medina and was now waiting outside a factory for a girl who might or might not be there. He thought of Betty, of all they'd shared. The tender nights they'd kissed and held each other hiding in the back of his parents' bakery. He remembered how she had come forward for him, putting her own reputation on the line, when the rest of the town shunned him. They were in love once. And he felt certain that once he found her and explained everything that had happened, she would marry him. He touched the ring box in his pocket. The diamond was large, clear, and beautiful, far more than most men would be able to afford. This was what he wanted. This was why he'd gone to work for Laevsky. So he could return not as the poor, pathetic Jew, but as a force to be reckoned with. He was looking forward to her reaction to his fancy suit and expensive car. If he closed his eyes, he could see her face. She would look at him with pride; she would be glad had defied society. That she was the only person who had stood by Samuel Schatzman, the Jew. Because now it was clear he had made something of himself, and he was going to give her a life most women only dreamed of.

As he waited for the end of the workday, his thoughts drifted to Chana. If there was anyone he wished he could talk to right now, it was her. He wished he could tell her how worried he was that he would never find Joan, and he was even more worried he'd never find Betty. But even if he and Chana were not angry with each other, he could never talk about Betty with her. Anything else, yes. But not Betty. Still, Sam had to admit, Chana had become his best friend. And when he needed someone to lean on, it was always Chana he turned to. *Well, once Betty and I are back together, Betty will be my best friend and my wife,* he thought. But when he closed his eyes, it was still Chana's face he saw.

The whistle sounded. Sam trembled a little because he knew the employees would be coming out of the factory momentarily. All he could remember about the girl he'd met with Betty was that her name was Joan and her hair was the color of his black shoes right after they'd been shined.

Groups of the girls were chatting loudly as they came pouring out the door of the factory. Some of them in twos, others in threes and quartets A few were alone. He scanned the crowd in search of that raven's-wing hair. But he didn't see anyone who even slightly resembled the girl he remembered. Then the employees stopped coming out the door. It seemed that the building was empty. Sam felt lost. There was nothing else to do but start his car and drive away. He turned the key in the ignition and the car rumbled. Sam was just about to pull away when he saw the girl with the black hair leaving the building. It was Joan. He was sure of it. His hands began to sweat on the steering wheel.

"Joan" he called out as she walked by him. The girl turned around.

"Do I know you?" she asked skeptically.

"You probably don't remember me. I'm Sam Schatzman. Betty Howard's friend."

"Oh yeah," she said. "I remember you."

"Well, I have been here outside the factory waiting for you. I want to talk to you. Maybe I could give you a lift home?"

"Sure," Joan said, getting into the car. Sam saw the look of admiration in her eyes as she glanced at his suit.

"So direct me to your house," he said.

"All right. Make a left at the corner," Joan said.

They drove for a few minutes, then Samuel said, "I haven't been living in Medina. I've been living in the city. New York City. But I came back because I am looking for Betty."

"Oh gosh," she said, her shoulders slumping in the seat. Then she shook her head. "You don't know."

"Don't know what? She's not dead, is she?" Sam stopped the car in the middle of the street and turned to look at her.

"No, it's nothing like that."

"Then what is it?"

"She's married," Joan said.

Sam swallowed hard. *She might as well be dead.*

CHAPTER SEVENTY-SIX

Joan asked Sam not to drop her off in front of her apartment. She had just gotten engaged. "Just let me out a block away. I don't want the neighbors to start talking. All they need to see is me getting out of a fancy car driven by a man wearing an expensive suit, and those tongues will be wagging."

"I understand, "Sam said.

"My fiancé is a very jealous man. I don't mind because when a fella is jealous like that it means he is really in love. Don't you think so? And I sure wouldn't want him to get the wrong idea."

"Yeah, sure," Sam said. He didn't hear what Joan said because he wasn't paying attention to Joan anymore. All he could think of was that Betty was married. Some other man has held Betty in his arms. *But she can't be in love with him. She can't. I won't believe it until I hear it with my own ears.*

"Sam, turn here," Joan said, but he kept going straight. "Sam!" She tugged at his sleeve. "You all right?"

"Yeah, I'm fine. I'm sorry."

"Turn here," Joan repeated.

Sam turned and drove up the street a few houses before Joan said, "All right, stop. I'll get out here."

"Thanks for the information," Sam said.

"Sure. And thanks for the ride," she said as she slammed the door.

Sam nodded and drove away.

Married? Sam repeated the word over and over in his head. He couldn't believe that Betty loved another man. *I'm convinced she did this because I disappeared, and she thought I didn't love her anymore. I must see her. Once I can hold her in my arms and tell her how I feel, she'll realize that her marriage was just a poor substitute for what we had. She'll remember how much she loves me. Then she'll leave him and go back to the city with me.*

It was getting dark. He needed a drink and a good meal before he could find the emotional strength to make his way to the veterinary office on the outskirts where Joan told him Betty lived.

I'll get a room for the night. It will give me time to steel myself for whatever happens. Then when I am fresh and ready tomorrow morning, I'll drive to Betty's home.

After Sam checked into the local hotel, he took a flask of whiskey out of his car and went upstairs to have a few shots. The liquor calmed him. He loved the way the warm liquid burned his throat. He thought about having dinner at a restaurant down the street. But the alcohol made him bold and nostalgic. So he decided to take a drive through his old neighborhood, the Jewish section of town. He would stop there for dinner. It wasn't far, a couple of miles at most. When he turned onto Gleason Street, he immediately felt the memories of his early life come flooding back. The school he attended was on the right, and the synagogue where he and his family had broken the fast on Yom Kippur four years ago was on the left. He stopped the car and tried to look through the stained-glass windows. But he couldn't see anything. Sam wondered how the rabbi and his wife were doing. And for a moment he considered going into the synagogue and saying hello. But he decided against it. He had changed, and he didn't want the rabbi asking him any questions about how he'd acquired the car, or the suit. He didn't want to explain the man he'd become. Or worse, listen to tales of woe about how the Jewish people in town were affected by the scandal between him and Betty. *No,* he thought. *Sometimes memories are best left right where they belong, in the past.*

Then Sam turned right and drove by the front of the bakery his father had once owned. A black-and-white sign that read Shlomie's Bakery hung there. He pulled over and stopped the car. Sam closed his eyes. In his mind he could still see the sign that had once read Schatzman's. A bittersweet memory tugged at his heart. How different his life had been then. As a child, Sam believed he would live his entire life in Medina. In those long-ago days, his future seemed preordained. He believed he would marry and have children and they would grow up in this little neighborhood surrounded by the love of his parents and his sister. Those days when he was still ignorant of what was to come were golden days in his mind. But now his mother was gone. It had been months, and there still had been no word from her. His father had lost his wife, his business, and his dreams. And . . . Sam? He'd lost his innocence.

On the corner was Mendel's deli. It had been there for as long as Samuel. His mouth watered as he remembered the delicious knishes. But when he thought about going inside and the possibility of seeing his old friends and neighbors, he drove away. Finally, he returned to the hotel, but before he went up to his room, he stopped at the restaurant down the street to have a sandwich which he ate quickly. Then he went upstairs to his room, took a bath, and drank the rest of the whiskey he'd brought with him.

CHAPTER SEVENTY-SEVEN

That night Sam was restless. He found it difficult to sleep. In the morning he got dressed, downed a cup of black coffee, and then got into his car and followed Joan's directions which led him to a winding road in a rural area. The rolling hills were covered in snow, and the trees had tiny icicles hanging from their branches. When the light hit them, they reflected like crystal rainbows. It was like a scene out of a painting. Beautiful, perhaps, but he wondered how Betty had ever come to meet someone who was an animal doctor living so far away from town. As he got closer, Sam's hands began to shake, and his heart began to beat faster. He had no idea how all of this would play out. All he knew was that he had to see her again. She was the reason he'd gone to work for Laevsky. She was the reason he was the man he was today. And he had to hold her in his arms again. *We are one. She is my bashert. I know she will feel it, too, once I take her in my arms. She will know beyond a doubt that we belong together, and she'll come back to the city with me. I must believe. I must, or I will go out of my mind after all that I have done to get to this moment.*

CHAPTER SEVENTY-EIGHT

R oland was awakened by a loud knock on the door of his house and someone calling out, "Dr. Horvath! Dr. Horvath."

The sun had just begun to rise and was peeking through his bedroom drapes. Glancing over at his wife, Betty, he longed to lean over and kiss her. But she was sleeping serenely with the two new kittens cuddled up into her arm, so he didn't want to disturb her.

"Dr. Horvath!" The knock was louder this time.

Roland forced himself to get out of his warm bed. The floor was cold as he made his way to the front door, careful to step over the two old dogs that slept on his bedroom floor. They both looked up at him. Then, although they were tired, both dogs got up and followed him. He opened the door, and there stood George Campton, a young man whose family bred horses. They lived two hours from Roland's veterinary clinic, but they liked him and trusted him, so even though there were closer vets, they used Roland as their vet for all their horses and dogs.

"Come in, George. You must be freezing out there."

"It's cold," George said as he walked inside rubbing his hands together.

"What can I do for you?" Roland asked.

"My folks need you desperately. Our prize mare is sick. She is lying down in her stall and she's rolling around. I'm afraid if we don't get back to her in a hurry, she may colic."

"All right. Let me put on some clothes, and we'll be on our way."

Within minutes, Roland had washed up and dressed. He was ready to go. So, although he hated to wake her, he leaned over his wife and kissed her gently. "Betty, sweetheart," he said, "I have to go to the Campton farm. One of their horses might be starting to colic."

Betty opened her eyes.

"By the way, have I ever told you how beautiful you are in the morning," he said, kissing her.

She smiled. "You tell me all the time . . . and I never tire of hearing it."

"I love you. I'll be home as soon as I can."

"Be careful. There's ice under that snow out there," she said, "and you're precious to me."

"Not nearly as precious as you are to me," he said, "and don't worry, I'm always careful. After all, I have you to come home to."

Betty gently moved the sleeping kittens and put on her flannel robe, then she followed Roland into the living room. "Hello, George," she said.

George nodded. "Good morning, Betty," he said.

"Would you two like some coffee before you leave?" she asked, but she already knew the answer. She knew her husband would deny his own needs for the needs of a customer or an animal.

"I'd love some, but I am afraid we should hurry and get on the road," Roland said.

"I agree," George said. "The sooner we can get to my farm, the better."

Roland planted a kiss on his wife's lips. "See you soon," he said.

"I love you," she answered.

CHAPTER SEVENTY-NINE

After Roland left, Betty put on a pot of coffee for herself. Then she began to feed the pets. They were all gathered around her as she put the full dishes down on the floor. Then she picked up the water bowls from the night before. After she washed them and refilled each one, she poured herself a cup of steaming hot coffee. *The first sip is always the best,* she thought. Betty was glad that when the harsh weather had set in, Roland had put a sign on the window of the clinic instructing clients to come to the house. Still, she had to be dressed in case anyone came. So as much as she would have loved to spend the day lounging in her warm nightgown, she washed up and got dressed.

With Roland gone and no patients boarding in the clinic, there was nothing do to. So she decided to put on a pot of lecsó, a rich vegetable stew and bake a kifli, a crescent bread to go with it, for Roland when he got home. *Even if he doesn't come back until tomorrow, I could keep this simmering.*

Betty sang softly to herself as she chopped onions, tomatoes, and peppers. A mutt that had been abandoned outside the clinic last week now sat beside her with his muzzle resting on her knee. She had become quite good at preparing Hungarian food, and Roland told her constantly how much he appreciated her efforts.

Every Sunday, Betty's parents came to the house for dinner. They finally forgave and accepted her. After all, she was a married woman now. And over time they, too, had developed a love for Hungarian food.

She filled a pot with water and added the vegetables. Then she put it on a low flame while she made the dough for the kifli. After she finished, she began reading her book. *It will be a lazy day,* she thought. *I think I'll take a nap after lunch.*

CHAPTER EIGHTY

A big wooden sign on the road read, Horvath Animal Hospital. Turn Right.

Samuel could feel his hands sweating on the steering wheel as he turned right. The road up to the hospital was lined with trees whose branches were still dusted with snow from the night before. At the end of the road Sam reached a fork with two newly painted signs, one pointed to the right. It said, Animal Clinic. "Please make sure all animals are on leashes or in some way contained. Please bring large animals, like cows and horses around the back. Thank you. Dr. Horvath." The other sign pointed to the left which read, "The home of Dr. and Mrs. Horvath."

Sam felt queasy when he read the words Mrs. Horvath. *Betty,* he thought. *Betty Horvath, I hope you still love me. I pray I haven't lost you. I hope it hasn't taken me too long to get back to you.*

He assumed Betty's husband was at the hospital, so he turned left to go to the house.

The white house with its red door had a warm, inviting glow to it, in the way that a home should be. There were evergreens dusted with snow on either side of the walk. And it was clear that someone had taken great care to shovel the walkway and ensure there was no ice.

His hands trembled as he knocked on the door. In a few minutes he would see her. Betty, the girl who had haunted his dreams. A cold wind whipped across his face. He held his breath. And then . . . the door opened, and there she was.

"Sam?" she said. Her mouth flew open and her hand went to her throat. A big yellow dog stood at her side.

"Betty . . ." he said, his breath turning to white smoke in the cold.

"C-come in," she stammered.

He walked inside the house. The furniture was large and comfortable with two handmade quilts draped across the sofa. A black-and-white kitten, who had been sleeping on the rug below the coffee table, yawned and let out a soft meow at having been disturbed by the cold air that came in when Betty opened the front door. A lovely fragrance of something baking wafted through the air. Sam swallowed hard as he looked into Betty's eyes.

They stood in awkward silence for several moments. Then Sam blurted, "My sister lied. She said that she saw you, and you told her that you never wanted to see me again."

"I don't know what you're talking about. I never spoke to your sister," Betty answered, flabbergasted.

"I know. She lied. Later she told me the truth. She finally admitted that she never spoke to you. But I didn't know, Betty. I would have come back sooner if I thought that you wanted to see me." He was rambling. "You see, I was in the hospital. Some of those KKK boys beat me up pretty badly. While I was in the hospital, I sent my sister to tell you to come and see me. I waited for you. I wanted to plan our future."

"No one told me anything. I waited for you too. I lost my job because of us. I prayed every day that you would come and take me away from Medina and marry me. I was shunned so badly. I needed you, but you didn't come. And . . . finally . . . I met Roland."

"Roland," he repeated.

"My husband."

Sam looked away. He couldn't meet her eyes.

He wanted to explain that he'd known the truth for a while, but he had to find a way to support her before he could bring her back to the city with him. He longed to tell her how he'd worked for Laevsky to ensure that when she was his wife, she would have anything she could ever wish for. But he couldn't find the words. Tears threatened to fall from his eyes. His body was trembling. He turned to look at her. She was still beautiful. She was still his Betty. Sam walked over to where she stood and put his arms around her. At first, she tensed up, resistant. But then Sam kissed her, and he felt her melt into his arms. He pulled her closer to him and kissed her again with more passion. His lips traveled to her neck and behind her ear. His breath was heavy with desire. He lifted her into his arms and lay her down on the sofa lifting her skirt.

She sat up suddenly. "I can't. I'm sorry." She touched his face gently. "I am so sorry. Our time has passed, Samuel. I'm married, and . . . I'm pregnant."

He sat up and looked into her eyes. "Pregnant?" he said. The passion dissolving almost instantly. Betty was no longer the young girl he had been in love with. She was now another man's wife with another man's child growing safely in her womb.

"Yes, I am pregnant. I haven't even told Roland yet."

Sam was confused. He was filled with so many different emotions. He felt sad at the death of a dream and happy to be free of it at the same time. Betty was right; their time had passed. And then he thought of Chana. He wished he could go to see her right now and tell her that he'd made a mistake.

Betty interrupted his thoughts. "My husband is a good person," she said.

"Not a Jew?"

"No, but he isn't a hater of Jews either."

"You're the only person who isn't Jewish that I've ever met who doesn't hate Jews."

"There are plenty more. There are good people who are Jewish and good people who are not."

"Whatever happened to that bastard you were engaged to? The one in the KKK?"

"John? He got married. He's living in town. He's one of the not-so-good people. There will always be those kinds of people who are filled with hate. But if you knew my husband, you'd see that he's a really good man, Sam."

"You love him, don't you?"

"Very much. And more every day," Betty said.

"I'm happy for you, Betty. And I know this sounds strange but I'm glad I came to see you. I needed to do this so that I could go forward with the rest of my life."

"You'll meet a girl, Sam. You'll see. You'll meet the right girl for you, and you'll get married."

"It's hard to believe that after all this time it won't be you, Betty. But I am pretty sure I know who it might be. That is if she can forgive me for being a real heel," he said, then he stood up. "I'm going to go now. I'd rather not meet your husband. I don't think it would be good for any of us."

She nodded. "It was good to see you, Sam. You look good. You look like life has been kinder to you since you left Medina."

"I have plenty of money if that's what you mean."

"Well, in this economy that's something to be very thankful for. Lots of people are in financial trouble. But anyway, my wish for you is to be happy, Sam."

"Things are much clearer to me now. And I think I finally know what I want. And if all goes well, I'll be very happy, very soon," he said, then he touched her cheek and walked to the door. Turning around for a second, he said, "Goodbye, Betty. I wish you happiness too."

She smiled at him and waved, then she wiped a tear that had fallen down her cheek. Sam stared at her for a moment before he got into his car. And at that moment he realized that until today, when he held her in his arms, and their childhood vows of love were broken, she, too, had wondered if by some miracle they would be together again.

CHAPTER EIGHTY-ONE

S amuel began driving back to the city. He had so many things he wanted to say to Chana. Tiny white snowflakes that looked like lace fell on his windshield. He felt a pang of fear. *What if Chana refuses to forgive me? What if she doesn't want me back?* He put his hand in his pocket and felt the ring box. *I bought this for Betty, but it was never really meant for her. It was meant for the woman I love and want to spend the rest of my life with. I know now that woman is Chana. But how can I ever explain everything to her? All the things I didn't say to her when I had the chance. Will she give me another chance? If she will, I'll get down on my knees and beg her to be my wife.*

CHAPTER EIGHTY-TWO

Chana was miserable. She couldn't eat; she was sick to her stomach after Sam told her about Betty. She'd given Sam her heart, something she'd never done with any man before. And he had broken it. She thought if she loved him enough and changed her life for him that he would see her as the kind of girl he wanted to marry. *What a stupid fool I am,* she thought. *He never saw me as anything but a tchotchke, a toy, something to be used and discarded.*

CHAPTER EIGHTY-THREE

The more she thought about Sam, the more furious Chana became. She left work that day and went home with fire in her heart. Ignoring her mother's invitation to eat, she went into her bedroom and got out her finest dress—a tight black satin low-cut number with a slit up the side that showed off her curvy legs. She washed her face and then carefully applied dark makeup around her eyes, and red lipstick. *If that bastard thinks of me as a whore, then I'll be a whore,* she thought. *This one is for you, Sam.* After slipping her feet into black high-heeled pumps, she grabbed her coat and handbag and made her way to the speakeasy where she knew she'd find her prey.

When Chana walked in Lenny let out a loud whistle. "You look like one hot tomato. Where's Sam?"

"Who knows? Who cares?" she said as flippantly as she was able. Then she went to the bar and ordered a glass of whiskey neat.

"It's on me, doll," a voice from behind her said. She whipped around to see Izzy.

"Thanks." She smiled.

"Sure. Why don't you come and sit with me at my table?"

A pianist played softly as they downed two more drinks. Chana was feeling more at ease. She leaned forward displaying her cleavage and enjoying Izzy's obvious reaction. Then she whispered in his ear, "Want to get out of here?"

"What about Sam?"

"Don't mention him."

"Everything all right?"

She was starting to become angry again. The last thing she wanted to think about was Sam. Taking a deep breath, she forced a smile. Then she let her hand softly graze his knee. Chana fixed her eyes on his, and with an intense stare that promised a night of wild pleasure she said, "You want me, don't you?"

He nodded, reminding her of a puppy.

"Well then, don't ask me any more questions. Let's go."

She took his hand and led him out onto the street. Then he flagged a car, and they headed to his apartment.

Once they arrived, Chana pulled Izzy into the bedroom. She pushed him on the bed and took off her dress. His eyes told her that she was still beautiful, still desirable, even if Sam didn't think so. Laying down next to Izzy she began to kiss him. He pulled away, breathless. Then he took her face into his hands and held it as if it were the most precious thing on earth. His eyes were glassy, and she thought he might cry. For several moments he just stared at her. Then in a soft voice, he admitted, "Chana, I've always loved you. I loved you from the day I first saw you. I don't care about Sam or about anything you did up until this moment. None of it matters. All that matters to me is you. Will you marry me? Will you make me the happiest man alive?"

The honesty in his voice sobered her.

She stood up and turned away from him. Then she picked up her dress and put it on. With tears in her eyes, she turned back to look at him. He was confused, and she felt bad. "I'm sorry, Izzy. I am really so sorry. I don't know what to do or say. I have to go."

CHAPTER EIGHTY-FOUR

The next morning Chana felt sick. But regardless of how terrible she was feeling, she had to get dressed and go to work because she knew if she lost her job, her family would starve and be on the street. She had spent the night confused, uncertain, and weeping. After she washed her tear-stained face with cold water, she got dressed and left for work. The sky was gray, with no trace of sunshine. Snow was falling, and the cold wind as it burnt her face, made her feel even more lost and abandoned. Her shoes were wet, and her feet were cold from the gray slush on the sidewalks. For a single second she thought about suicide. It would be easier to just give up. But she knew she would never do it. Chana was a strong woman. She'd found a way to support her loved ones when there seemed to be no way. And then when it became known that she'd sold her body, she faced the scorn of the entire town with her head held high. And now she would find a way to face the loss of her dream, the dream of being Sam's wife and the mother of his children. And she would do it with dignity.

Chana was setting up for the day in the front of the shoe repair store when the old cobbler let out a cry of pain. She ran to the back of the store thinking he'd hurt himself with one of the tools. But when she got there, he lay on the floor with his hand on his chest. His eyes were open wide. And even before the doctors came, Chana knew he was dead.

After the old man's body was removed, Chana was alone. She sat down in his chair and gently ran her fingers over his tools. Tears streamed down her face. *How could this happen today? What have I done to deserve all of this? My world is falling apart, and all I want is to be able to talk to Sam. Damn him.*

Just then the bell attached to the door rang, and for a moment Chana had hope it was Sam. But it was only Mr. Goldsmith's attorney.

"Are you Chana Rubinstein?" he asked.

"Yes."

"Mr. Goldsmith left this for you. I found it rather interesting because he recently revised this letter. Poor fella, he must have felt something coming."

"For me? I only work here."

"Yes, it's for Chana Rubinstein. I'm so sorry for your loss," he said, handing her a large envelope filled with papers. On top was a letter in a sealed envelope.

She was trembling. "Thank you," she said.

"I asked that you read the letter first. And I assume you might like some time to read it alone," the attorney suggested.

"Yes, I would."

The attorney left and Chana stared at the letter. It took her several minutes to find the courage to open it. It said,

Dear Chana,

If you are receiving this letter, I am on my way to meet with Hashem. I know I have made many mistakes in my life. I hope I can be forgiven. This letter should make a lot of things clear to you. I know I have been a difficult and sometimes cruel boss, demanding perfection in everything you did. There were times when we were busy, and I expected you to stay and work several extra hours without any extra compensation. That was because, although you didn't know it at the time, you were building your own business. I always intended to leave the store to you. It was yours even then. You see, you never knew this, but your father and I started this business. He was a skilled cobbler. Then when you were still very young, your brother was born. We knew right away that something was wrong with him. Then once the doctors confirmed it, your mother became depressed because she could not have any more children, and your father started drinking heavily. Our business suffered. I resented him for it. But I can't put the blame entirely on him. I was difficult, too, and it was hard for us to get along with each other. He didn't come into work most of the time, and I was frustrated and angry. I did something I should not have done. Something underhanded. I took more than my share of our earnings and hid them. Finally, I bought him out for less than half the business was worth. It was not right. Out of guilt, I kept watch on your family. And I saw how all of you were struggling. Then once you were old enough to work and needed a job, I offered you an apprenticeship so I would be able to help your family.

Then when the gossip about your prostitution ran rampant through our small community, I refused to listen. I knew it was true. But I also knew why you did it. You did it because you have a big heart, Chana. You always did for others before yourself. Even for me. And although you got yourself a hell of a bad reputation, those people didn't know you. But

I did; I always saw the real you. When I lost my wife seven years ago, you were the only person who I could depend on for emotional support. Remember that true love is a gift, and we might only find it once in a lifetime. I know how much you love that boy Sam. See, you thought I wasn't paying attention. But I knew all along. Don't be too hard on him, I know that he has hurt you plenty of times. He's young and reckless, but we all make mistakes. I figure you will probably consider sitting shiva for me. Don't. Keep the store open. There's no such thing as customer loyalty. If you close, they will go somewhere else. I've always loved you like a daughter. You were the child my wife and I could never have. In the envelope you'll find my life savings. Spend it well. I worked hard for it. Now that I am gone, I hope you will help me to make this right. Hire your father. Give him a reason to get up in the morning. I know he drinks, but I also have seen how well you can handle him. He needs this. It will breathe new life into him. Well, I have been rambling far too long. And I guess it's time to say goodbye. I'll miss you, my young friend. I wish you a good life. And always remember that I am looking down on you from heaven, and I am putting in a good word for you.

Harry Goldsmith

Chana felt her heart breaking. She was tired, very tired. It was late, nearly seven o'clock. Her eyes hurt from crying, and all she wanted to do was go home and crawl into her bed. She glanced inside the envelope. There was what appeared to be a substantial amount of cash. She held the letter to her chest and thought of the old cobbler. There had been times she was so angry with him that she could scream. But somehow, she'd always known he cared about her. "Goodbye, old friend," she whispered. Then she took the envelope into the back with her to get her handbag. She placed the letter inside her purse, took her coat and hat off the rack, and put them on. The bell attached to the door rang.

"I'm sorry, we're closed," she said as she came out of the back room without even looking up.

"Chana."

CHAPTER EIGHTY-FIVE

S he knew that voice. It sent waves of emotion flooding through her. Her body trembled. She felt goose bumps rise on her skin. The room went dark. She almost tripped over her shoes. Grabbing on to the wall, she looked up and said, "What are you doing here, Sam?"

He stood there for several moments, silent, staring at her. She felt uncomfortable. "Sam?" she said. "What do you want?"

"I-I-I made a terrible mistake. I love you. I have always loved you. But I didn't know it until . . ."

"Until you went back and saw your old girlfriend?"

"I spent less than an hour with her. It didn't take long for me to realize that she was someone from my past. But, you . . . you are my future, my bashert, the love of my life."

"You know Izzy proposed to me," she said, wanting to hurt him as she wrapped her arms around her chest.

"That rat bastard. I was gone for one lousy night and he moved in on my girl. And"—she heard the fear in his voice—"did you accept?"

She hesitated, enjoying his angst.

"Chana, I don't care if you did or not, just give me another chance. I love you more than I can say in words. Let me prove it to you. Please, I'm begging you." He dropped to his knees and took the ring out of his pocket. "Be my wife. You are the one. Betty means nothing to me now. She's just a memory from my past. You are the one. Marry me, please . . ."

But before she could answer, Irving burst through the door. The overhead doorbell rang wildly.

"Sam, I've been looking everywhere for you. Where have you been? Never mind, it doesn't matter. I need you to come with me right now. Your mother is in trouble. I got a letter from your sister in Germany. We have to decide what to do."

"Chana, I'll be back," Sam said.

NOTE FROM THE AUTHOR

Dear Readers,

I always enjoy hearing from my readers, and your thoughts about my work are very important to me. If you enjoyed my novel, please consider telling your friends and posting a short review on Amazon. Word of mouth is an author's best friend.

Please Click Here to Leave a Review

Also, it would be my honor to have you join my mailing list. As my gift to you for joining, you will receive 3 **free** short stories and my USA Today award-winning novella complimentary in your email! To sign up, just go to my website at www.RobertaKagan.com

I send blessings to each and every one of you,

Roberta

Email: roberta@robertakagan.com

Please turn the page to read the prologue of the next book in this series, *They Never Saw It Coming…*

THEY NEVER SAW IT COMING
EXCERPT

Berlin, Germany, February 1906

When the school bell rang, fifteen-year-old Luisa Eisenreich grabbed her books and ran outside as fast as she could. She was attempting to escape from the school grounds before her schoolmates could catch up with her. But, as always, they were right on her tail, calling out the hurtful things that burned inside her long after they were said.

"Hey, Luisa, how'd you get so ugly? You look like a rat."

"Luisa, I thought that you were a rat monster the first time I saw you."

"When was the last time you took a bath? You stink. You smell so bad you make me want to vomit."

She ran as fast as she could to get away from them, but it was the middle of winter and the sidewalks were covered in ice. The group of boys who'd been shouting insults were right behind her. Luisa gasped as a snowball whipped right by her face. Then another and then another. Finally, one found its mark and hit her in the back of the head. She felt hot liquid run down her neck. When she reached up and touched her hair, her hand was sticky. She looked at her fingers. They were red with blood. "Oh," she gasped, and tears began to fall down her cheeks, but she dared not stop. Not even for a second. With her heart beating wildly, she turned down a street. Now she was only a few houses from the house where she lived. When she walked in through the kitchen door, her mother frowned at her.

"What happened to you? What is with all of this blood? My God. Let me see."

Luisa stood still while her mother inspected her hair. Then her mother sat Luisa down in a chair and began to clean up the cut.

"Luisa! What is wrong with you? Do you want me to lose this job? Frau and Herr Horwitz were kind enough to let us move in here. It is because of their generosity that you are able to attend a good school. How do you reward them? By fighting?" She sighed. "And even worse, you could really get hurt from fighting. I don't understand you."

"I hate this school, Mutti. I would much rather go back to my old school. I fit in there. I miss my friends. Mostly, I miss Frida."

"For goodness' sake. Please don't mention going back there again. It is a terrible idea. We were so poor. Starving. The flat we lived in was filled with cockroaches and rodents." Her mother finished cleaning up her wound. Then she sighed and added, "I'm tired. I've been cleaning all morning. The Horwitzes are having a big party, and the missus wants the entire place spotless. She wants all of the closets cleaned out. All of the old chests up in attic cleaned too. I have so much work, I can't begin to tell you." Then she looked down and saw the blood on the floor. "Oh, Luisa, look at the mess you've made on the floor."

"A party? There's going to be a party here?"

"Yes, the Horwitzes are having a party for their son, who is coming home from the university in two weeks."

"Can I go to the party?"

"Of course not. We are the help. The Horwitzes are our employers. We don't attend their parties."

"I don't go to any parties."

"You're wearing my patience thin. Go and clean yourself up. Wash your face and change your clothes. Then come back to the kitchen, and I'll give you something to eat."

As Luisa walked out of the room, she heard her mother scoff, "I have to wash this damn floor again."

After Luisa was cleaned up and changed, she wasn't hungry, so instead of going to the kitchen, she went into her room and thought about her life. Everything had changed when her father died. Last year she and her mother had moved into this Jewish neighborhood. The Horwitzes were rich in comparison to anyone from Luisa's old neighborhood. They owned a home even if it was one of the smaller homes in the small wealthy area where they lived. And that home had a study and a ballroom. They owned nice things like china, silverware, pretty furnishings, and lovely orchid-colored drapes. Frau Horwitz had always been kind to Luisa. But Luisa felt uncomfortable around her. She always felt like Frau Horwitz pitied her. *Why wouldn't she pity me? I am pitiful. My father is dead. My mother is a maid. We have no money.*

Luisa and her mother were given a clean and modest room in the maids' quarters of the Horwitzes' home. It was nothing fancy, but it was warm in the winter, and they had plenty of food. These were things they'd lacked before they moved in with the Horwitzes. And Luisa knew she should be grateful for all that the Horwitzes gave them. But she had been much happier in her own neighborhood even if the winters were miserable and she and her mother often went to bed hungry.

Most of the time when Luisa wasn't in school, she was helping her mother cook or clean. Sometimes she was ensconced in her room doing her homework, but she found it hard to concentrate on her studies. Her mind was always drifting and because of this her grades suffered. Luisa was lonely. She often thought of her friends who she'd left behind. Unfortunately, her mother was too exhausted to take the time to talk to her. Even so, Luisa knew her mother loved her. She could feel it even when her mother was angry with her. It hurt to see how hard her mother worked. And although she never told anyone, she was angry at how unfair life was. *How is it that some people, like the Horwitzes, have everything, and others like my mutti and me have nothing?*

The girls who attended school with Luisa sat together in groups, none of which included Luisa. Some of the girls were very studious, others very wealthy, but the ones Luisa admired the most were the beauties. They were a small group of girls who everyone seemed to marvel at. All of them were pretty and charming, but one in particular was above the rest. Her name was Goldie Birnbaum. Not only was she beautiful, but her family was rich, perhaps the richest family in the entire school. The Birnbaums owned a large woman's clothing factory right in town. Luisa's mother knew women who worked for Goldie's family. But none of them had ever met the Birnbaums. Not even Luisa. She'd only watched Goldie from afar and gaped at her beauty. Goldie had hair that was the color of sunshine and always perfectly styled. Her clothes were tailored to her tall, lanky figure. And no matter what the latest fashion was, she wore it, and she wore it well.

When Luisa was alone in her room, she closed her eyes and imagined what it might be like to be Goldie. She thought about how it would feel to go to school wearing the prettiest dresses. *What would it feel like to be greeted by all the other girls, each of them hoping that I would choose to sit beside them. And the boys! I wonder what it would be like to have the boys sit up straighter when I walked into the room and speak respectfully when they talked to me. Instead of teasing me and calling me ugly, they would vie for my attentions.* She giggled when she thought about it. But a glimpse of her image in the mirror was a bitter reminder that she was not Goldie Birnbaum. She was Luisa Eisenreich, a skinny, frightened girl with no figure and a face that she had been told looked like the face of a rat. Her nose was long and pointed. Her brown hair was straggly. And sometimes she was lazy, and her hygiene wasn't what it should have been. Luisa threw herself on the bed and wished she could quit school and do something exciting, something that made her feel important. She fantasized about being an actress, or a singer. But she had no talent for either.

The following Wednesday was her sixteenth birthday. She didn't expect much from anyone because she had never received much. But to her surprise when she arrived home from school on her birthday, Frida was waiting in her room for her. Frau Horwitz had ordered a cake from the bakery for the girls. And she gave Luisa a small gold locket as a gift from herself and Mr. Horwitz. Frida and Luisa loved the cake. They laughed and talked until it started getting dark. Then Frida said, "I have to get going home."

Luisa hugged her friend. "I wish you could come and visit all the time," she said.

Frida squeezed her friend tightly. "I know. I'll try to come again soon. But you know how hard it is to get here. Frau Horwitz sent me money for transportation to come today. That's how I got here. This is really a wonderful place to live. I wish I lived here. Frau Horwitz is very nice to you, and the house is so warm," she said.

"I'd rather be back at home with you in the old neighborhood."

"I know." Then she handed Luisa a little box. "It's not much, but it's my birthday gift for you," Frida said.

Luisa opened the box. Inside was a small pin. "What is it?"

"It was my mother's nurses' pin. She gave it to me before she died. I wanted to give it to you because it's the nicest thing I have. And you're my best friend, and you always will be. So I wanted you to have it."

"I just made a decision," Luisa said, smiling. Then she pinned the pin onto her dress. "Someday, I am going to be a nurse."

"I believe in you. And I know you will," Frida said.

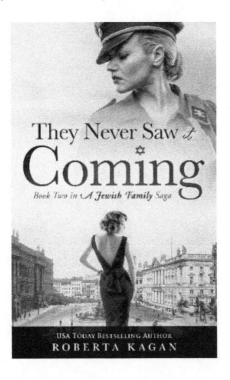

Click Here To Purchase They Never Saw It Coming By Roberta Kagan

ALSO BY ROBERTA KAGAN

Available on Amazon

A Jewish Family Saga

Not In America

They Never Saw It Coming

When The Dust Settled

The Syndrome That Saved Us

A Holocaust Story Series

The Smallest Crack

The Darkest Canyon

Millions Of Pebbles

Sarah and Solomon

All My Love, Detrick Series

All My Love, Detrick

You Are My Sunshine

The Promised Land

Michal's Destiny Series

Michal's Destiny

A Family Shattered

Watch Over My Child

Another Breath, Another Sunrise

Eidel's Story Series

Who Is The Real Mother?

Secrets Revealed

New Life, New Land

Another Generation

The Wrath of Eden Series

The Wrath Of Eden

The Angels Song

Stand Alone Novels

One Last Hope

A Flicker Of Light

The Heart Of A Gypsy

ACKNOWLEDGMENTS

I would also like to thank my editor, proofreader, and developmental editor for all their help with this project. I couldn't have done it without them.

Paula Grundy of Paula Proofreader

Terrance Grundy of Editerry

Carli Kagan, Developmental Editor

Thank you so much for reading my book. I am truly honored. In all of my novels I try to use factual historical events blended with fictional characters in order to educate the reader in an entertaining fashion.

When I first heard about the blood libel in Messina, New York, in the late 1920s, I was horrified and shocked. And I knew this was something that had to be brought to light. So I wrote this novel. Before you begin, please allow me to help you to decipher what was fact and what was fiction. As always, my dear readers, please know that I am truly grateful for your loyal support of my work.

The facts: The blood libel is not new. It has been a lie that has acted as a curse on the Jewish people for centuries. It is a very disturbing concept that states Jews use the blood of Christian children for religious rituals. It is absurd, dangerous, and horrific. As you will see in my novel.

In 1928, in a town called Messina in Upstate New York, a little girl disappeared. The incident occurred a few days before Yom Kippur. A rumor began and then spread throughout the town that the Jews had taken the child and were planning to use her blood for religious rituals. When the child returned the following morning, the horrific accusations did not cease. The little girl claimed she'd fallen asleep in the woods. However, a witch hunt had already begun, and now the Jewish citizens were accused of releasing the child unharmed because they realized the town's people were onto them. All of this caused rifts between the Jewish people and their gentile neighbors. The mayor put out statements against the Jewish people. The KKK became involved, and Jewish businesses were boycotted. If you would like to know more about the actual events, I recommend a book called *The Accusation*, by Edward Berenson.

The fiction: The characters in my book are all fictional. I've even renamed the town from Messina to Medina. Although the child who disappeared (in reality) was a four-year-old girl whose mother actually did send her out to look for her brother. I had to make that clear because I am still shocked by it. I am a mother, and I would never have sent a four-year-old into the forest alone for any reason.

My novel, *Not in America*, is a purely fictional story of what might have been happening behind the scenes. It's a sad depiction of how quickly and easily the Jewish people could be accused of horrific things just because they are Jewish. And how they could be made to suffer for crimes they did not commit. What I found most frightening of all was that the blood libel, a backward way of thinking, actually peeked its ugly head right here on American soil in 1928. Could it happen again?

www.ingramcontent.com/pod-product-compliance
Lightning Source LLC
La Vergne TN
LVHW040008040325
805046LV00038B/790